THE PROMISE

THE PROMISE

A Green Ridge Series - Book One

J.J. Marcell

To my husband and children, you are my world.
To my mom and dad, thanks for everything.
To Esther Rose, you bring sunshine to Lola's world.
To my extended family, I'm blessed to have you.
I love you all.

PROLOGUE

February 17, 2022

Was it possible to break an already shattered heart? Hannah Presten tried to conceal her emotions as she watched her husband in her favorite black slacks and a white button-down shirt stand in the middle of their bedroom. Ethan was finally letting go. The room seemed to close in each time Ethan took a step toward her. There was no stopping her tears. She didn't care. Her tears flowed as she held Ethan's hands to her chest. Hannah gazed into Ethan's equally mournful eyes and forced a smile. She exhaled after taking what she felt was the deepest breath she'd taken in her entire life. "It's Okay. You can go. I'll be alright." It was the right thing to do, knowing that Ethan would be happier where he was going, though it didn't make it less painful. Ethan stood there studying her face one last time as she held her breath.

Was there an easy way to say goodbye? He knew the answer to that, but there was no other way around it. Ethan had to say goodbye to the only woman he loved no matter how hard it would be. Forcing a smile, Ethan spoke, "You know, I will miss seeing you in this." He touched an image of a pug on the blue scrubs she was in. There was no hiding it-his heart ached.

Barely able to breathe as she buried herself in his arms, he whispered, "I'm sorry, babe." It was all he could say. What else was there? He *was* sorry and wished he didn't have to do this. He wished there was another way, but this just had to be. He needed her to be happy and keep his promise of letting her love and be loved again, the kind of love he could never give her any longer.

Hannah nodded, trying hard not to fall apart. "You don't have to be sorry for anything, Ethan. We both wanted this. I'd do it all over again if I had to." She squeezed his hand. "Listen to me. I love you *so* much, and *nothing* and *no one...* You hear me? *No one* could ever change that—"

"I know, but this whole thing seems wrong. Unfair."

She agreed. It was unfair. It was wrong, but it was out of their control. Why this way? She had no idea. All she knew was that everything happened for a reason. At least that's what her mother used to tell her when she was young, and her mother was right. Hannah had her sets of struggles and doubts in life, but every time she looked back, there was always a reason for why things happened the way they did. God was always in control.

"What we had-*have* is special and it will always stay that way."

"I will always love you, angel. You know that, right?" he said.

She nodded as she stared into his teary blue eyes, trying to write every detail in her memory. More tears fell on the floor as he kissed her deeply one last time. Their bodies pressed against each other, trembling as they breathed heavily in unison, savoring each rhythm their lips made together. Their hearts beat fiercely, and she could only take little sips of air as she wrapped her arms around his muscular body, pressing her chest against his; making him feel each painful heartbeat.

Ethan breathed in her familiar floral scent, her memory, her love, taking it all with him, memorizing her sweet taste, her gentle cries, her heartbeat. He breathed them all and took them in his heart. She bit her lower lip, and his breathing became intense. He pulled her in more, burying his fingers in her silky hair. He couldn't hold back any longer. He covered her mouth with his, letting his tears fall freely.

Time stood still and neither of them wanted to let go, but Ethan finally pulled back.

"I have to go, Han," he whispered. He stared at his wife, her eyes still closed, tears flowing down her angelic face. God, she was beautiful. He will forever carry that vision of her with him. She opened her eyes and more tears fell as she gazed at him. Hannah smiled with that sweet, innocent smile he loved so much. He took another deep breath as he brushed her tears away. "*Please* don't forget that feeling."

Ethan stepped back, and the thought of him finally letting go broke Hannah's heart into a million pieces once more. His hands slipped from her grip as he took another step away from her. Her heart thudded. He took one last deep breath, let it out, and gave her a smile that would forever remain etched in her heart. It wasn't goodbye. It was love. Hannah stood in the middle of their bedroom, unable to move, watching the love of her life walk away. Her heart ached, but somehow, there was also peace. She wiped her tears away, and when she glanced back up, like a puff of smoke, he was gone.

Thank you, Ethan, for everything.

Ethan was gone. What was she to do now?

Chapter One

September 2021

*W*here am I? Hannah wondered as she stood in the middle of what looked like a vast forest she'd never seen before where grownups she didn't recognize towered over her. "Hello, can someone tell me where I am?" she said in a soft tiny voice. She glanced around, trying to look for a familiar face. The air was cool, but she wasn't cold. In the center was a lake glistening from the shining sun. In the distance was a roaring waterfall. She should have felt scared, but she didn't. She didn't feel lost either. Whatever this place was, it was beautiful. "Excuse me, can someone help me?" she called out again. There were other kids running around the place. Finally, a familiar face.

"Jean! I'm so glad to see you! Where are we?"

"Hannah! What are you doing here?" The little girl seemed surprised to see her. "You can't stay here. You need to go back," Jean said. She didn't sound upset, but she did look concerned.

"Go back? Where? I don't even know where I am."

"Turn around and go back."

"I don't understand," she whined.

A man in a gray suit who looked to be in his forties approached them. He was tall, handsome, and had the most brilliant smile.

"Hi, Hannah."

He placed a hand on her tiny shoulder. "This is not a place for you yet. You need to go back. Your mom is waiting for you."

Who was this man? He seemed familiar and, she felt a connection with him as if she'd known him all along. There was something about the man's face and Jean's too. They almost glowed.

"*Yet? My mom?*"

"Yes." The man smiled.

She looked around for her mother. Now she was really confused.

"I really don't understand," she said. Tears welled up in her eyes, but she held them back. "Why don't you guys want me to stay? And where is my mom?"

"We do, Han, but not yet," Jean explained. There was something about Jean's smile as if she knew Hannah would one day come back.

"I want my mommy," Hannah cried.

Now, she felt lost. Why did they want her to leave? Didn't they like her? Hannah studied the people around her, and that's when she noticed everyone seemed to have the same glow the man and Jean had.

"You need to go back, Hannah. They're waiting for you," Jean said gesturing towards a path that Hannah hadn't noticed before.

Hannah took a step forward but turned back to face Jean. "Will I see you again?"

"Don't worry. I'll be around." She smiled.

Jean's words were the last she heard before everything went black. Suddenly, Hannah stood in the middle of what looked like someone's living room. A matching sofa and loveseat on one side and a fireplace on the other; on top was a family portrait which she could not quite make out. Whose house was she in? Nothing was familiar. Suddenly, she realized she was holding a baby sleeping peacefully in her arms. Somehow, she knew the baby was hers. How could that be? Hannah blinked. One moment she was a confused little girl, now she was an adult with *her* baby in her arms. A man stood next to her - a man familiar to her, but she couldn't make out who it was for sure.

"I love you," the man whispered as he walked past her, not looking back.

"I love you, too," she replied.

What the heck? She loved this man? Who was he? It had to be Ethan, who else would it be? They seemed happy together. The man held her hand and was about to turn around when her phone rang. Kate, her assistant, had babbled frantically, something about an accident, *the man didn't see it! You need to hurry! The poor thing is in terrible shape!* Her dream left her perplexed, but she quickly rolled out of bed, jumped in the shower, and got ready.

***

It was a few minutes after nine on a Tuesday morning, and Hannah was still in bumper-to-bumper traffic. After talking to Kate, she decided to leave earlier than usual. She thought about her dream as she sat in her car; it was the same dream she had when she was in a coma for three days, fighting for her life at six years old. Then there was that second dream that started a few months ago. The baby dreams. That was new.

She needed her caffeine, especially for a start like this. She thought she could make a quick stop at Starbucks and still make it to the clinic on time, but she changed her mind as she looked at the stalled cars in front of her and glanced at her watch. It was impossible. She had to let the clinic know. She pressed a button on the side of the steering wheel and commanded, "Call work." Tuesday was always a busy day at the clinic and the fact that she was late would only make it worse.

Sacramento Animal Clinic, this is Kate. How can I help you? The commotion in the background was evident as her assistant answered, yelling over the noise.

"Kate, it's Hannah," she said over the barking. "I'm only a few miles away, but I'm stuck in traffic. I think there's an accident in front of me."

"Oh boy," Kate responded.

"How's the cat doing?"

"It's doing ok, but the poor thing needs treatment ASAP. We're keeping it comfortable 'till you get here, but—"

"Push all my appointments. I'll be there as soon as I can."

She thought about her dream again as she sat in traffic, waiting for the cars to move. Why was she dreaming about Jean? Perhaps she missed her imaginary friend. They were inseparable for years, and then one day, just before she turned nine, Jean stopped visiting. She never saw her again. And what about that man in her dream? Why was she dreaming about that again? That was the fifth time in the past few months. She parted with her thoughts as the traffic started to move slowly. A green, circular emblem came into sight; another Starbucks was nearby. Suddenly, she wanted her morning dirty chai latte, but she would have to do without for today. *Fur babies come first.* That was her mantra. Papalo would be proud of her if he could see her now. She smiled at the thought.

Don't cry, sweetheart. I will be watching over you. She held on to that last statement Papalo said before passing on.

Like an angel, papalo? she asked.

Like an angel, sweetheart, he told her.

Her grandfather was her inspiration. He was the reason she became a veterinarian. She would be happy if she could at least be half as good as her grandfather was. *Pets are angels in disguise sent from above to give us unconditional love* he used to say. She believed Papalo wholeheartedly. Hannah missed him so much, and she missed Green Ridge. She was three when she first visited Papalo's farm, where she learned to love animals like he did. Every summer was special. She even made friends with a couple of girls named Anne and Ressa. There were others, too, but she couldn't remember their names. Green Ridge was where she first fell in love with a boy named Jody, it was also where she had her heart broken for the first time. Despite all that, she loved Green Ridge.

Twenty minutes later, Hannah pulled into the Sacramento Animal Clinic parking lot. She took her reserved parking spot and rushed inside. If there was one thing Hannah hated most, it was making her patients wait, especially if it was an emergency.

It took about two hours for her to tend to the emergency and slowly got back to her scheduled appointments.

"Excuse me," she said as she accidentally bumped into a man standing by the front desk. The clinic was small, and the waiting room was busy with pet owners and their fur babies.

"So, are we excited for Virginia?" Kate asked giddily from behind the desk, fixing the oversized eyeglasses on her face.

"Yes, we are," Hannah grinned and took the folder Kate was handing her. She was about to go into one of the rooms when a man's voice stopped her.

"You're going to Virginia? I used to live there," the man said, standing by the counter.

She turned and quickly glanced at the man. "Yes, my husband and I are going to Green Ridge for vacation," Hannah replied.

"Nice place," he added.

"Yes, it is. Sorry, but I must get back to work," she gestured at the people waiting at the lobby and smiled.

The man nodded.

***

A few hours later, Ethan strode into the clinic with a Starbucks cup. He nodded at Kate who was behind the front counter with the phone plastered against her ear. She looked a bit shorter today, he thought. Her face had a few strands of hair that had fallen from her pinned-up short red hair. She must have been in a hurry this morning because her makeup wasn't as elaborate as usual, but she still wore those godforsaken glasses that were too big for her face. Despite that, she looked better today. Kate gave him a weak smile and immediately gestured for him to proceed, signaling that Hannah was free. He returned the smile and moved straight to the hallway.

The door to Hannah's office was ajar, and the view of his wife sitting behind the desk, unaware of his presence, made him smile. After all these years, she still took his breath away. He stood by the door, watching Hannah tie her long, curly, brown hair into a ponytail. She dabbed powder on her slightly tanned face and tinted her lips with what he assumed was the pink drugstore brand lip gloss they bought yesterday. What was it called? Oh yeah, *"Drop It Like It's Hot."* Who comes up with these crazy names? *Beats me,* he recalled her saying. This time, she tended to her almond-shaped eyes, applying a subtle green liner on the bottom, which made her hazel iris glow under the fluorescent light. He still couldn't believe he was married to this goddess.

"Knock. Knock. Special delivery for the prettiest veterinarian in town," he announced as he entered the small room. Inside was a rectangular mahogany desk with two white chairs in front of it. On the right wall were Hannah's credentials and on the other was a collage of pets she'd treated over the years.

Hannah shot up, removed her lab coat, and tossed it on a chair. She strutted toward him in her black slacks and white sleeveless turtleneck. "In town?" she asked, drawing her brows together.

"In... the... *state?"*

"Give me that." She snatched the cup from his hand and leaned in for a kiss.

"Whoa. Slow down."

"Slow down? When a hot, lean, tall, blond delivery guy is in front of me? Not a chance." She took a sip and immediately tasted something very familiar. "Is this—"

"Of course, it is." As if he was going to make a mistake after five years of bringing her favorite dirty chai latte. He even made sure he got the ginger powder from home to surprise her. Though he often wondered how someone could like such a disgusting drink. Ginger? In a latte? Really? But all he knew was that it made her happy. So be it.

"Where did you get ginger?"

"I have my sources." He winked.

"You're a lifesaver. You have no idea what kind of morning I've had."

He took the cup from her, sat it on a small glass table on the corner before grabbing his wife around the waists. They stood in the middle of her office. They fit perfectly into each other's arms. Though he was six-one, and she was about five-five, the three-inch black stilettos she wore today almost caught her up to his height. She loved to bury her face in his neck and inhale his natural scent, but he was sure she was smelling the subtle hint of cedar and sandalwood from his cologne he put on earlier.

"I could've sworn you left in your blue scrubs this morning." He caressed her soft, naturally glowing, tanned shoulder as she nuzzled closer to him.

"I did. I had to change for a meeting."

Hannah ran her fingers through his chest, making him shiver. Her subtle touches still made him feel like an infatuated teenager. Yeah, it seemed crazy, but he didn't care.

Knowing he would be stopping to see her today, he intentionally wore one of her favorite outfits - black slacks with a slightly loose white button-down shirt, tucked in, fitting just right to show his well-defined muscles. His golden blond hair needed trimming, but he didn't have the time, so he let his mane flow just above his ocean-blue eyes, accentuating his strong facial structure. He did have time to trim his beard this morning. She loved his neatly trimmed, well-groomed blond beard, so he made sure he took care of that. Unaware of the day she'd had so far, he had planned to seduce her into having lunch with him.

"I needed my caffeine hours ago, but I couldn't find the time to even sit until now," she said as she pulled away.

"I suppose a lunch break is out of the question, then?"

"Oh honey, I'm sorry, but because of the emergency this morning and the meeting this afternoon, the rest of my appointments have been delayed."

He pouted.

"Aww, don't give me that look. Don't worry; you will have me *all* to yourself in a couple of weeks," she said and winked.

"Can't wait," he said as he pulled away, walked behind her and whispered in her ear, "I can't wait to have you *all* to myself, *doctor.* " Now facing her, he grinned and pulled her in for a hug. "As a matter of fact, why wait. I'm suddenly feeling a little sick now. *Cough. Cough.* Would you listen to my chest? I'm having a little hard time breathing," he said, as he pulled back and started unbuttoning the top of his shirt.

"I'm a vet," she said, laughing.

"And I'm a hungry wolf."

"Oh, stop it."

He leaned back on her desk. "Are you refusing to treat a patient, Doctor Presten? I'm shocked," he said, placing a hand on his chest. "Well, I suppose I could wait till I get you *all* to myself; *that way*, I won't have to fight for time with *Fido* or *Whiskers* or—What's the name of that overweight bunny you love so much?"

"Mr. Thumper." She snickered.

"Mr. Thumper. Yeah, *him.*

"Honey, *please* button your shirt back up. I have to get back to work." Hannah walked behind her desk.

"You're no fun, " he said as he sat on a chair and started buttoning up his shirt. "Hey, what's up with your assistant's hair and those gigantic glasses?"

Without glancing up, she asked, "What about it? I think they're cute. Anyway, have you spoken to Ol?"

That was a quick change of subject, he thought, but he didn't press; she had a lot on her mind. "I told Ol this morning that we'll be gone for a couple of weeks. He agreed to take care of the office while I'm gone. Of course, he whined, but he got over it."

"Good. I was afraid Ol would give you a hard time knowing that you guys are still trying to secure that sale in Tahoe. So, how's that coming along, anyway?"

"Well, I'm hoping he and I can close the deal before we leave. He did call earlier and told me he wanted to talk about something, but he wouldn't tell me what."

Hannah shifted in her seat. "I wonder what it could be? You think it's about Tahoe?"

"I don't know. Maybe."

"Anyway, before I forget, I already put a down payment on Serenity Manor."

"You did? I haven't even seen the place."

"I'll show you tonight after dinner. Can we finalize then?"

"Sounds great."

There was still a lot of business to take care of before they left, but Ethan needed to finalize the trip first, so working late was out of the question.

Hannah stood, glancing at her watch.

"Remember to pick up a bottle of chardonnay. We only have half a bottle left.

"Yes, ma'am." He saluted.

There was a hesitant knock on the door. Hannah slipped into her white coat, and just as she was about to walk to the door, he swiftly drew her into his lap and covered her lips with his.

Chapter Two

Ethan picked up a sandwich from a nearby deli before returning to work. As he returned to his car, he wondered what his best friend was up to. It wasn't like Ol to withhold information. Something was up. After almost twenty years of friendship, he should know. Wow, twenty years. Has it been that long? It felt like it was only yesterday when he had to rescue Oliver from a couple of drunk guys in college. Ethan was in his second week at his part-time job at a bistro near campus when he noticed a guy arguing with well-known troublemakers near the billiard table. Though he had never seen him before, he could tell he was a student at the university by the monogram hoodie he wore.

C'mon, rich kid, cough it up, one guy said.

You clearly cheated! the new kid argued.

Ethan knew the hustlers; he was warned about the Perry brothers on his first night at the job. They were regulars at the establishment and had never failed to have an argument or a brawl of some kind with other students. Sammy, whom he heard had just gotten out of prison for assault, was tall, probably six foot one, looked like a stick, and wore his blond hair in a ponytail. His younger brother, Steve, was a bit shorter, fit, and bald. They were known for hustling new students like Oliver. Oliver would not have left the restaurant in one piece hadn't he intervened. Before he could de-escalate the situation, punches were thrown all over the place. Two against one, which certainly wasn't fair, so he knew he had to help.

Hey, you two! Stop! Let him go!

Stay out of it, bartender, Sammy yelled.

Hey, scrawny! I said let him go, or I'll call the cops again.

The two brothers looked at each other, grinned and decided to ignore his threats.

He wasn't much of a fighter; he would rather talk things out most of the time, but when push came to shove, his black belt in taekwondo was always a big help.

I got this man, the new kid yelled out to him before taking a punch to the face. Ethan couldn't help but smirk. The kid was obviously out of his elements. These guys could smell the brand-new rubber sole of the two-hundred-dollar Nike shoes he was wearing. There was no way they would have given up easily.

The kid threw a punch back and landed on Steve's chest, sending him to the floor, gasping for air. The new kid was actually holding his own and Ethan thought about letting it go for a while, but before Ethan could blink, Sammy broke a bottle on the kid's head, and he came tumbling down. The brothers took turns kicking him until the new kid couldn't do anything but curl into a ball.

Stop it! Ethan shouted.

Or what? Steve taunted.

Ethan grabbed Sammy by the neck and gave him a rear-naked choke hold. Steve was quick to the rescue, but Ethan quickly dropped Sammy to the ground, spun and gave Steve a palm strike to the nose.

Sammy staggered up. *Let's get outta here, man!*

Both ran off before the police showed up.

C'mon, he offered his hand to the new guy.

Where did you learn to do that? the guy asked as he staggered up, holding his busted lips.

Taekwondo Class.

Dang, man. You acted like Bruce Lee there for a minute. Impressive, the guy said, dabbing his bloody lips with his hand.

Here, have a seat, Ethan said as he went behind the bar. *You need this,* he said, handing the kid a beer and a bag of ice.

Thanks! I'm Oliver. What's your name?

Ethan.

Before the night was over, they were both laughing at something he couldn't even remember. Oliver Keon Rossi quickly became Ethan's best friend, college roommate, and business partner. He'd even spent a couple of holidays with the Rossi's, and there was one holiday he couldn't forget- the very first time he'd met the family.

So, Ethan, what are you plannin' to do after you graduate? Carlos Rossi, Oliver's Real Estate mogul dad, had asked him during a Thanksgiving dinner at their home one day.

I'm not sure yet, sir; I'm thinking about opening my own business, though, he told him as he studied the large white plate with gold trim in front of him. On top was a matching smaller plate, and on top of that was a matching soup bowl. Next to his dishes were gold utensils. He picked up a fork and thought, *who needed more than one fork to eat?* His eyes had wandered on the dark, long wooden table with a sparkling white runner in the middle. On the runner, lined multiple candles in different sizes inside a gold holder, and on one end, in the center, was a massive carving of ham next to a bowl of green beans, mashed potatoes, and a basket of bread. The other end was just as crowded with a bowl of stuffing, cranberry, several plates of various pumpkin and pecan pies, and a large bowl of salad next to a gigantic turkey on a silver platter. He had never been to a dinner like that before. Everything seemed glistening, from the silver platters to the crystal bowls.

Carlos Rossi continued to grill him about the kind of business he'd planned to open. Thank goodness, Oliver saved him from his father's interrogation.

You see this house, Ethan? The tall, well-built man with silver hair continued despite Oliver's protests. *This is all from hard work.* The man looked at Oliver, then to Adrian, Ol's brother. Ethan couldn't help but study what the man was wearing, a designer green golf shirt and tan slacks. He looked very confident and dignified, though by the way he was acting he wasn't sure about the latter.

You kids, these days, take your sweet little time to figure out what you want to do, Carlos said.

Dad, really? Oliver finally chimed in.

What? All I'm sayin' is that you guys should know what you want to do by now. I knew I wanted to be in Real Estate before entering the university and look where we are now.

Yes, Dad. You've told us several times, Oliver said, shaking his head at Ethan.

More wine? Eva, Oliver's mother, a retired interior decorator, offered as she stood and grabbed her own crystal wine glass. She wore a baby blue casual dress down to her knees with a simple thong sandal and diamond stud earrings. The woman, despite her age, looked young. She was at least five foot six. Well-dressed all the time, as he remembered. Her soft, pale skin complimented her ebony-colored hair, which she kept in a bun every time he'd seen her. She looked expensive without trying to look as such. Eva Rossi was beautiful and simple. She reminded him of his mom, not as expensive looking but beautiful and simple. She smiled at him, but Ethan could tell she was getting uncomfortable with her husband's grumbling. Watching the couple had made Ethan wonder what his parents would have been like if they had stayed together.

How's the divorce coming along, Adrian? Is your social climbing ex-wife still giving you a hard time? The old man's baritone voice got Ethan's attention back and watched Carlos take a swig of his favorite Jameson whisky before glancing at Adrian. There it was. He knew there was something off about Oliver's dad's attitude.

Adrian shook his head, as if he'd heard the question many times before.

Poor Adrian, he remembered thinking.

So, Caleb, how's residency going? Eva asked her youngest son.

Last Ethan knew, Caleb was finishing residency as an ER doctor in South Carolina.

Everything is great. Just busy trying to get through the hectic schedule, the youngest brother, who looked like a younger version of Oliver - dark hair, tall, skinny, with visible signs of sleepless nights, explained.

You've met Caleb, right, Ethan? Carlos questioned.

Yes, sir.

He's an ER doctor, he announced proudly.

He knows, Hon, Eva said, giving Ethan a faint smile. There was a hint of embarrassment in her eyes, but he could tell, she knew how to handle her husband.

The Rossi family dynamic was very interesting. It sure made him thankful he didn't have to deal with family drama like that.

Then there was Olivia. Olivia was a female version of Oliver. If he didn't know any better, he swore the two were twins, but Olivia was two years younger than Ol. He liked Olivia. She was beautiful and simple like her mom, but mostly because she stayed away from nonsensical conversations her family seemed to have.

Ethan was surprised he and Oliver had gotten along all these years, considering their opposite personalities. He was more of a loner, and Oliver was very outgoing. Ethan was on a partial scholarship, had to work while in school, and Oliver was a trust fund kid, but Oliver was cool and there was something about him he really liked. During their senior year, they both decided to take their Real Estate exams and not long after graduation R.P. & Associates was born.

Their office was on the fifteenth floor of a twenty-floor high-rise in downtown Sacramento. The front office was designed with an open floor plan and decorated in a minimalist way: white walls, black leather sofa, and large landscape photography art of the Sacramento skyline. Ethan nodded at the older lady at the front desk and headed straight to his office. He noticed the door was half open.

Sitting on the brown leather sofa, legs crossed, holding up a manila folder, Oliver asked, "Are you up for a drive?"

There was enthusiasm in his partner's voice.

"Nice hair, by the way," he added.

Ethan snatched the folder as he walked past him to his desk. "Is this what I think it is?"

Oliver snatched the folder back.

"Hey."

Oliver held up the folder and grinned like the Cheshire cat. He couldn't help but shake his head. Oliver was a month older than him, but sometimes acted like a juvenile. The idea of him turning thirty-five in a few months interrupted his thoughts. Dang, he's getting old. He glanced at Oliver, who was still grinning. He couldn't blame the guy for acting crazy today; this was a big contract for them. If the folder contained what he thought it did, he probably would act the same. He felt a surge of excitement as he pondered the possibility, but he also didn't want to get the carriage in front of the horse, so he pushed aside his feelings for now - it wasn't a done deal until everything was signed by all parties after all.

He watched Oliver grin from ear to ear, but despite his attempt to look goofy, his friend was far from looking as such. No matter what the man did, he always managed to look his best. It was at times annoying, especially when they were in college, knowing Oliver could shop for designer clothes whenever and wherever he wanted; he, on the other hand, had to save up to buy a single pair of jeans. His best friend had always been a GQ type, and today was no different. He wore dark denim jeans, a light gray sweater under a navy-blue jacket, and tan loafers. His jet-black hair suited him, no matter how he'd styled it. Today, he had it slicked back.

"Nice hair," he said.

"Touché'," Oliver leaned on the wall with his legs crossed, making him look a little shorter than his six-foot-three.

He thought of how charismatic Oliver had always been despite the aloof look he had tried so hard to portray. The fact he had attracted many girls in college, nice and promiscuous, made Ethan a little envious, but because he drew more of the latter, it had solidified his thoughts about him - a playboy who will never settle down. The idea made him feel better, especially knowing that Hannah was married to him and not Oliver.

"Lake Tahoe properties, baby. We got it, E."

Oliver's reverberating baritone voice made him snap out of his thoughts.

Oliver slammed the folder on the table before him. "The Bradley brothers finally came to their senses. They're selling both. Both condominiums, brother, both. We are going to Tahoe to seal the deal."

"I can't believe they finally caved. This is great," Ethan announced.

"You mean, after months of driving back and forth to Tahoe, listening to both families fight whether to sell or not, spending an exuberant amount of dollars on expensive liquors?" He paused. "By the way, those brothers did have great taste in whiskey, didn't they?" He smiled.

"They sure did. Still have the receipts if you'd like to see them." Ethan teased.

"Anyway, they better cave," Oliver said.

"Well, after the latest Jerry Springer fights their wives had, I didn't think they would ever come to a decision," Ethan suggested.

"But they did, brother. They did. All our hard work had paid off. So, what do you say?"

"Can't they sign all the papers electronically?" Ethan asked.

Oliver toyed with a pen with his fingers. "The brothers wanted to meet in person and discuss a few things."

He wanted this deal just as much as Oliver. He wanted to be there when the brothers picked up the pen and finally signed the properties over to RP & Associates, but he made dinner plans with Hannah. Finalizing the trip tonight was important to her. He knew she would understand if he told her about the acquisition; in fact, she would tell him to go, but he had put off finalizing their trip for so long. Despite wanting to be there to ensure they close the biggest contract of the year, he knew he had to let Oliver seal the deal without him.

Oliver stood, pulled the key card to his Tesla out of his pocket, and waved it in front of him, "I'll let you drive," he grinned.

He leaned back and rubbed his temples. "Man. I really want to, but—"

"Wait. Wait. Are you for real?" Oliver's grin faded.

"Man, listen—"

"Dude. We worked hard on this deal for *so* long. I can't believe you're bailing out on me now. C'mon E." Oliver paused as if to give him time to respond, but Oliver continued, "This is what we've been waiting for. I thought you and I could make it an overnight thing and celebrate."

"Sorry, man. I told Hannah I'd be home for dinner. She's expecting me to be home early."

Oliver began to pace in front of him. He waited for him to protest some more, but Oliver held his tongue when it came to Hannah. Still, he waited for him to blast him with guilt trips; instead, his partner sighed and moved on.

"I still don't get it. Why Virginia? Of all places. Why not Italy, Greece, or even Hawaii?" Now leaning over with his hands on his desk, Oliver smirked. "You sure know how to pick the place, Mr. *Romance*."

"She had been wanting to go back there for a while. Not sure if she mentioned it to you. She used to spend summers there as a kid."

Oliver nodded.

Ethan continued without glancing up. "She found this Airbnb called *Tranquility* or *Serenity* something that captivated her. She swears up and down that she had dreamed about this place before and she just *had* to stay there." He gave a faint smile. "And...check this out." This time, he glanced up. "...Apparently, they say that Virginia is for *lovers*. Did you even know that? Mr. *Romeo*?"

"It is?" he questioned, wrinkling his nose.

"Yeah, so to the state for lovers we go. She has a long list of places for us to check out. It should be interesting."

"Exciting," Oliver said, sarcastically.

"You know how Hannah can be. She makes all the plans, and I am just happy to follow."

"You bet I know how Hannah can be. She's got you trained," Oliver jested.

"Can you blame me?"

"Eh, I suppose you're right. You're just lucky I didn't go after her back then."

Did he hear regret in Oliver's tone? He pushed the thoughts aside; it's been five years.

"Ha. She wouldn't have dated you, Mr. *ladies*-man. You change women like you change cars. Even when we were in college."

Oliver burst into laughter as he straightened himself before picking up a paper from his desk and crumpling it in his hand.

"Whatever, man. I can't believe you." He rose and shook his head. "I'll call you when I get back from Tahoe. Maybe, *just* maybe, we'll celebrate then. If the *wife* allows you - that is."

Oliver tossed the crumpled paper at him on his way out.

He caught it.

"Sounds good," he said.

Oliver peeked through the door one more time. "I'll be in my office for a few minutes if you change your mind."

He nodded in return, but before he could get back to the papers in front of him, he heard Oliver say,

"Tell Hannah I said Hi."

Chapter Three

O liver sat behind his desk, thinking about the conversation he had just had with Ethan. *Why Virginia?* He knew exactly why. He and Hannah had had this conversation when they were in college. Whatever time he spent with Hannah was hard to forget.

They were at Brewed Awakening, their usual meeting place. *Are you going anywhere for the summer?* he had asked as they sat by the window with hot drinks on each hand. He placed them on the table before taking a seat. She took a cup and sat across from him. *I thought about going back to Virginia, where I used to spend summer as a kid.*

You spent summer in Virginia?

Yeah, why is that so surprising? She brought the hot chai tea to her lips and took a sip. The simplest movements she made affected him so much. He smiled. *So, what's in Virginia?*

My grandparents used to live there before they passed away. He could sense the sadness in her voice.

I'm sorry.

Thank you. She took another sip before continuing. *Papalo- I mean, my grandpa lived in Green Ridge, Virginia.*

He was a veterinarian there, while Mamala stayed home and took care of the farm.

Oliver took a sip of his coffee. *Farm as in with horses and such?*

She smiled. *Yeah, and such.* She gave a faint laugh. The laugh that could make any man go crazy.

She continued. *I used to play with pygmy goats. Have you petted a pygmy goat?*

I have not petted any type of goats. He beamed. *I can't imagine you on a farm, I don't know why.*

Why not? I loved it there. I even had a donkey---

A donkey?

Yes, Ol. A donkey. His name was Tyler.

He let out a big laugh. *Who calls their donkey Tyler?*

Me! That's who, she said. *I spent hours at Papalo's clinic pretending to be his assistant. It taught me a lot.*

So that's why you wanted to be a vet yourself.

Yeah. After taking care of sick pets, we would return home, and Mamala would have this sandwich she called flying saucer waiting for us.

He laughed at that, too. *Really Han? Flying saucer?*

Stop it! She teased.

I'm just kidding. He loved teasing Hannah. Every time he teased her, her cheeks would get red, then she would pout like a little girl, which he thought was so adorable. Everything she did was adorable.

I want to go back to Virginia but not by myself. I wouldn't know what to do with all the memories if I return there alone.

Hannah was strong. Confident, no doubt about it, but he could feel she needed someone to be there for her.

Tell you what. When you're ready, you tell me, and you and I will go.

You'll go to Virginia with me?

Yea, why not? I've never been on a farm before.

You promise? She said excitedly.

I promise.

He smiled at the remembrance of how delighted she was about him going to Virginia with her. It was the first time she hugged him, and he knew right then that Hannah was special - someone he would want to spend more time with. As time passed, he'd realized she was someone he'd wanted to spend the rest of his life with, and then Ethan came into the picture. Sure, he and Ethan met Hannah almost simultaneously, but he'd met her first. He remembered that day vividly.

Hannah had caught his attention as soon as she walked into Brewed Awakening. Oliver couldn't help but watch her every move like a love-struck teenager. He remembered how she talked, how she moved, the way she laughed, he even remembered what she wore that day - a long, peach floral dress with an off-white cardigan and beige sandals. Boy, was he hooked. He couldn't get his eyes off her. Who could? She approached and addressed a girl at his table he was studying with. She met his gaze and smiled. He smiled back.

Hi, Hannah! I didn't think you'd come. This is Oliver. Oliver, this is Hannah, my roommate, Oliver's classmate had introduced them.

He stood, shook her hand, and his heart started beating fast. Gosh, she was beautiful. After a few minutes, their friends left, and he and Hannah stayed back.

Are you hungry? Would you–would you like to go to dinner? He had asked her.

I'm famished. What are you thinking?

How about sushi?

I love sushi!

They seemed to have hit it off. They went to dinner that night, walked her to her dorm, and promised to see each other again the next day. He couldn't get her out of his mind that evening or any time since, for that matter. He couldn't wait for the next day to come. Hannah was pretty. She was funny and was very smart. As time passed, he got to know her more; the more he got to know her, the more he liked her. He was sure she liked him, too.

Oliver recalled the night he would have finally told her how he felt; he had just gotten out of class and was on the phone with his mother. It had been a few weeks since they first met. When he had finished his conversation with his mother, he'd decided to stop by the church. He put his phone on silent as he entered in case others were praying. After his visit, he remembered feeling good, like he finally had the courage to tell Hannah about his feelings, and then she called.

Hey, rain check? Something came up.

Something was off. He knew it. She did tell him she had some news. He didn't know whether it was good or bad, though. He later found out and wished he hadn't.

The weekend had passed, and they met at their usual meeting place.

Where were you? she asked as soon as she arrived. She seemed a little more perky than usual.

What are you talking about? he asked.

I called you last Friday and left a message.

You did? He grabbed the phone and checked. Sure enough, there was a notification. He started to listen to it, but she grabbed his phone away.

Never mind. That's not important. I met someone, she had told him.

What?

He knew what she'd said, but he didn't want to believe it.

I said, I met someone, she repeated. *I called you last Friday because I was invited to this party, but you never answered. You were probably with one of your girlfriends, so I went with some friends.*

Wait, what? What girls? he said, confused, still reeling from the '*I met someone*' comment.

I met this guy, and he asked me out on a date, she announced.

Wait, what? His heart spiraled down to his stomach. This could not be happening, he remembered thinking to himself.

She shook him. K - are you not listening?

I am... You met a guy. His heart sank as he uttered the words. What happened? He was supposed to tell her how he felt. Now, it was too late. That's what you get for waiting too long.

What's his name? He didn't care for the guy's name. Who was he kidding? He was supposed to confess his feelings.

His name is Ethan.

27

He held his breath, hoping it wasn't him. *Does this Ethan have a last name?*

She smiled. Yeah. Presten with an E. He never thought her sweet smile could ever break his heart.

His heart exploded, shattering into bits and pieces. It was all the confirmation he needed to want to strangle himself for waiting too long. His friend Ethan beat him to it. He could have sworn he told him about Hannah, or did he? It didn't matter. He was supposed to tell her how he felt. But he didn't.

Ethan and Hannah became inseparable as time passed, and being the third wheel was no fun. He wanted to keep his distance, but Hannah insisted for him to stay around. She even called him her best friend. *Best friend!* He didn't want to be a *best friend*; he wanted more. Oliver wanted to love her and for her to love him back. He was sure she had feelings for him, too. Was he wrong? He shook the memory away. Hannah is with Ethan now, and she's happy. That's all that mattered, or was it? In the past few months, his feelings for Hannah had become stronger. Again. Not sure when it came back. Well, it had never really gone away, had it?

He knew getting over her was too good to be true. He wasn't sure he would ever, not when he was invited to every gathering at the Presten's house and witnessed how amazing Hannah was. Still. Sure, he had been dating here and there and even brought dates to their BBQ one day, but who was he kidding? He knew all his relationships were a band-aid for his feelings for Hannah, but it had been five years; why was it becoming stronger and harder to fight now? He needed to move on. Really move on. She's married, for crying out loud. And to his best friend. It was the same song and dance he did in his mind for the past five years, but this time, he was serious. He needed to move on. That was it. He was over Hannah. Starting now. Again. He grabbed his cell phone and dialed.

"Finally," a lady he dated a couple of times answered at the first ring. She sounded annoyed. But he knew better. "What are you doing today?"

"Was just about to head to the gym. Why?"

"I'm heading to Tahoe in an hour. Wanna come?"

Silence.

"Are you there?" he said.

"Is this going to be one of those trips where you make me fall in love with you and those beautiful green eyes of yours then vanish without any explanation? Because if it is, I don't think I could go through that again," she said flatly.

"Beautiful green eyes?" He chuckled.

"Well?"

"I'm so sorry about that. Things just got busy at work and there were things I had to take care of, but I took care of it, and now I can move on."

"Move on?" There was doubt in her voice.

"With work. I can *move on* with work. In fact, that's what I'm doing in Tahoe. I have to meet a client and after that, we can do whatever we want. I promise not to make you fall in love with me again if that helps. What do you say? I can pick you up in twenty."

Again, silence.

He sighed, suddenly unsure whether he really wanted to pursue the situation, but he found himself moving forward. "Still there?"

"Yeah. Make it thirty."

Oliver was used to women not being able to say no to him. He just wished he had given Hannah the chance to do so. At least it would have been easier to move on.

Chapter Four

Ethan wondered if he should call Hannah and tell her about the acquisition. It wouldn't take long for him to catch up with Oliver. But he ended up responding to emails, updating listings and ending the day by putting together an offer for one of his clients before leaving the office. It was close to seven in the evening when he finally pulled into the garage and immediately took in the wafting scent of garlic bread. Hannah was in the kitchen in her blue sweatpants and white tank top. She had her hair up - relatively simpler than what she looked earlier - more beautiful, he thought. She stood behind the white granite counter, holding a pot of pasta and draining it over the sink. The aroma of tomato and garlic sauce made his stomach growl.

"Hey, you're home. Dinner is almost ready. Why don't you freshen up while I set the table," she announced without glancing up, tending to the steaming spaghetti noodles in front of her.

"I'll help you," he offered as he carried a bottle of wine in each hand and gave her a quick kiss on the lips.

"Wash your hands, young man."

"Yes, ma'am."

"Oh, and a half bottle of chardonnay is chilling in the bucket. You can put those on the rack for now."

"Aye, aye, Captain."

Hannah placed two platefuls of steaming noodles topped with marinara sauce on the table. Neatly plated on a white ceramic plate, garnished with a basil leaf on top, their meal looked like it came straight from an Italian cookbook. She dimmed the linear, geometrically shaped chandelier above the table, placed a basket of garlic bread in the center, and lit the two votive candles before taking off her apron and setting it on the counter. Ethan pulled a chair back for her to sit before claiming the seat across from her.

Twirling noodles with his fork, he started the conversation.

"So, tell me about...Tranqui-li-ty manor? Was it?"

"*Serenity Manor.*"

"Ah, *Serenity Manor*, that's what I meant. Did you decide on this one, then?"

"Yes. This *is* definitely the place. I wish my grandparents' house was still available, but this house is the closest I could get; it's practically pulling me in. Honestly, Ethan. I've seen this house in my dreams."

The twinkle in her eyes made him feel much better about his decision not to go to Tahoe.

"You miss your Papalo, don't you?"

She brought the wineglass to her lips and took a sip. "Very much. He was the only one who understood me as a child. Remember, I told you about my so-called imaginary friend?" she said.

"Jean."

"Yes. My cousins used to make fun of me, saying I was crazy and everything. One day, Papalo saw me crying after my cousins were teasing me about Jean. He pulled me to the side and asked me if I wanted to know a secret. Of course, I said yes."

Ethan smiled.

"He pulled me closer, wiped my tears, and said, 'Ignore your cousins. They do not understand you because they don't see what you see.' I asked him if he could see Jean, and he said he did once. He then told me that Jean was my guardian angel. Papalo had a way of making all of us grandchildren feel better. I knew he made the story up, but even so, it made me feel better."

He took another bite. "So, you don't believe in guardian angels?"

"Well, I do. To some extent, I suppose. I don't believe we can see them, like my grandfather said. God protects us in different ways and perhaps sends angels to guide us. Papalo used to say pets are angels sent by God. I don't know." She shrugged. "All I know is that ever since my grandfather said that about my imaginary friend, I've always felt like someone was watching over me. I even dreamed about her when I was little. Remember, I told you I spent days in the hospital when I was little with pneumonia?"

"Yeah."

"I dreamed about Jean, then."

"Maybe your Papalo was right. Jean could be your guardian angel and maybe *he* is watching over you like a guardian angel, too."

She shrugged again. "Maybe," she said between sips.

"I believe in guardian angels, you know," he said, almost sounding like a confession.

"You do?"

"Sure. Do I see them? No. But I think they exist. You know I was raised catholic, and we believe in guardian angels. My mom used to tell stories about St. Michael the archangel. She used to tell me that he was a protector. Whenever I was scared, she would always remind me of St. Michael."

She absentmindedly twirled the noodles with her fork, pondering what he'd just said. "But Papalo also made up stories to make his grandchildren laugh or to teach us lessons," she said, smiling at the memory, finally bringing the twisted noodles to her mouth.

"Well, I know one thing that's true," Ethan said as he stood from the table.

"Oh yeah? What's that?"

"I will always be watching over you."

Hannah chuckled. "How cheesy."

"What? I'm serious."

"So, you're my guardian angel?" she said, squinting her eyes.

He walked toward her with an empty plate in his hand. "I can be your *anything*, babe," he whispered and grinned as he leaned over for a kiss.

Chapter Five

September 15

They arrived at the airport for their six fifty-five morning flight and thirty minutes later, they were seated in their first-class seats.

"Comfortable?" Ethan asked.

"Yeah, I just need to adjust this vent above me. It's blowing right on my face," Hannah responded as she stood and twisted the knob above her.

When she sat back, he lifted his glass and proposed a toast. "Here's to our fifth anniversary and many more years to come." As their glasses clinked together, a deep male voice came through the speakers, introducing himself as the flight captain. Ethan often wondered if the pilots altered their voices to sound more like radio hosts. Finally, the pilot announced their flight time of four hours and thirty-nine minutes and something about the weather being smooth all the way.

Hannah caught his gaze.

"What?" she said.

Ethan stared at his wife. After five years, he still could not believe she married him. His whole life, he had to work for everything he wanted. Raised by a single mother, he was taught to work hard. He was taught not to settle for handouts. He was taught that if he wanted something, he had to work for it. His mother gave him extra chores as a little boy so he could earn some money to buy the things he wanted. Determined to go to business school someday, he worked hard in high school, earning mostly A's and B's, and ended up getting a partial scholarship in college. His mother taught him well. He worked hard for everything, and Hannah was the only thing that came easily for him. He parted from his thoughts and smiled. "How did I get so lucky?"

Not waiting for a response, he leaned in and claimed her lips. He wasn't one to show public affection, but sometimes, he couldn't help himself. Her response was intoxicating. She met his wandering tongue, joining his rhythm, tasting the champagne off their lips. He had forgotten where they were for a moment, only to be interrupted by the sudden jerk of the plane as it started to pull back.

He was lucky, indeed.

***

Hannah enjoyed viewing the majestic mountains' slopes from their rented 2020 Toyota Highlander. She knew Ethan chose the scenic route, knowing she would appreciate it. The drive was serene and beautiful as fall arrived early this year, turning the leaves into mesmerizing splashes of yellow, red, and orange. They reached Green Ridge in Rappahannock County and, just a few miles in, spotted a sign that said *Serenity*

Manor. They slowly entered the stonewalled entrance and drove along the pebbled driveway.

"This place is beautiful," Hannah said as she took in the vast expanse around her.

"Look to your right. I think those are the Blue Ridge Mountains," Ethan announced.

As they pulled into the parking space, a lady who looked to be in her mid-fifties stood in front of the two-story white house. Though the lady was younger, her short and silver-colored hair reminded her of her mother. She was by the garden, smiling and waiting in her casual black jeggings, oversized gray sweatshirt and white tennis shoes.

"Welcome to Serenity Manor," the lady said, revealing a small dimple on her right cheek.

"Hi. You must be Mrs. Clark," Hannah replied.

"The one and only. But please call me Sally."

"Hi, Sally. I'm Ethan. Nice to meet you."

"Nice to meet you, too. I hope the trip wasn't too tiring," Sally responded.

"Oh, no, not at all," he said, looking around the massive well-maintained lawn around them.

"The room is ready if you need to rest," Sally offered.

"I don't think we'll be resting any time soon. I want to show Ethan Green Ridge right away," Hannah said.

"So, you've been here before, I take it?"

"Well, I spent a few summers here. My grandparents used to live down the road. I haven't been back for a while, but I wanted to show Ethan where I spent most of my childhood. Lots have changed."

"Oh, plenty has changed," Sally agreed.

Ethan took the last suitcase from the back of the car and sat it down in front of them. "Did you live here all your life, Sally?"

"Oh no. I grew up near DC, but my grandparents lived here. We came to visit, but not very often. Not sure why, really, the place is beautiful."

Sally led them through an old mahogany door. A bright open foyer greeted them. In the center was an oval Persian rug with a mixture of maroon, black, and beige foliate designs. The walls were cream, with a white baseboard that complemented the white balusters on the staircase. To the right was a gray carpeted staircase with wooden handrails that perfectly matched the front door and the wooden floor. Elegant crystal chandeliers hung from the center of the high-vaulted ceiling, shimmering from the sunlight peeking through the tall bay windows. The colonial revival-style house took Hannah's breath away. The photos on the internet did not do justice to the place. They continued to follow Sally as she passed by a large sliding window overlooking the expansive woods outside. A movement caught her attention, stopping her on her track. She squinted her eyes to make out the figure.

"Are you liking the place?"

She jumped. "I'm sorry?" she asked, a little dazed.

"I'm sorry. I didn't mean to startle you," Sally said.

"It's okay, was just admiring the lawn and thought I saw movement by the trees out there," she pointed.

"Probably a deer or two. We have all kinds of animals lurking around here," Sally explained. "Don't worry. They rarely come any closer."

Hannah gave Sally a faint smile, but she could have sworn she saw *someone* - not *something*. She knew about wild animals lurking around, she used to try and feed them, till Papalo warned her about the danger. Hannah peeked through the window again, but no one was there. Who knew, maybe it was a wild animal after all.

Chapter Six

Virginia. The thought continued to haunt Oliver as he stood in his boxer shorts in the middle of his glass walled apartment suite. Luckily, he lived on the top floor. No one could see him even if he decided to walk around naked in his living room. Not that he would ever do that, not his style.

He paced around with a crystal rock glass in his hand and thought about how he should have been the one with Hannah going to Virginia, after all, he promised her and knew about her wishes to go there before Ethan ever did. Heck, he knew much more about her; he knew her desires, her wants and plans in life before Ethan ever did. Now, she shares all those with Ethan when it should have been with him. The thought infuriated him, but what could he do? Ethan was Hannah's husband now. Hannah's husband. He let the statement play in his mind as he walked to the bar and poured another shot of whiskey into his glass. Looking through the window, he continued his thoughts. The streets below were surprisingly quiet. To the right were a few people sunbathing by the pool. Absentmindedly, he swirled his drink, wondering what it would be like being Hannah's husband. Would they stay in this apartment? He imagined what it would have been like having her around. Oddly, the thought made his chest tight. The idea that it could never happen now sent him into a dark mood. He downed the whiskey before parting from his thoughts, walked to the living room, and picked up the TV remote before flopping onto the brown leather sofa. Oliver flipped through the channels, hoping to find something to take his mind off Hannah.

He switched channels within seconds, not even seeing what was on. Finally, he tossed the remote on the sofa, changed into his running clothes, and went downstairs. Nothing seemed to get his mind off Hannah lately. Running should do the trick. After an hour, he returned to his empty apartment, dripping in sweat, still thinking about her. Her smile. Her laugh. Her face. Hannah was all he could think about. He needed to get a grip. She was in Virginia with her husband. *Husband. Ethan.* Not him. He needed to snap out of it. It will never happen. He needed to accept that. He slid off his shorts and tossed it in the laundry basket, got in the shower and let the cold water wash away his frustrations. By the time he got in his clothes, it was already nine in the evening. What now? Dinner? He didn't feel like eating. Liquor? He already did that. On his bed was his phone. He pressed a button. "Hey, want to come to my place and stay the night?"

Chapter Seven

Green Ridge 2001

There were two girls roaming around his neighborhood lately. He'd never seen them before. *Vacationers*, his mother had told him. Like any other twelve-year-old boy in middle school, he'd been attracted to a couple of girls in school, but unlike those boys, he couldn't get the courage to talk to any of them. These girls were pretty, but not his type. He decided to ride his bike around and noticed that the girls were checking him out. It felt good.

His bike chain came loose, and he stumbled to the ground. "Dangit," he mumbled as he discreetly checked if the girls had witnessed his demise. He quickly got up and dusted himself off. The girls were coming his way.

"Are you okay?"

He nodded. He didn't look up.

"My name is Ressa, and this is my cousin Anne. What's your name?"

He didn't know whether he should answer or run away. His knees started to buckle, and his palms began to sweat. He shrugged, got on his knees, and continued to mess around with the loose bike chain in front of him.

Maybe he's shy, he heard one girl say.

Maybe he doesn't talk, the other one added.

He did a quick glance. The girls exchanged looks and giggled as they walked away.

He couldn't seem to place the chain back the way it was. Frustrated, he stood, brushed the black oil stain from his hand on his pants, and glanced around to see if the girls were still there. Another girl stood across the street. She smiled at him. She was pretty. His type. He wanted to talk to her. As he was about to cross the road, he heard his mom calling. He dropped his head down and walked his bike home instead.

The girl, whom he found out later was named Hannah, became friends with Ressa and Anne. He waved at Hannah every time he saw her. Not until the following summer did he finally have the guts to say something to her.

Hello. That was it. *Hello.*

Each year, he couldn't wait for summer to arrive. Hannah got prettier each time she visited, and he got more attracted to her each time he saw her. One day, she came to the ice cream shop where he worked.

"Hey, don't you live in my neighborhood?" Hannah asked. Her hazel brown eyes sparkled as she asked him the question.

He nodded in response.

She probably liked me, too, he thought.

He handed her the order. She smiled, thanked him, and started to walk away. "Hannah," he called out.

"Yes?"

Gosh, her eyes, her lips, and her neck, they were all screaming for him to caress them.

"Did you call my name?" she asked.

"Ah, yes." He gestured for her to wait as he removed his red apron and stepped out of the small, red wooden ice cream establishment with a huge ice cream cone on the roof.

"Can you cover for me really quick?" he asked another girl in the shop as he hung the apron on the hook by the door and stepped out.

His heart thudded. After stuttering for a few seconds, he finally told her his name.

"I was wondering if you would. Maybe. Uhm. I was wondering if you would want to---"

Just as he was about to utter the words, Ressa and Anne approached.

"Are you asking her out? That's cute," Ressa said.

The girls started laughing.

"What's going on?" A young man asked as he got out of his red car. "What's so funny?"

He knew the guy as Jody. He went to high school with him. Jody was probably a year or two younger than him. He was a popular kid in school. Blond, blue eyed and looked like he spent every waking moment at the gym. He was the typical football jock. In fact, he was the quarterback of their high school football team, but that's all that Jodi had to offer. He knew Jody was all looks, no brains. Jody wrapped his arm around Hannah and took a bite of her ice cream.

"I think he was just about to ask Hannah out," Ressa said.

"Wait, who's asking my girl out?" Jodi tightened his eyes.

"No one," Hannah said before the girls could say anything else. "C'mon, let's go," she nudged, but Jody didn't move.

Jody stood in front of him. He could smell his pizza breath.

"Are you asking my girl out? Who do you think you are?"

Hannah grabbed Jody's arm. "No one," she said, pulling Jody away without even looking at him. "Let's go!"

He watched them walk away, laughing. Something inside him churned. No one. Her last statement echoed in his brain. It was like a knife to his chest. The words lingered in his mind for years. Her words made him feel invisible.

He planned to talk to Hannah again, but she never returned to the shop. The following summer, Hannah did not come. One day, a For Sale sign was in front of Hannah's grandparents' lawn. *Excuse me, ma'am, do you know where they moved?* He had asked the lady who placed the sign there.

Sorry, kid. I don't have any idea.

He went home angry. Frustrated. Cheated. He slumped onto his unmade bed and glared at the wall. *I will find you, Hannah. Even if it's the last thing I'd do. I will find you*; he said, admiring her photos.

✳✳✳

Years had passed and now he was married to Angela; a young woman he'd met in Roanoke during a job hunting one year. Still, he could not get Hannah off his mind. The twinkle in her eyes, her sweet smile, her beautiful cheekbones, he continued to crave them for years. His heart longed for her until he remembered her last words: *no one*. She thought of him as *no one*. How humiliating! Maybe he shouldn't think about her anymore now that he was married. He tried, but he just couldn't help himself.

One day, he stood inside a deli shop in town waiting for his sandwich. There were a few people in the shop, including a pregnant lady next to him.

"Hey, aren't you the guy who used to work at the old ice cream shop across the street?"

"Yeah, that was me." Who was this woman?

"I'm Anne. I used to live in your neighborhood."

He thought for a while, then smiled. "Oh yeah, I remember you. You're Hannah's friend, right?"

"Yeah. Wow, you look different," she said.

"Good, I hope," he answered confidently.

Anne smiled. If she wasn't pregnant, he would think she was flirting with him.

"Definitely. You must live in the gym nowadays. You look great!"

Yeah, she *was* flirting with him. He smiled back. "How's Hannah?"

"Oh, we haven't really kept up, but last I heard was that she just got married to a guy she went to college with, I think his name was Ethan Presten and she now has a veterinary clinic in California."

"Wow, she followed her grandfather's footsteps," he said.

"She sure did."

"Where in California?" he said, hoping not to sound too eager.

She squinted as if trying to recall. "Sacramento, I think."

He grinned deep inside. The universe had just given him another chance. Life was funny that way. *Sacramento, California*, he said in his mind. Right there and then he decided he would move there; there, he would make *Dr. Hannah Presten* pay for humiliating him all these years. Next thing he had to do was google her to find out exactly where she was.

Chapter Eight

"This house is gorgeous, Sally," Hannah said after taking in the beauty of Serenity Manor.

"Thank you," Sally replied, glancing around as if to admire her own house.

"Your website said the house is almost a hundred years old. I didn't expect it to be this modern, and honestly, I don't remember seeing this house here before."

"My parents died a few years ago and left this house for my children and me, and since my divorce a couple of years back, I decided to move back here from DC. However, the place was too big for me, so my kids suggested making it into an Airbnb. I try to make renovations here and there without changing the house's original structure. Trying to keep the nostalgia alive, I suppose. It sure kept me busy throughout the years," Sally said.

Hannah expressed some tenderness in her smile. "It's beautiful. I can't wait to see the rest of the property."

"Why don't I show you guys your room so you can drop all your belongings? Then we'll continue the tour?"

Just as they were about to head upstairs, a young lady walked in.

"There you are. This is Ethan and Hannah. Our guests for the week. This is my daughter, Nichole."

Nichole smiled. She tucked a piece of loose brown curl behind her ears before reaching out to shake their hands. Hannah guessed she was about her height, though she looked much younger. She wore ripped jeans, a white sweatshirt, and a pair of white sneakers. A few freckles were visible on Nicole's cheeks that somehow accentuated her light brown eyes. She was quite attractive, though she seemed timid, Hannah thought. Something inside her churned, and her longing for a sister came back. If she had one, she'd envisioned her to look like Nichole.

"I was about to show them their room, then finish their tour," Sally told her daughter.

"I can do that, Mom," Nichole said, revealing the same dimple her mother had; only hers was on the left cheek.

"Alright, I have a pie in the oven, anyhow. It should be ready by the time you guys get back," Sally said before shifting her attention back to them. "By the way, the last guests left yesterday, and the next ones are not arriving 'till next week, so the whole place is yours for the weekend."

Ethan beamed at her. "Wow, how did we get so lucky?" He winked.

Hannah gestured for him to behave.

Ethan reached for her hand, and they followed Nichole as she headed for the stairs. When they reached the landing upstairs, Hannah was so enthralled by the place that she hadn't realized she had let go of his hand and stopped following. She looked over the railing and continued to appreciate the house's grandeur from above. The foyer below was more captivating from where she stood now.

Her thoughts were interrupted when suddenly, a silhouette caught her peripheral vision. She diverted her attention to the door and blinked, trying to see through the blurriness of the rain glass door. When her eyes readjusted, whoever it was was gone. Something was ominous about this place, but it could also just be her imagination. Maybe it was just the unfamiliarity of the home. After all, it was an old house. She brushed the thought aside as her eyes drifted to the intricate designs and structure of the old mahogany door.

"Babe, you did good," Ethan announced.

"Oh, my goodness. You —"

"A bit jumpy, are we?"

She turned to face him completely. "Don't sneak up on me like that. You scared me."

"Sorry. What captivated your attention?"

"Everything"

"What was so scary?"

"Must be this ginormous house," she said, wrapping Ethan's arms around her as she continued admiring the space below. "Can you believe this place? It's beautiful, isn't it? The photos on the website did *not* do it justice *at all*. This is pretty amazing."

"It definitely is," he said, kissing the back of her neck. "Now, let's see the primary bedroom, shall we?"

She was excited for Ethan to see the room away from the others; he liked his privacy. It was a bit pricey, but she knew it would be worth it. Although, it didn't matter now that they had the place *all* to themselves - at least for the weekend. They walked through the short hallway that led to a double door at the end.

Ethan grinned when he saw where the room was situated. "You know me too well, Mrs. Presten."

Hannah smiled at his boyish smirk as she thought of what Mamala would have said to her: *well done, An-An.* The thought made her smile.

You have to be submissive to your husband, my dear. You need to know what makes him happy and ensure you try to accomplish that, Mamala used to say every time they talked about her getting married. *Yes, Mamala. Just like what you've done with Papalo, right?* She agreed with her grandmother to some extent and had tried to do what she had suggested, but Ethan wouldn't have any of it. Hannah learned that early in their marriage. *It is my job to serve you,* he'd told her once, so she made sure to be sensitive to his likes and dislikes and try to make him happy in other ways.

Remembering Mamala made her miss her grandparents a lot, especially Papalo. She knew he would have loved Ethan. He would have asked Ethan to tackle him so he could show him his Tae Kwon Do training and tell him *Don't mess with my granddaughter or else* like he warned every other guy who courted anyone in their family. Papalo loved to jest and make the suitors uncomfortable, but it was all a joke to him. He only did it to the guys he liked.

Nichole stood by another door, waiting as they entered the double doors. Fresh-cut grass wafted in the air as they entered the bedroom. The balcony door was wide open. She glanced around the room before entering, and even though it was her first time in the house, a feeling of nostalgia came over her. She entered and dropped her purse on the distressed, gray, pine king-size bed as she admired the rest of the area. On each side were two matching white wooden end tables. She grazed the massive bed, neatly covered with a white quilt detailed with embroidered flowers. Above the headboard was a framed photo of an old house next to a small lake. *Serenity,* she read quietly.

"This house I remember. I think," Hannah said as Ethan stood next to her.

"Wow, they made a lot of improvements."

"Still breathtaking," she said.

Ethan slipped his hand in hers and gently pulled her toward the balcony. The scent of fresh-cut grass was now more emphasized. In the distance was a man mowing the lawn. It must have been the guy she thought she had seen through the window and at the door earlier. She felt better knowing it wasn't some psycho lurking around. Breaking from her thoughts, she took in the expansive view before her, savoring the moment with her husband.

***

He heard Serenity Manor was expecting the couple to check in today, he'd already been there twice earlier to check if they had arrived. There was no way he would miss their arrival. Glancing at the cracked clock on his dashboard, trying to make out the time: 11:23 a.m. Who would have thought that it would all come back to where it all started - Green Ridge? Moving to Sacramento a few years before allowed him some time to follow Hannah and watch her every move. It didn't take long to find her, thanks to google. He had even stopped by her clinic several times, but she didn't recognize him. How sad. Maybe if she had acknowledged him, he would have changed his mind. But then again, maybe not. He left California thinking he would move on, but what were the odds that the universe would bring Hannah back to where it all started? Her last words: *no one,* echoed in the air like a mockingbird who lost its mate at night.

"I *am* someone, Hannah. I'll show you."

His co-workers would soon realize he'd been gone for a while. If not for that, he would sit there till they arrived, which meant he would have to return, but not much later, *that's* for sure. Missing their arrival was out of the question. He threw the binoculars he was holding on the passenger seat and picked up the stainless-steel tumbler from the cup holder. The hot coffee he poured this morning was now tepid. He didn't mind. He drank it and grinned before putting his car in reverse. The anticipation made him excited and nervous at the same time.

"I'll see you soon."

Chapter Nine

Somewhere in Rappahannock County, Virginia.

He couldn't wait to get out of work. He glanced at his watch; it was precisely three-thirty. He got in his car and was on his way back to check if the couple had arrived. He wasn't even past the driveway when he noticed a red flash on his dashboard. "Dang It." His gas gauge was below empty. Good thing the gas station was only a half mile away. After a few minutes, he pulled into the station and rushed inside. The store was quiet. A heavy-set young lady who always tried to flirt with him was behind the counter, talking to an older lady. They're gossiping again, as usual, he thought to himself. He overheard the conversation as he approached the counter to pay.

"I spoke to Sally earlier, and she told me the couple couldn't get their hands off each other. They must be on their honeymoon or something." The older woman was giddy as she described the couple's arrival.

Serenity Manor's visitors were always the talk of the town: *How many were staying there now? Where were they from? Were they friendly, and how did they look?*

The older lady left with a box of milk as he approached the counter. The attendant started twirling her blond hair. *Great.* Her eyes lit up like a star struck teenager.

"Hi, there," she greeted him with anticipation.

"Hi." He forced a smile but ignored her flirtatious vibes as usual. "Twenty on pump three," he said, handing her a fifty-dollar bill. He avoided using credit cards as much as possible.

"Sure thang," she replied.

Did she just bat her lashes at him? *Oh God*, the image made him shiver. He quickly decided to change the subject before the flirting went any further. "So, another couple is staying at the big house, huh?"

Still twirling her hair, she leaned forward, revealing her unsightly, pimple blotched cleavage, handing him his change. "Yes," she said with much enthusiasm. "A couple on their honeymoon is what I heard. Isn't that sweet?"

Sweet? Right. He didn't mind Jody then, why would he mind the husband now? But something deep inside him made him jealous.

She leaned forward some more. He could smell the cheap perfume she just sprayed on herself. "I would love to stay at the manor with someone someday," she announced.

He coughed, trying to discreetly wave away the offensive scent in front of him. "Is the Manor full? Or are there—"

"Nichole told me the last guests left a couple of days ago or last week, was it?" She paused, as if trying to recall. "*Anyhow*, all I know is that the new couple is so lucky to have the place all to themselves for the weekend. It's so romantic."

Perfect.

"Are you heading home? I'm off in a few. Maybe we could—"

"Sorry, gotta go. I'm in a hurry."

Obvious disappointment plastered on the attendant's face, but it didn't deter her enthusiasm. "Maybe next time, then?" she yelled out as he was reaching for the door.

He raised his hand in response and dashed out. Her giggle echoed behind him. So much for avoiding the bait. He arrived at his usual spot and peeked through his binoculars just as the couple walked out of the main bedroom and onto the balcony, holding hands. Something inside him wanted to explode.

She doesn't deserve you.

***

Hannah and Ethan stood on the balcony, taking in the majesty of the place before them. On their right was the lake, enveloped by two beautiful red maple trees.

Ethan let go of her hand and wrapped an arm around her waist. "Maybe we could swim in the lake tonight," he said.

"Are you kidding? Do you know how cold that water would be?"

"I'll warm you up. Remember, we have the whole place to ourselves," he said, as he pulled her closer and kissed her.

She was just about to shut her eyes when a movement caught her attention, making her jerk away. "Did you see that?"

"See what?"

"I thought I saw someone run behind those trees." She pointed toward the massive area across the lake.

"Hun, you really need to stop reading those thriller novels every night. I think it's making you paranoid."

"I swear I saw something. *No*, someone."

"I'm sure there are wild animals around here. A fox? A deer? Perhaps it's ---"

"I'm sorry to interrupt, but would you guys want something to drink before seeing the rest of the property? Nichole said, putting a halt to Hannah's thoughts.

Ethan turned to face Nichole, who stood inside the room. "Sorry, Nichole. Hannah thought she saw something or *someone* behind those trees."

"Oh, sometimes a family of deer lurks around here — Look. There's one right there," she said as a fawn peered through the forest area.

"See, it was a deer. Come on, Hun."

She saw the deer, but she remained unconvinced. But then again, it was just a glimpse. Now she wasn't sure. She peered back toward the wooded area, but it was gone. Whatever it was.

***

Thirty minutes later, they returned from their tour. The inviting scent of fresh-baked apple pie in the air welcomed them as they entered the kitchen.

"Just in time," Sally announced. "Hot apple pie with vanilla ice cream topped with homemade whipped cream is to die for," she added proudly. She pulled a chair and gestured for Hannah to sit. Ethan took the seat next to her.

"This looks delicious, Mrs. Clark," Ethan said.

"Sally. Please call me Sally."

"Nichole, why don't you join us?" Hannah gestured for her to sit next to them.

"Go ahead, honey, sit, and I'll give you a slice," Sally said.

The side door opened and a skinny young man in dark jeans, a white sweatshirt, and a red hat peeked through the door. His cheeks were flushed like he'd been under the sun all day.

Sally frowned. "Where have you been?"

The kid entered the kitchen with his eyes fixed on Hannah.

Ethan would have taken offense at his gawking, but he immediately saw a replica of Nichole standing before him and quickly realized who the young man was. He even had the same dimple Nichole had.

"This is my son, Dillon. These are the Prestens." Sally gestured towards them.

"He was supposed to be here earlier helping you guys with your luggage."

"Sorry, mama. I got caught doing something outside," he mumbled, eyes still fixed on Hannah.

"It's not polite to stare," Nichole finally said.

He lowered his gaze as if to realize the mistake he had made and quickly apologized, "I'm sorry. I didn't mean to. You just... You just look so much like someone I knew."

Hannah smiled. "It's okay."

"You have twins," Ethan said, directing the question at Sally.

Dillon took his hat off and turned on the faucet to wash his hands. "Unfortunately," he responded jokingly. He rolled his eyes at his sister, dried his hands before extending to shake Ethan's. "I'm sorry about the staring, sir. I'm Dillon. It's nice to meet you."

Ethan smiled. "It's all good. She's a beautiful woman; I'm used to it. I'm Ethan, and this is my wife, Hannah," he said, patting him on the back. Ethan picked up his plate and was about to pick up Hannah's when Dillon suddenly rushed to take the dishes from him and a twig fell on the table as he was reaching over.

"Are you roaming the woods again?" Nichole said with a smirk.

"No." Dillon snapped, then softened his tone, as if realizing they had company. "I don't roam the woods, Nichole. I look for birds," he said.

"Dillon likes to take photos of wild animals. He took that photo right there," Sally interjected, pointing at the framed photo of a family of deer on the wall.

"Impressive," Ethan said.

"Maybe it was you I saw moving around the woods earlier, then?"

Dillon returned his eyes to Hannah. "It's possible," he replied, the color leaving his face.

"You know, I convinced these two to start their own lives after college, but after my divorce, they insisted on helping me run the manor," Sally tried to conceal her emotions, but Ethan could see how proud she was of her kids.

"As much as I wanted them to get out there on their own, I'm glad they're here to help me run the place."

"Mama, our time will come. But, for now, we're here to help," Dillon said.

Hannah smiled. She thought of her mother. She missed her a lot. "That's so sweet. Not too many kids would think about helping their mothers nowadays."

"I am blessed, that's for sure. Even though we have a few staff in the manor, having a family run the place with me is better. "

Ethan stood from the table. "Thank you for the delicious pie, Sally. I think we'll get settled in our room before we drive around," he said.

"You're very welcome. We will head out as soon as we're done cleaning up. If you need anything, *anything* at all, you have our numbers. Or you could always stop by the house. We're just next door. Breakfast at seven," Sally replied.

Chapter Ten

Earlier in the afternoon, Dillon had suggested a few places for them to visit, and they decided to check out a pub downtown about fifteen minutes away from Serenity Manor. Hannah wore skinny jeans with a brown sweater and beige flats and placed her hair in a ponytail while Ethan slipped into his light denim jeans, paired with an olive-green shirt. He had just gotten a haircut before the trip, sides faded, and short on top, so he added a little gel, ran his fingers through it, making it wispy. He put on his brown suede sneakers before grabbing a black leather jacket, laying it on the bed and sat waiting for Hannah to finish getting ready.

"All day? And he never said where he would be. That's odd. Why don't you call me back when you hear from him?" Ethan said on the phone as he glanced at his watch. It was quarter to six, making it three o'clock in the afternoon in Sacramento. Shaking his head, he hung up and planned to call Oliver.

Hannah took in the confused look on her husband's face. "What's going on?"

"Sylvia said Ol never showed up for work today and told her to forward all his calls.

"That's odd."

"Yeah, that's what I said."

"Well, he probably had something important to do," Hannah reassured Ethan as she faced the mirror, dabbing on a little lip gloss.

"Yeah, maybe you're right. I'll try to call just in case."

He punched in Oliver's number.

"Voicemail," he said. "Hey, it's E. Call me back."

Ethan placed his phone in his back pocket, stood behind Hannah, and wrapped his arms around her. "You about ready?"

"Yes," she said as she turned around to face him. "Before I forget, let's check out my grandparent's old property tomorrow. Maybe we could ask to have a quick glance."

"Sure. Do you think they'll let us see it?"

"People here are nice. If I tell the new owners who we are, I'm sure they'll let us see the house."

"If you say so. It would help if we asked Sally who the new owners are. I'm sure she would know."

"Great idea! I know I married you for a reason."

He grabbed and gently kissed her, making sure not to mess up the lip gloss she had just applied.

The hell with the lip gloss. He pressed her harder into him and kissed her deeply.

***

Through his binoculars, he could see Hannah was just as beautiful as the first time they'd met; too bad she was heartless. He studied the man next to her. What was so special about this guy, anyway? His thoughts brought him back to Jody, what did Jody have that he didn't? He zoomed in, hoping to catch a clearer view of the man's face. He was good looking, very affectionate, but so was he. At least that's what his mom told him and believed her until Hannah called him: *No one.*

"She doesn't deserve you," he muttered. Just when he was about to zoom in on Hannah again, she turned, went inside the room, and pulled the curtains closed.

"Damn it." He groaned, slamming his hand on the dashboard as he took his hat off and threw it in the backseat. His breathing accelerated as his anger rose. Remembering the technique he'd learned from his therapist, he took a deep breath and tried to calm himself down. If there's one thing he took away from the overpaid shrink, it's breathing and counting backward from ten to control his anger. He grinned, exhaled, and peeked back through his binoculars.

"Wanna play? Let's play."

He tossed the binoculars on the passenger seat.

"I'll see you soon, honey."

He glanced around, making sure the path he'd made by the abandoned property behind the manor was clear before driving off. He drove with his windows down, enjoying the fall sunset that magnified the beautiful combination of red, yellow, and orange glowing from the trees surrounding him. Blasting and rocking to the sound of Kansas "*Carry on My Wayward Son,*" he felt the vibration from the road. He pressed harder on the gas pedal, singing and playing drums on his steering wheel as he drove away, thinking of the next time he'd see Hannah. The thought got him excited. Then, just as he was about to change lanes, he glanced at his rearview mirror, and there it was... blue lights flashing behind him. "Crap." *How long has he been there?* He slowed, pulled to the side of the road, and lowered his window. A young state trooper in a dark blue uniform approached.

"License and registration, please," the officer commanded.

"What seems to be the problem, officer?" he asked as he rummaged through the untidy glove compartment, trying to act as calmly as possible. When he finally found what he was looking for, he handed the cop a crumpled paper with his driver's license.

"I clocked you at sixty-five in a forty-five zone," the officer informed him as he examined the documents he had given him. "Looks like you've been traveling. Are you here on vacation?"

Vacation? Why would he think I'm on vacation? Suddenly, it dawned on him that the car registration was not in Virginia. He quickly thought of an answer. "Actually, I just moved back here," he said.

The officer glanced at the paper in his hand and then looked at him. He wondered if the officer recognized him. His heart started to thud a bit, but to his surprise, the trooper handed the paper and driver's license back to him.

"I'll let you go with a warning this time," he announced.

Relieved that he didn't get a ticket, he thanked the state trooper. He was about to push the button to roll up the window, but the officer had not moved. Had he changed his mind? Sixty-five on a forty-five would certainly earn him a ticket. Not what he needed right now. Nervous and slightly annoyed, he asked, "Anything else, officer?"

"Yes. Slow down. You're not in California anymore."

Chapter Eleven

The clock on the dashboard showed 6:43 p.m. when Ethan pulled into the parking lot of Royal Pub.

"The lot looks full," Hannah said.

A car pulled out of its spot and Ethan immediately flicked his turn signal on and waited for the car to back up. The pub looked like an abandoned industrial building with its red brick exterior and a glowing yellow sign on top that flashed *Royal Pub.* Downtown was quaint but very much alive.

"The place looks busy for a Wednesday night," Ethan said as he parked the SUV.

A few young men were roughhousing as they walked toward the entrance, so Ethan rushed to Hannah's side as he exited the car, reaching for her hand. "Stay next to me," he muttered, putting his arm around her.

"I'm okay," she said.

"I know, but just in case, stay close."

"Look who's paranoid... but thank you." She gave a small smile.

Hannah clasped his hand as they walked toward the pub's entrance. The place was packed. Laughter and chatter from every corner reverberated throughout the room. Luke Combs'

"Honky Tonk Highway" blasted in the background as they stepped in. Everyone seemed to be enjoying their time.

"Maybe we should have made a reservation," Hannah said, glancing around and stepping aside as more people came in behind them. "Should we wait here, or should we just go in and look for a table?"

"Let's give it a few minutes," he said.

A blonde-haired hostess approached. She wore tight jeans and a red T-shirt with the restaurant's logo on the right chest.

"Hi, there. Sorry for the wait. Table for two?"

"Yes, please," Ethan answered as he gently pulled Hannah next to him.

The hostess grabbed the menus from behind the counter. "Please follow me." She took a quick glance at Hannah and smiled. "That's a nice sweater you're wearing, Hun," she said.

As the hostess led them to their table, she and Hannah talked about sweaters and blouses as if they'd known each other for quite some time. He wasn't surprise; Hannah was always that friendly to everyone. The hostess stopped in front of a round table in the corner by the glass window where two bar stools stood empty.

Hannah pulled the wooden stool and sat, crossing her leg over the other. She glanced out the window as laughter erupted. Outside was a covered patio with a few more occupied tables. A few steps down, to what she assumed was an artificial grass turf, were a group of people who seemed to be having fun watching each other take turns tossing bean bags into a hole in a wooden platform.

"What's the name of that game?" Hannah asked.

"Corn hole. You play?" The hostess said.

"Oh gosh, no, but I'd like to try one of these days."

"Server will be with you in a moment. Enjoy." The hostess said before walking away, swaying now to Keith Urban and Carrie Underwood's *"Fighter."*

Hannah continued to take in the pub's atmosphere, nodding her head to the beat of the music. Ethan wasn't surprised. On their second date, he discovered that his California goddess loved country music. Ethan had never listened to a single country song until he started dating Hannah in college. To his surprise, he learned to like country music, too. He grew to love it, in fact.

"Keith Urban," he said.

"Great job." Hannah grinned and patted him on the shoulder.

Hannah ordered a Chardonnay while Ethan tried one of the IPAs everyone was raving about in the reviews. As the night went on, Hannah talked louder, faster, and with more hand gestures. He knew it was time to switch to water, remembering their first meeting.

Luke Combs' *"Beautiful Crazy"* played in the background. He glanced at his wife. *God, she's beautiful.* He couldn't help but think of how madly in love he was with this woman after all these years.

With a wide grin, Hannah reached for his hands and started singing. Hannah could sing, but he knew it was time to go.

When they arrived at the manor, he led Hannah toward the lawn. There were a few lit lamp posts lined up heading toward the pavilion. Yellow light was bouncing off the pavement leading to the lake ahead. The lake was still, and the woods were silent as if the whole place awaited them. It was a gorgeous night, especially with stars filling the sky like sparkling dust, and the moon, not quite complete, also released enough light, adding romance to the night. He turned to Hannah, squeezed her hand, and stared deeply into her eyes.

His wife blushed.

He gently touched her face. "Are you okay?"

"Yeah, just remembered what you said earlier...about swimming in the lake," she smiled, blushing some more.

"Don't worry, I'm not going to take advantage of you, Mrs. Presten," he said as they reached the pavilion. They sat on the black wrought-iron bench beside the matching lamp post. For a few minutes, they watched the lake in silence.

"This place is gorgeous," Hannah said, breaking the stillness between them. She laid her head on his shoulder.

"Are you sure you're okay? You're not feeling woozy?"

"I'm sure," burying her head deeper into his shoulder.

Ethan pulled away.

She knitted her brows together as she lifted her head "What's wrong?"

He held her face with both hands. "Nothing at all."

Her eyes sparkled under the moonlight, and he could feel the burning passion emanating from his body. He leaned in to kiss her, and she welcomed him by parting her mouth slightly, letting him explore. The floral scent from her hair wafted in the air, merging with the fresh scent of the breeze as he pulled her closer; he couldn't help but deepen the kiss as if there was no tomorrow. Hannah reciprocated his every move. She met his passion as he gently caressed the back of her head.

She inched away and unbuttoned her blouse, not removing her gaze from his piercing blue eyes. He immediately stopped her. "No, not here, sweetheart." He loved that she was always ready to give, but he wasn't going to make love to her in the open. Not his style. Hannah was a giving person, that's for sure, and he loved that about her, but these traits also made his wife vulnerable. The thought made him clench. Hannah had had her share of people taking advantage of her, and he needed to make sure she knew how much he respected her as his wife. As a woman. He gently kissed her neck, lifted her, and carried her back to the house.

The next day, Hannah woke with the alarm. Still groggy, she reached for Ethan, only to feel the cold and empty space beside her. The shower was on. She picked up her phone to check the time; it was just a few minutes after six. *Breakfast at seven;* remembering what Sally told them earlier, she sat up and did a quick leg stretch when she heard the shower shut off. She pulled the white robe from the chair beside the bed and flushed, remembering what had happened the night before as she saw their clothing sprawled all over the room.

"Not so fast, Mrs. Presten," Ethan said as he pushed her back onto the bed. He kissed her forehead and her nose before claiming her mouth. His tousled blond hair dripped water all over her face.

"Hey!" she grumbled, but Ethan ignored her half-hearted protest, so she pulled him closer, wrapped her legs around him, and gently bit him on the neck, taking in his floral scent. His wet body glistened from the sun shining through the window.

She ran her fingernails through his body and played with a few strands on his well-sculpted chest.

"You smell good," she mumbled, kissing his neck.

"I used your body wash."

"I can tell."

"Do I feel silky smooth?" he chuckled under his breath.

"You sure do. You know there's soap and shampoo in the bathroom, right?"

"Yeah, but yours smells better, " he said, eyes shut, savoring her little nibbles on his neck.

Hannah could feel Ethan's body tensed through her slightly parted robe. She glanced at the clock on the side table and decided she didn't care what time it was. Before he could even protest, not that he would, his towel was already off his body. He stared at her smiling, and she gave her husband a devilish look. Hannah didn't have to say a word. Ethan was ready and quickly took over the situation, untying her robe and kissing her shoulders. He took his time nibbling on her neck, before slowly turning her on her stomach. He traced his fingers up and down her spine and kissed her sensitive back, sending chills all over her body. Hannah was lost in his touch. As usual. She whimpered each time his hot lips touched any part of her body. Their connection was strong. Deep. Ethan took one look at her and knew she was ready. He entered her gently and made love to her. She cried as she felt their bodies and souls collide. She could feel his passion in each thrust, in each move. In each breath he took. It was mind-blowing, earth-shattering, nerve-pulsing love. She couldn't help but let some tears fall. This man loved her, and she loved him.

Chapter Twelve

Sally and the twins were in the kitchen, tucked in the back of the house, when he and Hannah finally walked in. The kitchen was a good size. A long, rectangular, light-grained counter with a white marble top sat in the middle. On the other side was a farmer's sink where Nichole stood cleaning dishes. Sally was in front of the stove, flipping pancakes.

As they came closer, the mixture of bacon and pancake permeated the room. A plate of bacon, a bowl of assorted fruits, croissants, a pitcher of orange juice, and neatly plated sliced bread were on the table. A bouquet of mixed-colored tulips was the centerpiece.

Nichole walked to the table with a coffeepot in her hand. "Good morning," she said.

"Good morning! Smells good in here. We thought we were gonna miss breakfast," Ethan announced. He glanced at Hannah and grinned. "Hannah slept in," he added. He winked at her before pulling a chair for her to sit on.

"Is there something we can do to help?" Hannah offered.

"You're here on vacation. Leave meal preparation to us. Did you reheat the coffee, Nichole?"

"No, I made a fresh batch," the daughter replied.

71

"How would you like your eggs?" Sally asked, but before she or Ethan could answer, Sally added, "You two need to eat a substantial breakfast this morning. I'm sure you need to replenish your energy."

"Mom!" the twins shrieked in unison.

Dillon shook his head as he carried a plate of muffins to the table. "Please excuse our mother. Sometimes, she thinks she's being funny."

He and Hannah exchanged looks and smiled.

"What? I only meant they needed the energy for their adventure. Didn't you say you will be sightseeing today?" Sally said, not looking up as she continued flipping pancakes.

"Yes, we thought about checking out a couple of hiking trails," Hannah said.

Sally walked around the kitchen counter and placed a plate of pancakes on the table. "You two need to get your minds out of the gutter," Sally addressed her kids.

Ethan brought the white mug to his lips and sipped the hot coffee. "By the way, Sally. Do you know the family at 98 Chonokis Road?"

"Yes, why do you ask? Is that your grandfather's old house?" Sally turned her attention to Hannah.

"Yes, it was."

"That's Karen's house, isn't it?" Nichole looked at her brother.

"Yes, that's the Jensen's house," Dillon said. "Your grandfather used to own that house?"

"Yes, I used to spend summers there before. Who's Karen?" Hannah said.

"A girl I went to High School with," Dillon replied.

"More like the girl who broke Dillon's heart," Nichole added.

Her brother just rolled his eyes.

"Do you think they'll let us in?" Hannah said.

"I don't see why not. I'll call Mrs. Jensen. I'm sure she'll be glad to show you your old grandfather's home," Sally said smiling.

"Thank you! We would appreciate that," Hannah said.

His wife needed this. He hoped Sally was right and Mrs. Jensen would let them in. The vacation would be a memorable one if Hannah could at least see her Papalo's farm. He glanced at her innocent face as she took a bite of her pancake. He would do anything to make this woman happy.

They just turned onto Chonokis Road, and Hannah could already see her grandparents' residence. The tall Red Maple tree she used to play around still stood firmly next to it, almost covering the house with its lush, bright orange leaves.

"The Jensens painted the fence white. It used to be brown," Hannah said absentmindedly through the window.

They pulled into the driveway and got out of the car. The house - a white two-story farmhouse with a stone chimney sticking all the way past what used to be red shingles still looked exactly the way she remembered it even though the roof was now metal. A woman, maybe in her seventies, who she assumed was Mrs. Jensen, stood at the porch where Papalo and

Mamala used to sit on their rocking chairs, talking the night away. The woman looked eager for them to approach.

"You must be the Prestens," she said warmly.

"Yes, I'm Hannah, and this is my husband, Ethan."

"It's nice to meet you both. I'm Holly. Sally mentioned your grandparents used to live here," Holly said.

"Yes. I spent a few summers here with them. I hope we're not too much of a bother," Hannah said.

"Nonsense. I don't get many visitors, so this is refreshing. Come, let's go inside."

Hannah and Ethan followed Holly, but Hannah studied her surroundings each step she made, trying to bring out some memories from the past.

"Come on in. We've renovated some, but I'm sure there are still a lot of things you'll remember from when you were here."

The woman was very inviting. She reminded her of her Mamala a little.

Hannah held Ethan's hand as she followed Holly into the living room. It looked different, but she could still envision how her grandparents' living room was. It was hard to forget.

Mamala didn't have many things. She didn't like clutter.

Ethan looked at her as if to ask if the place was how she had expected it.

"There was a red sofa in that corner against the brown wall," Hannah pointed to where Holly's pink floral living room set was now neatly placed.

"There was a wooden table here with a vase of fresh flowers from Mamala's garden. She loved fresh flowers in the house. There was also a matching loveseat that sat across. I used to sleep on that loveseat," she said, smiling. "Next to the fireplace was Papalo's brown recliner. On the other side was a wooden cabinet full of books and where that flower art hung was my grandparent's wedding photo." Hannah touched the wall as she moved along. She looked down at the gray carpet under her feet; it used to be bare, solid wood. She could almost see Mamala placing a quilt on the floor as Papalo prepared to tell her some of his famous tales.

"Bringing back some memories?" Holly said.

"Oh, lots of them," Hannah answered.

"Good ones, I hope," Holly said.

"Great ones," she said, almost choking on the words.

"May we?" Hannah gestured as she stood by the narrow hallway that led to the bedrooms. "We won't go in the bedrooms. I just want to check something by the bathroom door."

"It's still there," Holly announced. As if she knew what she was looking for.

As she stood by the bathroom door, she was suddenly overwhelmed with emotions.

Holly urged her to go in. "Please, go ahead."

She went inside and pushed the door halfway, and there it was on the door jam. Written in pencil was her name- *An-An.* She touched it as if feeling to see if she could feel Papalo's presence. Next to it, below her name were numbers - her height for every year. Some were Papalo's handwriting, some were Mamala's, and some were hers. Each year was scribbled next to each mark, beginning with 1994.

"I was three years old when we started this," Hannah said as she continued to study the writings on the wall. She brushed her hand on the last dash.

"2008-17 years old," she read.

"When I turned twelve, I told Papalo I was too old for this. I might have given him an attitude that year, too, begging him to stop measuring me."

"You were too cool," Ethan said, teasing her a little.

"Yeah. I'm sure I thought I was, but Papalo said *Nonsense!*"

Her chest tightened as she fought back the tears threatening to fall.

"I couldn't find it in me to paint over it. I knew there was a beautiful story behind it. I thought maybe someday, this day would come," Holly said.

Hannah blinked the tears away. "You have no idea how much this means to me," she said, choking on her words and Ethan was quick to hold her.

They went through the rest of the house, and it brought so many memories, but what she couldn't wait to see was the back of the house. The three-acre fenced-in farm was just as she remembered. A red barn, though newly painted, was still there. A couple of horses stood by the fence, feeding on grass. She saw herself as a young girl, running around this very farm. Pygmy goats climbing around, ducks waddling, chickens clucking, and Tyler - her donkey following her everywhere she went. The nostalgia was so strong it was overwhelming. She missed her grandparents very much. She turned to Ethan, who knew right away to hug her tight.

Suddenly, she saw a glimpse of another animal from afar. *It couldn't be.*

Hannah placed her hand on her chest. "I can't believe it."

"What?" Ethan said, following her gaze.

"Tyler?" she called out.

"Oh, you mean the donkey," Holly said.

"I thought... I thought they found him a new home. That's what Mamala said."

"Oh, he stayed here when we bought the farm. Together with the rest of the other animals. We've sold a few, but most of them are still here."

"Can I pet him?"

"Of course. We call him Benjie. We didn't know he had a name." Holly announced.

They walked toward where Tyler was nibbling on some grass under the tree.

"Hey, Tyler." Hannah bent down to touch the donkey. Tyler turned around as if to respond to her voice. The animal came and stood next to her and started nuzzling.

"He remembers you," Ethan said.

"That is just the sweetest thing I've ever seen," Holly said, placing a hand on her chest.

She wanted to hug Tyler like she used to do. She wanted to sit on a bale of hay and just talk to the donkey for hours.

"I can't believe you still have him," she said, brushing away the tears on her cheeks. Are the goats still here? Ethan has never petted a goat before," she said as she forced a faint smile looking at her husband.

"We have a few pygmy goats, but I'm afraid they're not the ones you had. Let me see, they must be in the pen."

They spent a few more minutes petting the goats and then she said bye to Tyler. Again. But this time, she promised to visit.

"See you soon, bud."

***

"Are you okay?" Ethan asked as they got in the car.

"I'm more than okay. I'm so glad we did this. Thank you." She leaned over to kiss Ethan's cheek.

"Glad we've made it work. I can't believe I petted pygmy goats. Highlight of the trip so far," he said, giving a faint laugh.

"Are you ready? We have at least a three-hour drive not including stops for photo ops," Ethan said.

Hannah glanced back one last time and said, "Yes, I'm ready. Do you want me to drive?" She offered teasingly.

"Good gracious, no!"

"Hey, I'm a wonderful driver. Thank you very much!"

"Sure, you are, but not as good as I am."

"Whatever!"

Hannah rolled down the windows as they entered Skyline Drive, listening to country music. The weather was clear, and the breeze was invigorating. They stopped at every possible overlooking sight, enjoying the views of Blue Ridge Mountain. They took as many pictures as possible, something he had to get used to since they started dating. Hannah loved taking pictures, while he avoided it at all costs. Growing up, he was shy, and for the most part, kept to himself. He had avoided having his photos taken except for special occasions, but that all changed when he met Hannah. They pulled into another scenic viewpoint, and Hannah had her phone ready. "More pictures?" He teased. Of course, more pictures. Who was he kidding?

"I told you, Hun, I want to preserve as many memories as possible so we can show them to our children in the future.

How was he supposed to argue with that?

After admiring the scenery and a few snaps here and there, they returned to the road. It was past noon, and their stomachs growled in unison. How could that be possible after the breakfast they've had? They found a restaurant and pulled over for a quick bite. He didn't want work to interfere with their vacation, but since he hadn't heard from Oliver for a couple of days, he decided to call him again before they got back on the road.

Odd. Oliver always answered his calls, especially if it was him calling. He shook his head at Hannah, responding to her unasked question.

"Maybe he met someone. Remember that day in college when he went MIA for days, and we were so worried about him?"

Yes, he remembered. He remembered very well how *she* worried so much about him to where it made him uncomfortable, knowing that his best friend was probably somewhere gallivanting with a girl. She was frantic over nothing. He knew how Oliver operated. When things got hard, he ran away and hid. "I wouldn't be surprised," he said.

He left another message. "Dude, you better tell me you found your future wife, or you're lying in a hospital somewhere," he managed to end with a chuckle. "Anyway, call me when you resurface on Earth."

An hour later, they were back on the road, once again stopping at every spot they could snap a selfie from or ask strangers to take a picture of them. The area had several beautiful waterfalls, but some required long and intense hikes. They hiked a few easy ones and took lots of magnificent photos. Another hiking spot was just around the corner, and they decided to explore it. At the end was a waterfall that led to a beautiful lagoon. Surprisingly, there was no one there but the two of them. Hannah dropped the backpack she was carrying and stripped into her bikini.

"What are you doing? Wait, you have a bikini on?"

"Live a little, would you?"

Before he could protest some more, Hannah plunged into the water. He shook his head in disbelief. "You're going to get hypothermia— what the heck?" He undressed down to his boxers and jumped after her. When he reached her, he pulled her closer. "You're nuts. You know that?"

She giggled. "Only nuts about you."

Ethan shook his head, annoyed and amused at the same time—nothing else to do now but kiss her, forgetting how cold the water felt on his body.

***

It was almost midnight when they arrived back at Serenity Manor. The moon was complete, and the scattered stars shone brightly in the whole place. The manor was indeed a magnificent sight, especially at night. Ethan's yawn broke the silence as they strolled toward the house, both taking heavy steps as if not wanting the night to end.

"Gorgeous night, isn't it?" Ethan said in between enormous yawns.

"Absolutely beautiful."

"Can you see yourself living here?" he asked.

"Honestly? I could, but not anytime soon. I like the peace here. Plus, I'd be close to Tyler."

He smiled at her last comment. "Yeah, me, too. This is a good place to retire. Maybe we could buy your old grandparent's home or build a house with a good-sized yard for all our grandkids to play in."

Grandkids. They haven't even talked about their own kids, but the thought of kids running around the yard, watching them as they laughed and played, made him yearn for them. It was time to have *the* talk with his wife.

Chapter Thirteen

September 18

I t was the morning of their anniversary, and Hannah woke up from another dream; this time, the man was holding the baby. Who was this man, and why did she keep dreaming about him? Why couldn't she see his face? The wind started to rumble, snapping her away from her thoughts. The weather had gotten colder the last few days. She rolled out of bed, grabbed the quilt from the chair next to her, wrapped herself in it, and closed the sliding door they left opened before going to bed.

Her phone buzzed. She snatched it before it woke Ethan up and slowly climbed back to bed. Several text notifications showed up, but Ethan groaned before she had time to read them. She did notice a text from K. K- *Keon* was what she called Oliver when they first met. She quickly glanced and read the message: *I'm all right. Happy Anniversary.*

"What are you doing?" Ethan mumbled.

She contemplated telling him about her dreams. Maybe some other time.

"The wind woke me up."

"Go back to sleep," he said, placing his arm over her.

THE PROMISE

"It's almost six, Ethan." She didn't mean to whine.

"Shh... fifteen minutes."

She would have to remember to check her messages later, but knowing that Oliver was OK, was a relief. She was starting to worry. She decided to close her eyes and enjoy her husband's warm embrace. She didn't mean to fall back to sleep, but she did. Suddenly, the sun shining through the window woke her up. She pried her arm out of Ethan's embrace and grabbed the phone from the chair beside her. It was eight twenty. How could she had fallen back asleep for two more hours? She knew exactly why. His embrace had always had a calming effect on her. She always felt protected in Ethan's arms.

"Fifteen minutes over?" he mumbled.

She could feel Ethan grinning behind her as he asked the question. She pictured his dreamy blue eyes, messy blond hair, strands falling on his face, that boyish smile that could make any woman fall head over heels in love with him. Oh yeah, and his firm naked body. She could feel all of him. He was ready. She shimmied around to face him. He pulled her closer.

"Not yet," she said.

"Ugh, why not?"

She smiled. Softly, she kissed his sleepy eyes, nose, and his pouty lips. She kissed his chest, his stomach, then moved between his legs. Ethan was suddenly alert and pulled the white sheet over them and gently slammed her on the bed. She wasn't going to protest. She was ready, too. She wanted him to claim her. All of her. And he did. Twice.

***

83

Both dressed in denim jeans and sweatshirts; they were off on a trail ride across a working cattle ranch nestled in the foothills of the Blue Ridge Mountains that Ethan had booked before their trip. They arrived at the farm and were greeted by an expansive fifty-acre spread surrounded by trees and mountains. The fog was thick, but she could still make out a stable in the distance. There was some commotion in the field as they walked toward the enormous red colonial-style house in front of them. Several people were walking about the large foyer area as they entered. Just as they approached the counter, a man came rushing toward the front desk.

"Is there another number for Dr. Bill?" he asked the lady behind the desk.

"Yeah, it should be in the system. Let me look."

The man shook his head as he peered at the computer screen. "We already called that number, but it's not going through. We left a message on his voice mail, too, but he hasn't called back," he said. The man seemed frantic.

"What's going on? Is one of the horses hurt?" The lady behind the counter said.

The conversation caught Hannah's attention.

"It's Freedom; she's been in labor, but something is wrong. We need Dr. Bill ASAP," the young man explained as he tried to dial the number again.

Hannah leaned in closer, addressing the man behind the counter. "Excuse me, I didn't mean to eavesdrop, but did you say something's wrong with a mare in labor?"

"Yes, one of our horses is pregnant, and we expected to wake up with a foal this morning, but I guess something went wrong," the lady behind the counter said.

"Can you take me to the stable? We don't have much time if something's wrong, especially if the mare has been in labor for a while. I need to deliver fast if we want to save both the mother and the foal."

Still holding the phone to his ears, the man addressed Hannah. "Are you a vet?"

"I wouldn't *dare* suggest helping if I wasn't one," she said with a smile.

The man dropped the phone and gestured for her to follow. "This way, please."

When they got to the stable, Hannah found a large, dark chocolate Arabian horse lying on its side on a bed of hay. *She's beautiful,* Hannah thought at first glance, but immediately swallowed the thought, knowing that there was a more pressing matter at hand. The mare suddenly got up and started pacing. A few minutes later, it laid back down and started to roll side to side. The mare performed the ritual a couple of times - a sign of distress. Based on the mare's actions, she knew she was likely dealing with dystocia, a difficulty in foaling. The foal was not in its normal foaling position, which is typically front legs first. Here, she may be dealing with a breech pregnancy. She cautiously approached the animal to look closer and quickly realized that the amniotic sac had already ruptured. She needed to act fast.

"How long ago did the sac rupture?"

"A few minutes before you got here," a young lady answered.

Hannah slipped on the long plastic gloves she was given, "Can you stand by her head and try to calm her down as I check her?"

The lady nodded and rushed in front of the horse as two older men assisted her.

"This is my dad, Eugene." The lady pointed to the older man with gray hair. "And this is Gilbert," she announced, gesturing to another older gentleman. Gilbert took her position and started stroking the mare's head. "They take care of the horses here. They can assist with the delivery if you need them."

While the mare stood still, Hannah lifted its tail and examined the animal. "As I suspected, the foal is not in its normal delivery position," she announced. "But it's not as bad as I thought. I can manipulate the body parts to get the legs to come out first, but I would need someone to keep her standing for a while," she added as she continued to prod inside the mare.

The horse protested with abrupt movements, but she was thankful it cooperated and remained standing for a while. "I would need some hands to keep her still while repositioning the foal inside the womb. I need to find the head for safe delivery. We need to act fast. The foal could lose oxygen, and we don't want that."

"Is it breach?" The young lady asked.

"Well..." Hannah paused as she felt inside the horse, trying to pay close attention to the task. "One of the feet is turned back," she said.

"I had a feeling," Eugene said.

Hannah gave the men directions on how to assist before she carefully manipulated the foal. Gilbert stood by the mare's head as Hannah pushed the foal back into the mother's uterus, carefully making sure she didn't tear it. She shifted the foal inside its mother's womb to locate the missing leg. The mare was straining, making it difficult for all of them, especially for her. But she wasn't about to give up. Her large animal training kicked in, and she was surprised at what she remembered. After a lot of pushing and shoving, she located both limbs. She grabbed both legs into the birth canal and correctly positioned the head. It was time to pull. The giant animal's uterus contracted again, and Hannah finessed the forelimbs. Now exposed, she held onto both legs and pulled hard as the mare continued to push. As the head came out, she gave the mare more time to go through her contraction. She tore the rest of the amniotic sac, giving the foal some oxygen. The foal finally dropped to the ground, and she tended to the ebony colt, removing the film from its limp body.

The mare licked the colt, cleaning and aiding her baby, but it didn't move. Hannah had to do something fast. Covering one nostril with her hand and ensuring the mouth was shut she blew into the other nostril and waited for the chest wall to rise. Nothing. She did it again. *C'mon,* she thought as she did the procedure one more time.

"It's alive," Eugene called out as the colt's chest moved.

After making sure the newborn was healthy and alert, she gave the mom some time to bond with it. "Great job, momma," she whispered, stroking Freedom's back. Freedom was still panting but thanked her with a *neigh.* "Aww. You're welcome."

"His name is Reign," the lady announced.

"Freedom and Reign. I like that," Hannah replied.

Reign eased up little by little, lifting its front, then his hind legs, trying to get up while his mama continued to clean him up. Hannah had delivered many animals before, but they never ceased to amaze her every time. As she watched the mother and child exchange, a longing for her child came over her, absentmindedly touching her belly. She told Ethan that she wanted to enjoy marriage before having children. Perhaps it was time; it's been five years, after all.

"Thank goodness you were here," Eugene said as he reached out to shake Hannah's hands. "You are Godsent," he added, gently pulling his daughter beside him. "My daughter and I stayed and watched Freedom throughout the night, thinking she would have started labor, but she didn't start pacing till this morning. We knew something was wrong."

The young man who was at the front desk earlier interjected. "We probably would have lost one of them, if not both. If you weren't here, ma'am - I mean... Doctor."

"You were amazing, Hun. I can't believe you delivered that foal," Ethan said as he stood beside her.

"I did what any vet would do," she said, wiping off the sweat from her face.

"Well, thank you so much for helping us out. I'm sure Freedom thanks you, too," Gilbert said.

"It was my pleasure."

"Hun?" Ethan said.

"Yes?"

"You never cease to amaze me. I don't know how you do all that," kissing her head.

She smiled.

"Hun?" Ethan repeated.

"Yes?"

"You need to shower. You kind of stink." Ethan chuckled.

She pushed him to the side jokingly.

A man in a dark suit approached the group, making both stop jostling around.

"Do we have a fresh addition? Healthy?"

"Yes, thanks to Doc–" the young lady started to say.

"Hannah, please call me Hannah."

The man pulled out a business card that said *CEO* from his shirt pocket and handed one to her. "See to it that Dr...?" He glanced at her again.

"Hannah," she replied. "...and this is my husband, Ethan. We're the Prestens, with an E," she smiled, looking at the business card he had just given her.

"Well, how about that? Pres*ten* and my name is Pres*ton*," the man responded with a noticeable twang. He turned around and addressed one of the staff standing in the corner. "Make sure The Prestens..." he glanced at Ethan and winked before continuing, "...with an *E* are enjoying their stay here. See to it that they are well taken care of." He then turned his attention back to her and Ethan. "I hope you enjoy your stay here at the ranch, and again, thank you *very* much for your help today, Hannah."

Chapter Fourteen

It had been a couple of days since the patrol officer pulled him over, but he still needed to lie low, so he called in sick and stayed home. His house was small but cozy- he liked it that way. From his kitchen window, he saw the neighbors entering their cars and heading to work every morning. Sometimes, he waved at them, but for the most part, he kept to himself. Today was one of those days. He sat at his small dining table, enjoying a hot cup of coffee while he watched the neighbors leave.

"When are you going back to the manor?"

Startled by the woman's screechy voice, he jumped and whirled around to face her with annoyance.

"Don't scare me like that."

"I'm sorry, but you were just staring into space. What's so enchanting out there, anyway?" The woman asked, peeking through the window in front of him. Her hair was short, naturally gray, and teased at the top to make it look fuller. The wrinkles on her face showed her age. She was in her late seventies, short, thin, and she wore an unflattering long white dress. Yet, despite looking like she had just woken up, she still exuded beauty. People had always found his mother gorgeous in her younger years, but in the last few years, he'd noticed the sparkle had vanished from her once tantalizing eyes.

"So... I see you found Hannah?" she asked in a monotone voice as she continued looking outside the window, trying to figure out what intrigued him.

"Yes, I did."

"And?"

"I will take care of it. I had to lie low for a while," he said coldly. He wasn't going to bother explaining his encounter with the police. That would only rile her up.

"You need to move fast," she snapped.

"You can't rush this," he snapped back. "I need to make sure I do things right."

"What are you waiting for?"

That was the last thing he heard, and she was gone.

He thought of Hannah and immediately felt exhausted. "I am tired of you invading my thoughts, hurting me repeatedly. I will show you just how important I am when I have you begging me to let you live."

He approached the fireplace, picked up a photo frame from the mantle, and stared at the woman in the photo with a longing that immediately turned into condemnation. His eyes burned as he stared at the picture. The lady in the photo stared back at him, smiling with her long, curly brown hair, tanned skin, and enticing brown eyes. Standing in the middle of the vast green lawn in her crisp white wedding gown, she looked stunning, about to toss the bouquet in her hand. "Why do you torture me, Hannah? I tried to move on, but even the woman I married reminded me of you."

He brushed a finger on Andrea's face on the photo. He needed a plan. He couldn't afford any mistakes like the last time. He had to get rid of Hannah, and maybe his memory of her will finally disappear. But now, there's a man with her. That infuriated him.

Hannah destroyed him all these years, and now he will destroy her. He brought the frame to his chest and hummed the wedding march tune. He closed his eyes and began to sway. Lost in his world, he relived his first dance with his wife, Andrea. "Don't worry, baby. It's almost over, and we'll be together again," he said coldly.

The high-pitched sound of the doorbell jolted him back to reality, and he accidentally dropped the frame he was holding.

"Damn it."

"How pathetic!" His mother smirked.

Great, she was back. He ignored her and glanced at the shards of glass by his feet. He shook off the glass fragments that landed on his foot, walked to the door, and peeked through. It was the woman next door. What was she doing at his house? He had only spoken to her once since he moved into the neighborhood; it's not like they were friends. He contemplated walking away from the door and not answering. Instead, he opened it.

"Hey, there," she said.

"Hi," he replied, acting nonchalantly as he glanced back over his shoulder.

"Shella." She reminded him.

He nodded.

"I'm sorry to bother you, but could I borrow a cup of sugar? Silly me, I was baking upside-down pineapple cake for the kids only to find out I ran out of sugar, and my husband took the car," the woman said, shaking her head and rolling her eyes as if embarrassed by the whole sugar demise.

"How cliché," his mother said.

He glanced over his shoulder and gave his mom a stern look. "Sure, come on in."

"What?" His mother shrieked as Shella entered the house.

"Stop," he said, gritting his teeth.

"I'm sorry. But I thought you said to come in?" Shella said, confused.

"Yes, I did." His tone was harsher than he intended it to be. "I'm sorry. I - I didn't mean to snap at you."

"Don't worry about it. Long day?" she said, smiling.

He didn't reply; instead, he took a deep breath before addressing her again. "Please stay here," he said in a more placid voice. He headed to the kitchen.

"I'm sorry. Did you say something?" Shella said. "Hello?" she called out as she walked toward the voices.

"Stop it, Mother," he said, gritting his teeth, just in time for him to see Stella watching him with a confused look on her face. *Dangit.*

Shella quickly turned around and headed for the door.

"Shella! The sugar." Who was he kidding? He heard the door shut. "Look what you've done." He cried out, but when he turned, he was alone. *Great. Just great.* He tossed the sugar can into the sink and returned to the living room. He picked up the photo from the floor and brushed off the shards of glass stuck to it.

"Son of a---"

A piece of shard cut his finger. He instinctively sucked the blood as he glared at the photo. "Don't worry, babe. I'm coming for you after I take care of Hannah. Maybe when she's gone, we can finally move on."

Chapter Fifteen

"It's good to see you again," Dr. Cavanaugh said as she watched him enter the room, glancing at her watch. Then she stood behind her desk and offered the chaise lounge for him to sit.

He studied his therapist from head to toe. She differed from his wife and Hannah - not in a bad way, but in a more contrasting way. There was something about her that he found attractive. Dr. Linda Cavanaugh was slender and tall and knew how to dress to complement her features. She stood with confidence and class. Today, she wore gray slacks and a loose-fitting black, long-sleeve blouse. She was click-clacking around with her three-inch black stilettos, slightly towering over him. He was unsure how he felt about that.

He met Dr. Cavanaugh at a mandatory psych evaluation at his work last year. Not long after they'd met, he paid her a visit, which was also her recommendation. They've been friends since then, though Cavanaugh clarified that she was his therapist first.

"I have a few minutes to spare before my next appointment. What brought you here today?"

He claimed the sofa, slumped down, and once again studied all the plaques and accolades hanging on the wall as he always did. Maybe it was strategically placed there for clients to know who they were dealing with, he thought. She was impressive, that's for sure. His constant resistance did not stop Dr. Cavanaugh from offering the chaise lounge every time he came in, and today was no different.

"Here, have a seat," she said.

"No, I'm good here." He sat on a different chair.

"You look stressed," Doctor Cavanaugh said as she took the chair across from him, opened her notepad, and waited for him to start talking.

"This week has been *very* stressful. The dreams are more vivid and keep me awake at night," he said, fiddling with his thumbs, a nervous mannerism she'd noticed from the first meeting.

She assessed his appearance today, took notes, and listened to him simultaneously, something she always did without letting her patients know. When she first visited his work, she had taken a mental description of each worker she spoke with, including him. He was about five feet and ten inches tall, give or take, and his whole being screamed masculinity and confidence.

The man was fit. He once told her that eating healthily and working out was not only required at his job but also something he valued and enjoyed. As she recalled, his light brown hair was always shaved on the sides and brushed back on top. Today, his hair was a bit shaggy and all over his face, like he didn't care to fix it. She remembered his vibrant blue eyes that radiated mildness, making him an attractive man, but today, they were empty. He looked more ragged than usual like he hadn't slept for days. Despite the crisp white sweatshirt and the denim jeans he wore today, he looked untidy. She noted his unshaven face, bloodshot eyes, and messy demeanor. Flipping through her notes, she reminded herself of his progress from the last time they met; she read: *Sleeping better, exercising more, fewer nightmares.* Something has had to happen recently for him to look like a mess today.

"Why do you think you're having these nightmares again? What's been going on?" she asked, catching the red marks on his wrists as he continued to play with his thumb. She took note of it.

"Hannah is back," he said, looking down as if embarrassed to admit something he didn't want to.

"Is she now? Tell me about it."

Raising his voice, he looked up, stared at her with bloodshot eyes, "Yes. She is. With a man."

Keeping her composure, she noted, *Agitated.*

"And the last time you saw Hannah was when you were in California months ago, am I correct?"

"Yes," he gritted his teeth in response, touching the marks on his wrist.

She could sense his contemptuous attitude. "Okay, why don't you take a deep breath? Remember the counting technique I taught you?"

"I've been doing that, but honestly, Linda - *doc*, I don't think it's going to work much longer."

His disdaining tone piqued her interest. She pressed him. "Why wouldn't it?"

His voice rose an octave higher. "My mother won't leave me alone, and I have been counting backward from one hundred. *One hundred*, Linda!"

Restless, jittery, "mother" is back, she scribbled down. The timer went off, but before she could end the session, she needed an answer. "How long has your mother been back? What are you doing about it, and what are those marks on your wrist?"

"One at a time, will you?" He sighed as if not wanting to go there at all, but he divulged anyway. "I don't know... seems like forever," he said, more calmly this time.

"If you could give me a time frame, when did she return?"

"A few days ago."

She made a note. *Why? What brought his mother back?* "And your wrist?"

"I started using a rubber band to snap away my negative thoughts. My *irrational thoughts*, as *you* called them. I saw it in a movie once," he said, rolling his eyes. "I guess I snapped too much. Too hard. Don't know," he grumbled.

They were out of time, but she had to be careful how she told him about it. The last time she did, he got very agitated, saying he was just as important as everyone else.

"I'd like to explore these negative thoughts you've mention some more, as well as your mother's visits," she said. "Unfortunately, I have another client waiting outside and we are out of time, but I'd like to see you soon. Can you come back tomorrow morning? Better yet, this afternoon? I have four o'clock open," she said, glancing at her schedule.

He stood and headed for the door.

"See you tomorrow," he said in a detached voice.

"Call me if you need to talk before then."

He needed her help. He was a mess. It was the only reason he showed up unannounced.

Without glancing back, he extended his arms above his head and gave her a thumbs up. Then, just as he was out the door, he paused, turned around, and said, "You look lovely today, Linda."

Chapter Sixteen

"I need to get out of these clothes. I smell like a horse." Hannah said as she and Ethan walked toward the main building.

"Why don't we finish checking in and see if there's a room you can use to clean up?"

The young lady behind the counter was almost giddy, waiting for them to approach. "Hi, Dr. Hannah. *Mr. Presten.*" She nodded as they reached the counter.

The lady was probably in her early twenties. She gave them the welcome speech, then praised her for helping Freedom with the delivery.

The news did travel fast, Hannah thought. She was flattered by everyone's enthusiasm at the ranch, but as far as she was concerned, she simply did her job. She glanced down at her clothes before addressing the young lady.

"Is there a place I could clean up before the tour starts?"

"Actually, I have a packet here for you, Doctor. The Ranch's manager, Mr. Monroe, instructed me to give you a room along with free access to all the ranch's amenities," she said, handing her the key to their room. "Your stay includes all the activities, Ethan..." she paused as if suddenly embarrassed, quickly took her eyes off Ethan, and corrected herself, "I *mean* Mr. Presten... booked and whatever else you guys would like to do on your stay here."

That was odd. Hannah was always used to young ladies flirting with Ethan, but for crying out loud. Why was this lady so flustered?

"Also, breakfast and dinner are included," the lady added.

"Wow, that's very generous, but we're only here for the day," Hannah said.

"I believe Mr. Monroe has invited you guys to stay for the weekend."

"What?" She turned to Ethan.

"What do you mean what?" he said.

Hannah rolled her eyes. "Mr. Monroe's invitation? For us to stay for the weekend?" she said, sarcastically.

"Oh, that. I'm good if you are." He turned around as if looking around for something.

"Really? What about the manor?"

"I'll call and explain later," he said, took the key from her and thanked the front desk clerk.

"You're acting weird," she said.

"Me?"

"Yeah, you. *Ethan. I mean, Mr. Presten.*" She whined, imitating the lady behind the counter. "What was that?"

"What? I don't know what you're talking about."

She punched his shoulder. "You're such a flirt."

"Can't blame me for being irresistible now, can you?" he said before giving out a boisterous laugh.

"Are we really going to stay for the weekend?"

"Well, since the vet emergency took some of our time here, we could at least take advantage of Mr. Monroe's offer and enjoy it. What do you think?"

"I suppose we could," she said, getting excited about their weekend adventure.

***

Ethan caught Preston Monroe's gaze from the corner as they walked from the front desk. He discreetly nodded at him and mouthed the words, *Thank you.* The man winked in return.

He wasn't sure if it would have worked, but while Hannah was busy aiding Freedom, he had a conversation with Mr. Monroe. He told him about his surprise for Hannah and how she had never ridden a horse before. Preston then offered for them to have the whole ranch experience. The manager gave them a suite for the weekend as a gesture of gratitude. That's when he decided to take the entire plan to the next level and conspired with the workers at the ranch. They were all happy to make it happen for him. Good thing the ranch was not as full as they thought it was.

A concierge led them into the back of the main house, where they followed a long, pebbled pathway leading them to a private cottage nestled between two large maple trees. In the distance were two other villas with pebbled garden paths.

The man stepped aside as he opened the door to their villa. The massive four-post king bed in the center, covered with a fluffy white comforter, four gigantic white pillows, and a crystal chandelier hanging on the ceiling, greeted them.

"This is beautiful! You did this," she said, turning to Ethan.

He held her hand.

"Wait till you see what's outside."

"Enjoy your stay with us, Mr. and Dr. Presten. Please don't hesitate to call us if you need anything," the concierge said before excusing himself.

Before the young man stepped out, Ethan slipped a twenty into his hand and thanked him.

They proceeded to the open patio at the back of the cottage. The earth-toned, slate-tiled, bamboo-fenced patio with towering pine trees outside was just as charming as the rest of the villa. There was a large jacuzzi in the center under the bright blue sky filled with bubbles - *pièce de résistance*.

"Dip after horseback riding?" he asked.

"It's a must." She hugged him tightly.

He enjoyed watching Hannah taking in the richness of the place. He wasn't much for extravagance, but Hannah deserved the occasional pampering, which he ensured he did the last five years.

"There they are." He wiped her tears and kissed her.

Hannah was strong. She was a fighter. No obstacles were too big for her, but she was also soft, fragile, and sensitive. He was very much aware of that despite the hard-shell exterior. Everything he did was for her, and he loved that she appreciated every effort he made - big or small- that made her who she was. Those traits are what made him fall deeply in love with her.

"I better get ready before we miss the horseback riding." Hannah reminded him.

"Oh yeah, I forgot to tell you. I booked a private tour for us at sundown."

"Really? Just the two of us? You did that?"

"I would love to take the credit, but it was the front desk clerk's idea."

"Was it now?"

He chuckled. She wasn't jealous, but he enjoyed riling her up sometimes.

"Yeah, she was pretty accommodating—"

"I bet she was."

"She was accommodating, trying to get the rest of the plan in place. She also got the other workers to help, which was pretty cool."

"Uhuh." She had her arms crossed, giving him the look that said *don't mess with me.*

"Oh, c'mon. You're not jealous of her, are you?"

"Me? Jealous?" she rolled her eyes. "As if."

He pulled her to him and kissed her forehead. "You know, you are cute when you pretend to be jealous."

"Gosh, you know me so well." She wrapped her arms around him.

"Thanks to Freedom, it all worked out for the best," he said.

"Yes, thanks to Freedom and I guess, thanks to the front desk clerk, too." She smiled and squeezed him tight.

His phone vibrated in his pocket, and she pulled away so he could get to it. He glanced at the number.

"Ol! Where have you been?"

Hannah stepped out of the room.

After a few minutes, she came back in the bedroom.

"That was Ol. Remember that girl he brought to one of our BBQs last summer?"

"The teacher? I forgot her name. What about her?" Hannah questioned.

"Apparently, she went to Tahoe with him a few weeks ago and now they're in Arizona together."

"Interesting. So, Sylvia was definitely confused then. He's in Arizona, not Virginia."

"Looks that way," he said.

"Glad he's back dating again, though. I forgot to tell you, he texted this morning, greeting us with a happy anniversary."

Something inside him felt uneasy.

"I meant to tell you earlier, but with all that has happened... I guess it had slipped my mind."

If he didn't know any better, he'd say he was getting jealous, but why? He couldn't be jealous of Oliver and Hannah's friendship, plus he wasn't the jealous type. And not with his best friend. If anything, it would be the other way around, but Ol had gotten over Hannah long ago, or had he? For crying out loud, it had been years since Oliver had confessed to him about his feelings for Hannah. But recently, something had changed. He could feel it.

Chapter Seventeen

Despite his brief session with Dr. Cavanaugh, he somehow felt uplifted. Whistling behind the wheel, he drove back to Serenity Manor to get a glimpse of Hannah. He pulled into his usual spot. It was 9:43 p.m. He lowered the window and brought the binoculars to his eyes. No movements. He knew they spent most of their time out and about, but they should be back by now. He decided to wait. As the night got deeper, his frustration got stronger. Still, no sign of the couple - it was already 11:55. Counting backward wasn't helping anymore, so he resorted to the rubber band on his wrist again, despite Linda's order to stop using it. He grew weary so he rested his arms and head on the steering wheel before jerking his body away instantly and stepping out of the car.

"WHERE ARE YOU?"

He kicked the tire then the twigs on the ground. He checked the time again; it was past midnight, and there was still no sign of them. The outside of the manor was well-lit, but there was no movement inside. He got back in his car and rubbed his temple. What should he do? He could go to the house and check. No, he shouldn't do that. Taking a deep breath, he started to think; he needed to make sure he wasn't hasty with his decisions. He did have to go to work early the next day. So, he decided to leave when a familiar voice startled him.

"Are you leaving without seeing her?"

He cursed at the sound of his mother's voice.

"Gosh. I told you not to scare me like that. And yes. I have no choice. Please leave me alone."

"Excuse me? Is that how you talk to me now?" she asked, shaking her head as if offended. If there's one thing he didn't like doing, it was upsetting his mother.

"I'm sorry, but you scare the crap out of me when you show up like that."

"Is there any other way?" she said flamboyantly, fluffing her hair in the mirror as she toyed with him.

"I don't know. Give me a sign or something."

"Fine, I'll blow in your ears, then I'll show up. *Poof!* How's that for a sign?" she said, laughing at her ridiculous statement.

She seemed amused by his reaction, which calmed him down. He lowered his voice, "I'm sorry, Mom. I'm just exhausted." He forced a smile.

"You know, you always take things so seriously, even when you were a kid, but I always know how to snap you out of it, don't I?"

"You do, mother. That, you do."

"Well, it was always just the two of us, so we had to make sure we took care of each other."

"I know, Mom and we did."

"I know things are tough for you lately, son, but it will all be over soon," she reassured him before vanishing again.

His mother had been making her dramatic appearance more often. He knew deep down inside that if he wanted to live a normal life, he would have to do something for her to stop showing up the way she did. But did he want to? Was he ready? Sometimes, he wondered if he could go on without her presence. It was ridiculous, he knew, even so, seeing her was his only comfort. He loved his mother. She always had his back. She ensured he was cared for and got him out of trouble. Always. Even when she found out she had cancer. She stayed strong till the end, fighting for him. She was the only one who knew about his feelings for Hannah, and she was the only one there when he got his feelings out of hand, but sometimes, her meddling was too much, especially during his marriage to Angela, but what could he do? He knew the right answer to that question. The only way she would go away was for him to do what his mother wanted all along and that was to get rid of Hannah once and for all. At least in that way, she would leave happy. Maybe. But it was the least he could do for everything she had done for him.

Chapter Eighteen

The weekend at the ranch was perfect. It was more than Hannah could ever wish for their anniversary and she finally rode a horse today. She was a little scared, but Ethan was with her, and she always felt safe when Ethan was around. When they entered the stable, her eyes immediately darted toward a gorgeous white horse in its stall. *Annabelle* was the name tag attached to its door. She knew she was the one.

"Great choice." Gilbert said. "Annabelle is a Missouri Fox Trotter. She is about ten years old and was born here at the ranch."

"She's beautiful," she said as she admired the horse.

Ethan had chosen the horse across from Annabelle's stall. It was a massive, dark-brown stallion with light-caramel legs that faded to ebony from its knees to its hooves, matching its mane.

"That's Amaro - a Tennessee Walker," Gilbert said. "Tennessee Walkers are known for their great disposition, making them suitable for riding. You guys seem to have an eye for magnificent horses," he said, pulling Amaro out just in time for the young lady who helped her with the delivery yesterday to walk in. Gilbert gestured to the young lady to take Annabelle out.

"You picked a great horse, Doctor," the lady told Hannah as she slowly guided Annabel out of its stall.

"That's what I was told, but I actually don't have any idea about horseback riding."

"Well, you'll have a great ride with Annabelle, that's for sure. She's a gentle giant... one of my favorites."

"Glad to hear. How's Freedom and Reign?"

"Oh, they're doing very well, thank you. You guys should see them before you leave the ranch."

"For sure."

Ethan aided her in mounting Annabelle before climbing onto his own horse. They rode the trail and caught the sun setting beautifully. The blue sky had faded into a flaming orange, a glorious scene. They rode around the ranch's massive estate surrounded by the breathtaking beauty of the Blue Ridge Mountain, serving as the backdrop to the stunning landscape. Hannah could feel the soft breeze as the wind whistled through the impressive trees that enveloped them. There was calmness in the air as the horse trotted, making the leaves rustle with each step. Nothing else could have described the moment but pure romance. On their way back, Ethan stopped and unmounted his horse. He gestured to the young lady who was not far behind, to take his horse. Ethan mounted Annabelle and rode back with Hannah.

They were back at the cottage just as it turned dark outside. Moments later, Hannah had her hair up in a messy bun, revealing a pair of white pearl earrings her mother had given her when she graduated from college. She toyed with one of them, wondering how her mother was doing these days. It had been a couple of weeks since she last spoke with her. She missed her mother so much. She wished she lived closer. Guam was just too far away.

The hidden memory of the night she had finally asked about a well-kept family secret suddenly resurfaced. Sitting in the dining room, preparing her wedding invitations, she had asked her mother.

Mom, I've been meaning to ask you something.

Yeah, sweetheart, what is it? You know you can ask me anything.

Are you sure?

Of course. What kind of question is that? Is it something about the wedding?

No, it's about my sister, she said.

Her mother was obviously taken aback by her question and had absentmindedly stopped what she was doing. *Your sister? What are you—* She sounded like she didn't know what to say. *Papalo told you,* she said, blankly.

Hannah suddenly felt unsure whether she should proceed with the conversation. She could tell her mother felt uncomfortable, but she needed to know. She needed to understand why. Why would her mother hide it from her? It bothered her. It bothered her a lot. All those times, she thought she was an only child, and she had a baby sister named Jean. *Jean,* as in her imaginary friend.

No, mom. Mamala did.

Her mother regained composure and continued slipping the cards into the envelopes. *And why now? You've known for years apparently.*

Mom. Why didn't you tell me?

Let it go. It was a long time ago, her mother said, not looking at her, instead she stood, grabbed the Chardonnay bottle, and refilled her glass.

I don't mean to upset you, but don't you think I have the right to know?

Her mother slammed her drink like a shot of tequila. She took a deep breath and sat back down.

I supposed you do. I was young. I had just discovered that your father had been living a double life, leaving us... leaving me while I was pregnant with your baby sister to do whatever it was he was doing. I was already four months pregnant when I found out. I knew about the other women---

And you put up with it?

Yes, I put up with his infidelities; what was I supposed to do? I was young. I thought all those out-of-town meetings were just that - out-of-town meetings, but then he would miss holidays. He even missed a couple of your birthdays.

That's why he wasn't in some of my birthday pictures, she said, remembering how she would ask where her father was then. She would always get the same answers from everyone around: he was busy with work, but he's thinking about you and left you presents. There were multiple birthdays presents whenever he wasn't around. She should have known; they were her mother's doing, covering her father's flaws.

Her mother nodded.

Anyway, time went on, and I confronted him. He got agitated and left. I was devastated. I loved your father very much and was willing to forgive him, but he chose to stay away for a while.

With another woman, she said, her chest tightening.

I'm sure.

Hannah could not believe what she was hearing, and she was pretty sure her mom had not gotten to the worst part yet.

Mom, it's fine. You don't need to continue. I understand.

No, it's okay. You have the right to know, like you said, and I have kept this away from you for a very long time. It's time.

Her mother continued. *I went into depression. I cried every day. Despite my attempt to take care of my pregnancy, I was lost. I was sad. I needed your father, and he wasn't there.*

Hannah could swear she saw a tear escape her mother's eye. It had been years, but she could tell the pain was still there, both for her dad and her baby.

Mom—

It's okay, her mother said, brushing the wetness off her face before continuing. *I tried to find your dad to let him know that it was okay. That we would work it out, but he never came back till I was already in the hospital giving birth to your sister, but he was too late. The baby was rushed to the ICU. She had difficulty breathing and after a couple of hours...*

Mom, we don't have to, she said, feeling the tightness in her chest, but it was too late. There was no stopping what she had already started.

Her mother's voice quaked. *She stopped fighting. My baby stopped fighting. Jean was gone.*

Why did she have to ask? Her heart spasmed as she hated herself for making her mother relive the worst day of her life. Why didn't she just leave it alone? She held her mother's shaking hand. *Mom, I'm so sorry. I didn't ---*

It's okay, sweetheart. You could not have known. It's not that I didn't want to tell you—

You wanted to forget, she interjected.

Her mother nodded. *Don't get me wrong, I have never forgotten about your baby sister. I thought about her all the time. I even wondered what she would be like standing next to you as your maid of honor. See, Han, I blamed myself. I blamed myself for what had happened to Jean. Maybe if I just took care of myself more. If I just let go of your father and focused on me, maybe she would be alive today.*

It wasn't your fault. It was never your fault, Hannah said firmly.

I know that now. But for a long time, I didn't. Even when the doctors told me she had a congenital heart defect, I still blamed myself. I felt as if I had given her that condition. It wasn't until I learned to forgive myself that I could move on. Then I vowed not to ever speak of what had happened again. I had to bury the pain deep down where it couldn't be reached...For you, her mother said, squeezing her hand.

For me? I don't understand.

Han, I was so consumed with guilt, anger, and pain that I had almost forgotten that I still had you, her mother confessed, finally letting the tears fall.

I don't know what to say.

Tell me you understand and that you forgive me.

She stood fast and hugged her mother tightly. *Of course, I understand, Mom, and I'm sorry for everything you went through. I'm sorry for letting you relive the worst moment of your life.*

I'm sorry that I kept it from you. I was ashamed.

You have nothing to be ashamed of, Mom. It was not your fault.

Hannah could almost feel the burden lifted from her mother's shoulders as she sighed deeply, hugging her back.

Her mother broke the hug first. *Now, we let the past stay in the past and never talk about it again.*

They hugged each other for a long time, but she wasn't prepared for what would come next.

Han, what did she look like?

She wasn't expecting that at all.

What do you mean?

I know you've seen her, her mother said softly, almost unsure whether she should continue.

How do you---

At the hospital when you were little. You know I never left you, not even a minute when you were there fighting for your life. The day you finally opened your eyes... You mumbled about Jean. I don't know what your conversation was about, but since then, she has been your constant friend. I knew then, her mother said, beaming.

Hannah didn't have to make sense of it all; she let it be. *She was beautiful, mom, Jean looked like you. She had a dimple on the right cheek, just like I do.*

Her mother touched Hannah's face and kissed her on the forehead, just like she used to do when she was a little girl.

How about we open another bottle? she said, as they both wiped their tears off their faces.

Sounds like a great idea. These invitation cards will never make it to the mail if we keep on with our drama, her mother said.

I love you, mom.

I love you more, sweetheart. Now, let's get all these cards put in the envelopes. I can't believe you're getting married soon. You will be a gorgeous bride. I can't wait.

The memories made her miss her mother more. She made a mental note to call her when they returned to Serenity Manor. She shook the memories off as she slipped into a simple, light pink floral maxi dress that accentuated her curves and matched it with a beige cardigan and tan sandals.

"Are you almost ready?" Ethan asked as he sat on the edge of the bed dressed in his white long-sleeve shirt and khaki pants, putting on his brown leather sneakers.

She nodded as she grabbed her purse and headed toward the front door, but Ethan walked the other way.

"Where are you going?" she said.

"Come." He extended his hand for her.

What was he up to now? She reached for him, and he led her to the patio.

Under the moonlight was a candlelight dinner for two. Next to the table was a silver ice bucket with a champagne bottle beside a tiki torch that added light and elegance to the outdoor dinner setting. Ethan picked up a bouquet of a dozen plump red roses from the table and handed it to her.

"Ethan...This is gorgeous."

"Only the best for my wife. Happy anniversary."

"Happy Anniversary, hun."

Ethan pulled a chair for her to sit. Along with the breeze under the moonlit sky, music suddenly wafted through the air. She turned to look at where it was coming from. She was familiar with the tune, *The Nearness of You* - her favorite song. When she turned back to look at Ethan, he was already on his feet.

"Dance with me," he said.

They danced to the mesmerizing voice of Frank Sinatra, feeling the brisk breeze as they swayed gently. She looked up at the sky and swore she could see the stars dancing with them. She buried her face in Ethan's chest, feeling every beat of his heart.

Ethan kissed her head, and she glanced up, meeting a satisfied sparkle in his eyes. Ethan knew how to please her in simple and grand ways. He lifted her chin to kiss her longing lips. The music stopped, but they continued to sway into their own melody as their tongues intertwined, earnestly finding a way to satisfaction.

***

As he clasped his wife, his body writhed, not sexually, but in a deep gut, unexplainable feeling.

"I love you so much, Han."

"I love you, too, babe."

Could he love someone so much that it's almost painful? Hannah was his first love. The only love he'd ever known. He didn't think he could love anyone the way he loved Hannah.

A sudden feeling of guilt came over him. He knew he wasn't Hannah's first love, but he won fair and square. At least, that's what he kept telling himself. Oliver didn't fight for her; instead, he ran away. Oliver couldn't blame him for that or for them simultaneously falling in love with the same woman. She was perfect, and they both knew it, but he was willing to do anything to have her, even if it cost him his best friend. Thankfully, it didn't come to that.

He gently pulled away, ending their long, passionate kiss, and stared deeply into Hannah's eyes. "Please don't ever leave me," he whispered.

"Never," she whispered back.

He gently placed her hands over his heart and covered them with his.

"I will never leave you, Hannah. No matter what happens, I will always be with you. That's a promise."

Ethan could read the confusion on her face as if wondering what was going on, so he took her slightly parted mouth into his before she could ask. Pulling her back and gently turning her, he planted his warm lips on her neck as he breathed her in; Ethan could almost see her eyes closed, anticipating each kiss he planted on her shoulders. He turned her back to face him and continued kissing her neck; she leaned back as he worked his way back to her patiently waiting lips. Her soft purr made him tense and rigid. He needed to have her tonight, and he needed her for the rest of his life.

The night air felt chilly. Suddenly, he was reminded of the jacuzzi waiting for them. He ended the kiss, surprising Hannah.

"Follow me," he said.

She nodded, took his hand, and they walked back to the patio.

As soon as they got inside, Ethan pulled her dress over her head, leaving her with a matching black lace bra and panty set he had never seen before.

"I love them," he whispered.

Her perfect, silky body shone under the moonlight. Ethan wanted her; he wanted her badly. He lifted her into the tub and handed her a glass of champagne, then kicked his shoes off, undressed within seconds, and climbed into the tub with her. He took the champagne glass from her hand, downed what was left, and set it aside.

"Come here," he said as he pulled her closer to his wet body, facing her away from him, and wrapped his legs around her. He kissed her wet shoulders as she rested her head on his neck. She whimpered. He cupped her bosoms, playing with the wetness of her nipples. She cried; oh, how he loved hearing her cry in euphoria. He teased her briefly before turning to face him and immediately claimed her throbbing mouth and pulled her legs apart to wrap around him as his manhood writhed in desire. He buried his face into her neck, kissing, biting, and loving her. He traveled down her petite, well-sculpted breasts and brushed off some bubbles before claiming each, making her arch her back.

"I want you. I want you now," she begged.

He parted her legs and slowly entered her. She cried. She moaned, she cried, and she moaned some more. He did the same, claiming her lips.

As soon as her tongue played with his, he almost lost control. Her kiss, her hot, wet kiss, was all it took. He was ready. He gently made love to her, waiting for her to reach oblivion.

When she did, he continued making love to her; this time, he didn't hold back. They groaned and whimpered in unison, clinging to each other like their lives depended on it. He could have sworn he had tears in his eyes.

***

Hannah followed Ethan to the villa. She knew what was waiting for her. She had prepared for this. She even purchased a new lingerie set, as she always did for the last four anniversaries. There was something sexy about a man who takes charge, and she always loved that about her husband, especially when it came to making love. Not that she'd never initiated anything first, but she always felt wanted when he did.

"Do you like them?" she asked teasingly when Ethan finally pulled her clothes over her head and tossed them to the side.

"I love them," he whispered.

He lifted her into the tub, and the hot water immediately felt good on her body.

"Here," Ethan handed her a glass of champagne, which would be her third glass of the night. She was feeling good. She looked up at the night sky full of sparkling stars as Ethan climbed in with her, asking her to get closer.

"I love it when you do that," she whispered as Ethan planted kisses on her shoulders.

"That's why I do it all the time."

"You need to do it more," she said.

He explored her body down, kissing every inch of her. Her breasts started to ache, waiting for him to get there, and when he finally did, she had to bite her lips to stop herself from screaming.

"I want you. I want you now," she begged.

His gaze almost penetrated her soul; they were fiery, full of desires. Desire for her. Her body. Her love. He kept his eyes on her as he pulled her legs apart and made love to her.

"Let it go, baby. Let it go," he said.

"Ethan..."

"Yes, angel?"

"I love you," she said as she gave up control and released herself onto him.

Chapter Nineteen

The following day, silence enveloped Ethan while driving back to Serenity. Their weekend at the ranch had revealed some intense feelings he never knew he had for his wife. He knew he loved Hannah; there was no question about that, but this feeling was more profound than love if that could ever be possible. Ethan didn't want to scare Hannah with his intense emotions; he wouldn't want her to think he was becoming obsessed, but the feelings intensified each day; it even scared him. Then there was the fear, somehow, the fear of losing her to Oliver had resurfaced. Why? He had no clue. It just did. All he knew was that he wouldn't want to separate from her. His heart ached for her constantly, and he never thought he would ever find a woman he would love more than life itself, that he would give anything and everything never to leave her side or for her to never leave him, for that matter. Ethan glanced at his wife sitting next to him in the car and was reminded of their wedding day, watching his bride march down the aisle. It was then that he realized that breathing was useless without her. He promised himself that he would do whatever it took to stay by her side no matter what. He was there to take care of her, to always make her happy, to love her. Not even death could separate them; that was his promise to her.

The blue lights flashing around the manor pulled him away from his thoughts. He was suddenly alert.

"I hope everyone is okay," Hannah said as they pulled behind a distance from the ambulance.

"Someone's inside, but I couldn't see who it is," she said.

They hurried toward the house.

A young, uniformed officer was quick to stop them.

"Excuse me. You guys can't be here."

Did he really just puff his chest at him?

"We are guests here. Is everything... everyone alright?" Ethan asked, ignoring the officer's perceived arrogance.

The officer lowered his dark aviators halfway and studied him before answering.

"I'm assuming you're the Prestens?" he said, placing his glasses back on.

"Yes, we are. I'm Ethan and---" The officer seemed to have moved on quickly and was already looking at Hannah. Ethan placed his hand on Hannah's back. "...and my wife, Hannah."

Silence.

"Excuse me, officer?" Ethan said firmly.

The officer straightened up and cleared his throat. "Deputy."

"I'm sorry?"

"I said, *Deputy*," he confirmed, not looking at him. "I understand that you guys were supposed to be staying at the Serenity Manor. So, where were you this morning?" The officer took a notepad from his shirt pocket.

Is this guy serious? He acted like Ethan couldn't hear the squeaky voice this man tried so hard to conceal. He could even tell Hannah was trying not to laugh. Ethan had to be polite. This is an officer of the law, after all. "We stayed at a ranch over the weekend. Have you spoken to Mrs. Clark? The owner of the manor? Is she okay? "Ethan didn't mean to sound brusque but wasn't sorry either. The deputy seemed to act like they should not have left the place. Who was he to judge? He asked again, "Is *anyone* hurt?"

The officer continued to scribble on his notepad. "You mean to tell me you guys came to Green Ridge, stayed at Serenity Manor, and then stayed in another place for the weekend?" This time, the officer looked up, staring straight into Ethan's eyes. Frustrated eyes.

What's up with this guy's ass? He thought. Did he have to be so condescending? His eyes landed on the officer's name tag: *Deputy Christopher Jacobs.*

Another officer approached. He was much older.

"What did you say your name was?" the Sherriff asked.

Ethan took a deep breath and shook his frustration aside, "Ethan, and this is —"

"Hannah," Deputy Jacobs interrupted enthusiastically like a little know- it- all kid during a pop quiz.

Seriously? This time Ethan didn't hide his irritation and glared at the Deputy.

"Ethan and Hannah Preston," the deputy added.

He nor Hannah tried to correct him. He tried to make sense of the deputy's attitude. He remembered Hannah's words: *perspective. Always try to see the other person's perspec-*

tive. So, he did. Maybe this guy was new and trying to impress the sheriff.

Sally and Nichole came. Thank goodness they were safe. Sally told them everything and that everything was fine, nothing was taken, and nothing was damaged.

"Is that Dillon in the ambulance?" Ethan asked.

"Yes," Nichole answered.

"Is he all right?" Hannah asked, looking toward where Dillon was getting treated.

"He's doing better."

"What happened?" Ethan asked.

"He fell and hit his head. He lost consciousness for a bit. Good thing I checked on him as I did. I called the ambulance, and they came right away. He's okay, but he needed to get checked to make sure," Sally said.

"Well, Sally, we've taken all the information we need for now," the Sheriff announced. His tone suggested they'd known each other for a while.

"Nothing seemed to imply robbery. However, we didn't really look into the Preston's belongings. Would you guys like to check if something is missing?"

"Good idea," Ethan blurted, and immediately started for the house with Hannah on his side.

He and Hannah surveyed the room.

"Nothing seemed to be missing here. Everything seemed to be in place," Ethan informed the deputy, who stood waiting to see if they revealed anything significant, he supposed.

"Wait," Hannah alerted. "I could have sworn we locked the sliding door." She slid the slightly opened glass door and walked outside. There was a vase on the table. Now it was on the ground, broken in pieces.

"The wind had picked up lately. That must be what Dillon heard," the Sheriff suggested.

Ethan surveyed the surroundings just to make sure. It was possible the wind could have knocked the vase off the table. Convinced that everything was fine, they all returned outside to join Sally, who was waiting by the ambulance where Dillon stood.

"Sally, if you notice anything else out of the ordinary, please don't hesitate to call Deputy Jacobs or me," the Sheriff said before turning around to address the rest. "That goes for all of you." He gestured toward Ethan and Hannah, tipping his hat before getting into his squad car. His young deputy followed and left the premises.

As they all started back for the house, Ethan noticed a guy standing across the manor. It was one of the paramedics standing by the ambulance. Something about the way he stood there bothered him. He wasn't just there assisting or getting ready to leave, he was staring at something. *Someone.* He followed his gaze and sure enough, the guy was staring at Hannah. Despite all the commotion earlier, he did notice the guy's odd interest in their every move. He thought it was just him, so he quickly brushed it off.

Finally, their eyes met, and the man quickly shifted his attention to the other paramedic next to him.

"Are we all good?" he heard him say.

A younger female paramedic was climbing into the driver's seat of the ambulance. "We're all good, Lieutenant David."

The man took one long gaze at Hannah before climbing into the rig.

Ethan watched him settle inside, fixing the rearview mirror. Why would he fix the rearview mirror when he wasn't driving? Was he still watching Hannah? Their eyes met. No, he was watching him.

Chapter Twenty

His heart pounded as he drove back to work. He finally got close to Hannah, yet she still didn't recognize him. The thought made his blood boil. It took all the control he could muster not to grab, kiss, and strangle her all right there in front of everyone, but he knew it wasn't the time. He felt high from being so close to her. He wanted to say *hi*, maybe she'd remember who he was, but as time passed, he realized she did not recognize him. Not even one bit.

Something was off. His mind was playing tricks on him; one moment, it was an excellent idea to make Hannah pay, the next, he'd feel guilty. One moment he'd see Hannah as some innocent girl, the next, he'd see her as the bitch who ignored and hurt him. Hannah's face flashed before him again. She was still as beautiful as ever. A voice inside his head told him to let go, to leave her alone, but the other voice, a much louder voice, screamed *she needed to pay,* especially when he watched her husband next to her. He quickly snapped out of his pity for Hannah. Why should she be happy when he's miserable? Why should any other guy be happy with her when he didn't even get the chance? She needed to pay for making him miserable all these years. That would show her just how much she needed him, maybe then, she'll remember who he was, someone she should have paid attention to then.

Chapter Twenty-One

Ethan rushed to where Hannah was standing. "What was that?"

"What was what?" Hannah said.

"Didn't you see how that paramedic looked at you? He was practically drooling the whole time he was here. Then I saw him glance through his rearview mirror to take another look before they drove off." Ethan was frantic. Something in his gut didn't feel right about what he'd just witnessed.

Hannah placed a hand on his shoulder. "Hun, it's okay. They're gone. Maybe he was just trying to make sure everything was alright before they left. Let's go inside and see if the Clarks need our help."

He took a deep breath and followed her. He'd have to deal with this later. Something was off with the that guy, but Hannah was right, they needed to check on the Clarks first.

The Clarks were all sitting at the dining table sipping hot tea that Sally had prepared for everyone.

"Is everyone alright?" Ethan said as they entered the room.

"Yes. We were just processing what had happened," Sally said, standing with a teapot in her hand. "Would you like some tea?" she asked, holding the pot in front of Hannah.

"That would be lovely," Hannah replied as she sat beside Dillon.

"Do you mind telling us the entire story, Dillon?" Ethan said. He wanted to ensure he didn't miss anything, especially now that he felt something was amiss. Did Hannah notice the guy looking at them? He wondered. Could the Deputy and the Paramedics be in cahoots about something? He was being paranoid; he knew, but his feelings were never wrong. Something about them didn't seem right, especially the paramedic. Dillon spoke and forced him to move away from his thoughts.

"I was walking toward the barn around ten this morning when I heard a crashing sound coming from the house. At first, I thought you guys were back, but I saw the car was still gone. I was sure someone was there, so I ran in to check and I swear I heard footsteps upstairs, so I grabbed the baseball bat in the kitchen and went up. I was in the hallway when I heard the door slam downstairs, or so I thought. So, I rushed down, and that's when I slipped, fell, and lost consciousness."

"Was the front door open when you got here?" Hannah asked.

"No, but I wasn't sure if I left it open after I came in. Everything happened so fast."

"Anything else?" Ethan pressed on.

"Well, unless you guys left your bedroom door open when you left, that's the only thing I thought was odd. I didn't think you guys would do that," Dillon explained as he rubbed his head.

"I think that's enough. I suggest you get a head CT just to make sure," Hannah said as she noticed the concern etched on Sally's face. "He'll be alright," she reassured her.

They were just about to head back to their room when the doorbell chimed. Nichole walked into the room, and trailing behind was Deputy Jacobs. Ethan studied the deputy as he walked in. Deputy Jacobs was tall, looked much younger than him, and was not a bad-looking guy.

The officer glanced at his direction. His pale blue eyes didn't match his demeanor. Maybe Hannah was right; he was just trying to prove something to his boss. Ethan placed his arms on Hannah's shoulders as the Deputy approached. He wouldn't usually be this protective, but something about this guy made him want to punch him in the nose. The Deputy looked at him again, and this time, they exchanged looks. Did he just see kindness in the Deputy's eyes? This guy's personality was all over the place, confusing him.

"Hey, bud. How are you feeling?" the Deputy asked.

"I'm okay. My head still hurts a bit, but we were just about to head to the clinic."

"I won't take long, then. I forgot to ask you earlier. What were you doing in the house this morning if the Prestens were *supposedly* gone for the weekend?"

Supposedly? His irritation was back.

"I've been doing some work while the Prestens were away. I was there much earlier in the morning but went to the barn to get a ladder. One of the lights up front needed changing," Dillon explained.

What the heck? Was he talking to Dillon or to Hannah because his attention was on her. He was about to say something, but the officer beat him to it.

"Mrs. Presten, help me understand why you would stay at another B&B when you're already staying here? It just doesn't make sense."

Hannah leaned over and placed the teacup back on the table.

Ethan's jaw muscles tensed. He gave Hannah a sideway glance and was about to answer for her, but Hannah spoke, squeezing his thigh in the process.

"It wasn't actually in our plans, Deputy," Hannah replied and proceeded to explain the events at the ranch. "My husband decided to take advantage of Mr. Monroe's gift," she finished.

The deputy smiled.

"Anniversary? How long have you guys been married?"

Ethan would have thought it was a gracious gesture, that he was excited for them, but his line of questioning irritated him.

"What does that have to do with anything?" he finally interjected.

He felt Hannah shift next to him, squeezing his hands.

"Well, I suppose, nothing," the deputy replied as he closed his notepad. "I'm sorry, Mr. Presten. I just wanted to make sure I had all the information before leaving. Thank you for your time." This time he smiled at Ethan.

It must be done soon, he thought as he drove away into the abyss.

Chapter Twenty-Two

He sat in his living room, formulating how to eliminate Hannah once and for all. All these years, he had tried to prove to women that he was somebody, but somehow, they all left him, including his wife. It was all Hannah's fault. All the pain he endured was all because of Hannah, and she needed to pay. It wasn't right that she got to live a happy life while he struggled.

"So, what's the plan?"

His mother was back! He lowered his head and rubbed his temples. Migraines had been terrible lately, and the screeching sound of his mother's voice made it worse. He took his time trying to comfort himself from his pounding headache. He lifted his head, looked his mother in the eye, and spoke softly, trying not to get more irritated by the sound of his own voice.

"Let me think," he said, gritting his teeth.

"Think? What is there to think about? So, you're going to let her go?" She started pacing, breathing heavily, and giving him a look that could set someone's soul on fire. "You're a coward," she yelled out.

He shot right up and lunged toward where his mother stood, forgetting the reality of it all.

"I am not a coward!"

"Sure, you are," she screamed back, now standing behind him.

He needed his rubber band. Dangit! It wasn't on his wrist. Where the heck did it go? That's right, it broke the day he stood close to Hannah. He walked toward his room and rummaged through his bedside drawer to find another. He rubbed his wrist where the red mark was visible. His wrist was on fire, but he didn't care; the pain in his heart was far worse than the one on his wrist. He threw everything on the ground, and the crumpled stationery landed on the carpet next to where he was kneeling, quickly recognizing what it was. As much as his soul told him not to go back there again, he couldn't help himself. He brought the paper next to his nose and smelled the faint scent of lavender that still lingered on the sheet after all these years, just like the pain she had left him. He opened the letter and started reading it. Again.

Dear Matt,

I don't know where to begin. We used to be so in love; I don't know what happened. I've tried to talk to you so many times about how I felt, but you've always dismissed me. Your priorities have changed. You've become obsessed with finding revenge, and you left me in this house with your mother. I tried to understand. Trust me, I tried so hard. I'm sorry, but I needed someone to take care of me, too. I needed someone to love me and be there for me; I needed a husband, not a mother, especially not your mother. I told you she scared me, but you never listen. I've given this marriage time to work, but I have had enough. So please don't come after me; there's no saving this marriage any longer.

Andrea

He sat there with the crumpled paper still in his hands. He let the tears of anger flow, remembering the day he walked into this very bedroom and saw the letter waiting on his empty bed. His world was turned upside down the day she walked out on him. He really did love her. He had tried to reconcile, but as she had said, she had moved on. She wouldn't return to him, no matter how much he had pleaded. *It's not just you; it's also your mother. She controls your every move, and you gladly let her. You're such a mama's boy,* he remembered her saying one day, and just like that, he whacked her across the face.

He couldn't believe what he had done. He had never struck a woman before. How could he have done it to the woman he loved? He tried apologizing and consoling her, but she wouldn't hear any of it; her last words reverberated in his brain. *You're crazy. You're just as mentally unstable as your mother. You are both crazy. Maybe Hannah was right!*

Andrea called him *crazy,* and she thought Hannah was right. The words kept him awake ever since. He placed the letter in his pocket and returned to the living room.

"You done wallowing in self-pity, boy?" his mother said.

He walked toward the door, grabbed his keys, and walked out. He could still hear her yelling behind him, but he didn't look back. Instead, he got in his car to find her waiting inside.

"Why won't you leave me alone?" he yelled, looking straight ahead, hoping she would vanish in thin air like she always did and never return.

"You think you can just ignore me and leave me in the house?"

"NO. You aren't real. YOU ARE NOT REAL."

He banged his hands on the steering wheel so hard and blasted the horn, startling the kids playing by the side of the road. He raised his hands to apologize to a group of mothers now giving him a dirty look. He looked in the rearview mirror and she was gone.

As he passed by the women who were now standing next to their children, he lowered his window and apologized once more. He drove slowly at first getting out of his neighborhood and as soon as he was out, he pressed on the gas pedal with intensity, ignoring all the stop signs. He drove, not knowing where he was going but somehow ended up outside Dr. Cavanaugh's clinic.

He pulled over in front of the small white building but took his time to go in. His heart pounded and his mind raced. He wasn't sure whether to stay in the car, go in or go somewhere else. *You're crazy. Hannah was right*, the words kept repeating in his mind. He pulled the paper out of his pocket, and right there and then, he knew where he wanted to be. He arrived at his spot just in time to see Ethan walk out of the manor in his joggers and sweats. The clock on the dashboard said five forty-six. The sun was still out, but not for long, so he waited.

Chapter Twenty-Three

Hannah sat by the lake, reminiscing about the night she and Ethan were there. She couldn't help but smile. Her heart ached for Ethan, and her love for him grew daily. The anniversary getaway was perfect, and she couldn't help but feel a little melancholy thinking this was their last night at the manor. Even the Clarks had become close to them. Something about Virginia made her feel at home, but she also hadn't forgotten the eerie feeling she had had the first day they'd arrived. Then, that whole thing with Dillon, the house, the deputy, the paramedic, and her dream. Something just didn't feel right, especially about her dream. She planned to tell Ethan about her recurrent dreams, but how could she do that now after seeing what it was all about? Last night's dream was the same as it had been, but this time, the man had finally shown his face. Oliver held her and her baby in his arms. The whole thing baffled her. She quickly brushed the thought aside as she saw Ethan approach.

"Did the nap help with your headache?" she asked as Ethan got closer.

"It sure did." He gave her a quick peck on the cheek. "I thought I'd go for a quick run under this beautiful scenery one last time. Wanna go?" he asked as he bent to tie a shoelace that came undone.

"I think I'll stay, watch the sunset. I might call Kate and check on the clinic and the young Dr. Reed."

"Alright then, enjoy the last few hours of peace and quiet. We drive out to DC early tomorrow," Ethan reminded her, then kissed her on the forehead. "I'll be back in an hour or so. Love you," he said as he jogged toward the side street.

Hannah watched her husband fade out of sight. She grabbed her phone and made her call.

"I was just about to call you, Dr. H."

"Hi, Kate. How're things at the clinic?"

"Everything is fine. The other Dr. H. Dr. Hotness - *that is,* is doing great." Hannah shook her head and smiled, remembering Kate's crush on the new young vet. Dr. Reed was a new veterinarian Hannah left in charge while she was away.

"How's that stray cat someone brought in last week? Did the guy ever come back?"

"We are still looking. Honestly, I don't think he's coming back. We've been calling the number he gave us, but it doesn't seem to work. Hey, doc, if no one claims Maroon, can I keep him?"

"Maroon? You've named him? And what kind of name is *Maroon*?"

She told Kate not to get too attached to the animals, but she always fell in love with them. Kate walked into the clinic one day looking for a job. *Anything. I would do anything even clean cages or something.* Kate seemed desperate, she remembered. They immediately hit it off a few weeks after Kate started working at the clinic. They were close in age, and

Hannah treated her more like a sister than an assistant, and Kate did the same.

"Maroon, you know? Like Maroon Five?"

Hannah could hear her giggle like a teenager over the phone.

"Gotcha."

"Anyway, the guy probably gave us a fake number."

"What's the name on the file?"

"Let me look. No name. Nada. No address, either," Kate said.

"That's odd. Well, it's probably one of those who can't pay the bill and decided to take off."

"Yeah, too bad. He was kind of good looking."

"Kate, you're crazy."

"I know. I know. I was just joking."

They talked for a few minutes longer before getting back to the book she was reading, enjoying the breeze and the sunset. Time went by fast, the wind got colder, and the sun disappeared. She glanced at her phone. It was almost eight, and Ethan should be back very soon. That's when she heard the uproarious sound of a speeding car. She spun around just in time to see a vehicle strike a man and fly up in the air.

"ETHAN."

Chapter Twenty-Four

He did it. His heart raced at the thought. He couldn't believe he had done it. He was there watching Hannah, not the husband. Surely, he wasn't planning on hitting him with his car, but something else took over as he watched him kiss Hannah. Suddenly, the circumstances were just right. Before he knew it, his foot connected with the gas pedal and didn't let up. He pressed hard and went straight for Ethan. He watched his back hit the top of his hood, crack his windshield, fly up before hitting the ground, and roll over into the ditch. The poor guy didn't see him coming. He looked through his rearview mirror and saw her run toward her husband's body. His heart stopped. He wanted to go back and console her, but he also knew how stupid that would be, so instead, he cried. He cried, and he laughed, then he cried some more.

He drove straight into the open barn behind his house, sat inside his car, and thought about what to do next. *Your sobbing is not going to do you any good,* he told himself. He needed to clean and get rid of the car. That's what he needed to do and *fast.* He stepped out of the vehicle and immediately searched for the black drape to cover it. There was blood on the hood, but he would have to deal with that later. First, he needed to find out if Ethan made it. Before he could take out his radio, his mother's voice reverberated in the barn.

"You tried to kill the wrong person, you imbecile."

The tears started flowing again.

"I didn't mean to. Oh my gosh, I killed him. What have I done?"

"You don't know that yet, so you got to go back and finish it. You need to clean up your mess, boy."

"NO. This must stop, mother."

Chapter Twenty-Five

Hannah ran to where Ethan was sprawled, covered with blood. She screamed for help as she tried to feel for her phone. *Dang it.* She must have dropped it. She screamed as loud as she could.

"Please help me. HELP!" She looked around to see if the car that had hit Ethan was there or if anyone else was there, but she was all alone. In the dark. Ethan was covered in blood. Her hands were covered with *his* blood. She tried to feel a pulse, but there was none. "No, baby, please no. Hang on, Ethan. Please don't leave me. Baby, can you hear me? Ethan, please." She pleaded as she started CPR. She knew she shouldn't panic, but this was Ethan. Her emotions were in turmoil, and her thinking was everywhere.

Nichole and Dillon appeared from behind.

"Call 9-1-1 hurry. Please call for help," she pleaded.

Within a few minutes, she could hear the sirens approaching.

"Let us take care of him, ma'am," the paramedic assisted her to the side as they performed their life-saving rituals. One continued CPR. Another stabilized his neck with a brace. Everything was blurry; she didn't know what to do. The sirens, the lights, and the uniformed people talking simultaneously were overwhelming. She felt helpless. She dropped to the ground and watched the paramedics try to save her husband. With Sally beside her, she waited for Ethan to open his eyes. She waited for the paramedics to say he was alive.

He's not breathing. Come on, man, breathe. She heard one paramedic say as the man administered chest compressions. Finally, after what felt like an eternity, the man yelled, "I got a pulse!"

Hannah rushed to where Ethan was laying, only to be pulled away by another paramedic.

"We got a pulse. Weak, but we got a pulse. Let's go." The man announced to the rest of the team.

She knew his head trauma was severe and was sure there were several broken bones. She watched the paramedic transfer Ethan to a gurney as Deputy Jacobs approached.

"Please, I need to go with my husband," she pleaded.

The officer nodded. "I will see you at the hospital."

She climbed into the ambulance and held her husband's hands as the EMT tended to him. Her heart dropped every time she heard the ominous beeping sound of the machines attached to Ethan's severely injured body. Her tears flowed like a fountain as she watched the barely recognizable love of her life. "How far is the hospital?" she asked the EMT sitting closest. The ambulance wasn't running fast enough for her. She would take over the ambulance if it meant getting there quicker and saving Ethan's life.

"Not far; we're almost there," the EMT replied.

Before the lady could give her more information, the radio came on. She gave Hannah a sideway look. "Yes, LT. He's hanging on--- Can't say."

She knew the paramedic was being cautious, making sure not to give her false hope.

While the paramedic was on the radio, she tried to focus on Ethan, watching his chest go up and down. *Keep breathing baby, please keep breathing*, she begged as she watched the machine. The paramedic was still on the radio. Finally, the ambulance stopped, and she was asked to disembark. She didn't go far. The paramedics rushed Ethan through the doors, where trauma doctors and nurses were waiting by the entrance. She heard them inform the receiving trauma team, *male, 35, MVA, GCS 3, multiple rib fractures, pulse is weak...*

Hannah knew what it all meant, but she had to remind herself that Ethan was a fighter. Before she could tell him to hold on, she was pulled away by a nurse as they wheeled his body into the operating room. "I'm sorry, ma'am, but you have to stay out here."

She didn't want to, but she let go of his hand and fell apart. It was all she could do.

***

Deputy Jacobs came alongside Hannah as the ER door closed behind her.

"I'm so sorry about what happened. Why don't you have a seat, and I'll get you something to drink. Would you like water? Coffee?"

She absentmindedly took the deputy's hands and had him lead her to the waiting area, where she sat, utterly drained. *Where did that car come from? Where did it go? Was it an accident, or did someone deliberately want to harm Ethan? But why?* So many things were going through her already exhausted mind.

"I can use some water, thank you," she finally said without looking directly at the deputy.

Deputy Jacobs returned and sat beside her as he handed her a Styrofoam cup.

"Mrs. Presten, I'm sorry. I know you're tired, but I must ask you a few questions while it's still fresh in your mind."

"I understand," she said.

"Did you see the car that hit your husband?"

"No, it happened so fast," she said, sniffling. "I just heard a loud screeching sound, and when I turned around, I saw Ethan tumbling through the air," she explained as she tried to brush the unstoppable flow of tears down her cheeks. "Oh my gosh, who would do something like this?"

"I'm sorry, ma'am, but did you see anyone parked around the street or lurking around the house?" the deputy asked as he handed her a tissue.

"No, but I really couldn't tell. I wasn't paying attention. It was dark, and I was getting ready to go back inside the house. When I ran to where Ethan was, I looked for the car, but no one was there. So, tell me, deputy, was this an accident?"

"We won't know for sure until we conduct a proper investigation. It is possible the driver was drunk and fled the scene," he informed her and continued. "I heard he decided to go for a run before your trip back home tomorrow. Who else knew he was going for a run?"

She didn't understand why he would ask such a question. He must think there's a possibility that this was intentional. "Yes, Ethan wanted to enjoy the fresh breeze before heading home tomorrow. I don't know who else knew he was going for a run. I suppose only *I* knew, unless the Clarks were there, and he talked to them."

The OR door opened, and Hannah rushed up to meet the nurse.

"He lost a lot of blood, but the doctors are doing their best, Mrs. Presten. I just wanted to give you an update. He is still in surgery. Your husband is in skilled hands." The nurse reached for her hand, trying to reassure her.

The Clarks rushed through the entrance and stood next to her.

"Oh, dear, how are you doing? How is Ethan? Have you heard from the doctors? Sally said as the nurse excused herself.

"He's still in surgery," was all Hannah could say.

"We're so sorry, sweetie. Who would do such a thing? Anything we can do?"

"Thank you, Sally. I don't need anything but prayers for Ethan to pull through."

"C'mon sweetheart, let's get you seated." Sally hugged her and said a quiet prayer as they sat in the waiting area.

Deputy Jacobs asked the Clarks a few questions before talking to her again.

"If you remember anything, *anything* at all, don't hesitate to call me. I will be heading back to the station. I'll talk to the Sheriff and update you as soon as we find something pertinent," he said.

She did notice the deputy's caring tone. Perhaps he was friendly, after all. She thought of Ethan. She would tell him about the deputy's kindness later when he felt better.

"Thank you, deputy."

"Deputy?" Dillon rushed up and stopped the officer in his tracks.

"Could this be related to what had happened at the Manor?"

She waited for the deputy to answer. She had forgotten about the possible break in at the manor.

"We didn't really conclude that there was, in fact, a break in." He paused. "But considering the timing of it all...I don't want to speculate, but it's possible. We really wouldn't know until we investigate further."

Was that a good thing or not? She was too exhausted to ask. She laid her head on Sally's shoulders. Then she remembered her dream. She was going to tell Ethan about her dream but decided not to. Suddenly, she felt guilty.

Chapter Twenty-Six

Detectives Reagan and her partner, Ardy Shikadans, were called to the scene.

Detective Reagan flashed the light on the road as she and her partner inspected the area where Ethan was hit.

"What made you guys call us for a hit and run?" Reagan asked as she continued studying the area.

"Something about it just didn't seem right to me," Sheriff Rodgers said.

"Is that so?" Shikadans said, turning around and looking at the Sheriff.

"You called us on a hunch?" Reagan said.

"I am ruling this as a first-degree aggravated assault... and, depending on if the victim pulls through. I pray he does. This could very well become a homicide," Rodgers said.

"I'm sorry. I didn't mean disrespect, but you know what I mean, Sheriff."

"Yes, I do, and I'm telling you something about this just doesn't seem right. Trust me."

She chose not to respond to the Sheriff's comment but continued looking around. In her experience, the small-town police department would usually want to solve the crime themselves, but for the Sheriff to call them, that said a lot.

Reagan and Shikadans continued to assess the scene. Under the naked eye, there wouldn't be much to go with, but this wasn't Reagan's first rodeo. The fact that there weren't any tire marks on the road suggested exactly what the Sheriff suspected; this *could* be intentional. Now, who would want to kill a random vacationer, and why? Or...was it a random act?

Detective Shikadans interrupted her thoughts, "Whoever was driving the car intended to kill Mr. Presten. He must have known he was going for a run tonight."

She nodded, still examining the scene. "We need to know more about the couple. Maybe someone followed them from..." she paused and looked at Rodgers for an answer."

"Sacramento," the Sherriff provided.

"All the way from California?" Shikadans blurted.

Reagan looked at her partner. "Detective, make sure we call SAC PD to see if there are any reports relating to the Prestens."

Detective Shikadans nodded and quickly made a note of it.

"Tell me about the family who owns the Manor, Sheriff. Where were they when it happened?" Reagan asked.

"I spoke to the Clarks earlier, and they told me they were at home when it happened. I also checked their cars; both were parked in front of the house when we arrived minutes after the accident. I'm sure it couldn't have been them. I know the family; they're good people."

"Well, we would still need to speak to the Clarks again. Could *you* and the deputy canvas the neighborhood and see if anyone was around when this happened? Maybe someone was out, saw, or heard something. Let's hope we find a witness," she said, facing the Sheriff, but she made herself loud enough for the entire team to hear.

"On it," Sheriff Rodgers said as the other officers started to move.

Reagan and Shikadans headed for Serenity Manor just as Nichole and Dillon exited their car.

They both flashed their badges. "Hi, I'm Detective Reagan, and this is Detective Shikadans. We're here to ask a few questions about what happened tonight." Detective Reagan couldn't help but notice Nichole holding her reaction at the mention of Shikadans' last name. This was not the first time someone chuckled when they'd heard *Shikadans.* She shook her head.

"Please come in, detectives," Dillon led them to the living room. "Please have a seat. My mom isn't here right now. She's at the hospital with Mrs. Presten, but we'll be glad to answer your questions."

Detective Shikadans spoke first. "What are your names?"

"I'm Dillon, and this is my twin sister, Nichole."

The detectives took notes.

"Where were you guys when the incident happened?" Detective Shikadans continued.

"We were both at home."

"Tell us what you witnessed," Reagan said.

"Not much, really. Nics, my sister, was watching TV, and I was reading a book. Then I heard a loud engine roar outside. At first, I thought it was the TV, till I looked up and saw she was watching a talk show, so I stepped outside to check. That's when I saw and heard Hannah screaming for help down the street. We both got up to check." Dillon glanced at Nichole, who was nodding in agreement.

"Did you notice anything odd? Maybe heard someone or *saw* someone outside?" Detective Reagan asked as she took mental pictures of her surroundings. There was really nothing out of the ordinary.

It was Nichole who answered this time. "No, ma'am. I mean, detective. I was even planning on stopping by to say goodbye to the Prestens. They were going to drive back to DC early tomorrow for their flight back to California," she explained.

"Did you know if the Prestens got into an altercation with anyone while they were here?" Reagan asked.

"Not that we know of. The Prestens are good and mild people. They are easy to like. Actually, we got so close to them in the short days they've stayed here. I don't know who would want to hurt Ethan. This is just crazy. Nothing like this happens here," Dillon said, shaking his head.

"Did you guys see a car or anyone lurking around the neighborhood earlier tonight? When they first arrived or any time after that?"

"No, ma'am," the twins said in unison.

"How about the last few days? Anything out of the ordinary?"

"I don't think so, not that I've noticed." Dillon looked at his sister as if to ask if she had, but she shook her head.

"With all due respect, ma'am, why are detectives involved? Wasn't it a stupid drunk driver or something?" Dillon asked.

"We are looking at all angles," Detective Reagan said.

The twins nodded.

"Wait," Nichole said abruptly and looked at her brother. "Could your incident be tied to this?"

"What incident?" Reagan's curiosity heightened.

It was Dillon who answered. "While the Prestens were away. I came here to fix a broken light, and I thought I heard something upstairs, so I rushed up there but found no one—"

"But then he heard a commotion downstairs, so he ran back down... but fell down the stairs and lost consciousness," Nicole finished.

"Is that how you got that?" Shikadans pointed at Dillon's forehead.

"Yes sir," he said as he absentmindedly touched his bandage.

"Did you call the cops?" Reagan asked.

"Yes, ma'am. I mean... detective. Yes, we did. The Sheriff and his Deputy came to investigate, but they didn't find anything.

Reagan gave her partner an inquisitive look. "I wonder why the Sheriff didn't mention this earlier?"

"As I said, they didn't find anything wrong or suspicious. It was just a broken vase from the balcony. The wind had picked up the last few days," Dillon explained.

"Still worth looking into," Shikadans said.

"Absolutely." Reagan glanced at her watch. It was almost midnight. She nodded at Shikadans, confirming they were done for now, and both stood at the same time.

Detective Shikadans handed Dillon his card as they started for the door.

"Thank you for your time. Please don't hesitate to call us if something else comes to mind."

Reagan made a mental note to talk to the Sheriff and his deputy later and find out more about this *incident* they failed to mention.

Chapter Twenty-Seven

It had been almost two hours, and Hannah still had not heard from the surgeons. Nurses came out several times to give her some vague updates, but nothing reassured her that Ethan was out of the woods. Sally never left her side, despite her persuasion for her to go home. In all honesty, Hannah was thankful Sally decided to stay. If she hadn't been there, she would not have known what to do with the uncertainties, the quietness, and the fears she had; she would have lost her mind.

She managed to call Oliver to let him know what had happened. Oliver quickly offered to fly to Virginia, but she told him not to. Not yet, at least; she would have to face this on her own and figure out the details of them flying back home as soon as Ethan was safe to travel. She needed to have faith. She looked for a chapel. *Hospitals still have chapels, right?* Hannah spotted a small prayer room, decided to step in, slid between the pews and said a quiet prayer.

Lord, God. I know you are listening. Please take care of my Ethan. Please don't take him away from me. I need him. I still need him. Please.

A few minutes later, she went back to the waiting area not wanting to miss any updates from the surgeons. It took another good thirty minutes before a man in blue scrubs came out looking exhausted as he pulled his cap off. Hannah's heart pounded with each step the surgeon took toward her. She rushed to meet him; Sally was right behind her. Hannah saw the mournful look in the surgeon's eyes as he lifted his head. She held her breath as her heart tightened.

"I'm sorry, Mrs. Presten. We did all we could. He was touch and go for a while, but his heart couldn't handle the trauma. It finally gave up. There was nothing more we could do."

"No. No. Please, NO."

The surgeon caught her as she collapsed in front of him, sobbing.

When she somewhat regained composure, Hannah was finally taken to see Ethan's body. Aside from the bruises and bloodstains on his face, he almost looked like he was sleeping. She wobbled as she approached the bed. Thank God for Sally aiding her and keeping her steady.

She held his hand before glancing back to address Sally. "Can I have a few minutes alone with my husband?"

"Of course, sweetheart. I'll be outside if you need me."

Her knees buckled as she stepped closer to his body. Her heart wanted to give up right there and then. She closed her eyes and stayed in the room without saying a word, praying that this was all a terrible nightmare, that she would open her eyes and all would be back to normal, but it didn't.

"You promised not to leave me, remember?" she managed to say softly between sobs. "You broke your promise." She stroked his hand, then his face. They were still warm. She tried to keep her composure, but there was no stopping her emotions. She fell on him, hugging and shaking, hoping for a miracle that he would wake up.

"You can't leave me. Please, baby, don't leave me. You promised. Remember? You promised," she screamed, hugging Ethan's lifeless body.

Sally walked back in and tried to pull her away, but she just couldn't let go. She wanted to go with Ethan, wherever that may be.

"He's gone, sweetie. I'm so sorry. Come on, let me take you home."

"A few more minutes, please," Hannah pleaded. She knew she had to let go, but how? How could she let go? How can she live without him? He promised.

"I love you, baby. Promise you'll wait for me."

She kissed his still warm lips and tears fell on his face. "I love you very much; don't ever forget that." There was nothing else she could do but face reality. "Goodbye, Ethan." Her own words stung like a knife twisting in her gut. Suddenly she felt an icy touch of air brushing her shoulder. She looked back at Ethan and felt the coldness again, this time on her cheeks. She touched her face and felt a surge of unexplainable feelings. That's when her heart knew he had kept his promise. *I will always be by your side no matter what happens,* she remembered him saying.

Hannah kissed her husband on the forehead as he used to do to her. "I feel you, babe. I know you're here."

She kissed him on the lips one last time before walking out of the door.

***

As soon as Matthew learned about Ethan's passing, he got into his truck and headed for the hospital. He needed to see her one last time. He walked in just as Sally and Hannah walked out of the room.

"Lt. David," Sally called out.

He was caught by surprise. He wasn't expecting anyone to remember him.

"Hi," was all he could muster.

"Thank you again for taking care of my son."

"I'm sorry?"

"My son, Dillon? At Serenity Manor?"

"Oh yes, Dillon," he said, trying to see if Hannah was listening, but she wasn't. He stood next to her, and she still did not remember him.

"Please excuse us. I need to take Hannah home so she can get some rest."

"Of course," he said.

Hannah looked up and gave him a faint smile. His heart skipped a beat, unsure whether it was from excitement or fear of her recognizing him as the person who killed her husband. *She couldn't have. I was going too fast;* he tried reassuring himself. He felt as if time had stopped as he watched her walk away, seeing the sadness in her eyes. Suddenly, he wanted to comfort her.

"Hey, Matt, are you working today?" A familiar voice shook him back to reality. Dr. Cavanaugh stood in front of him.

"No. I mean, yes, well was supposed to, but something came up, and I needed to check on something here."

"Are you Ok?"

"Yes. Of course. Why would you ask that?"

"Are you sure you're, Okay? C'mon, it's me."

"Yes, Linda, I'm Ok. Anyway, I gotta go, and I probably won't see you for a while. I have to go on a trip."

He didn't give the doctor a chance to respond. Instead, he hugged her and said, "Thank you." He could sense his therapist watching him as he walked away; he didn't look back. He knew he needed to leave Virginia ASAP, but he still needed to take care of the car in the barn and get rid of all the evidence that would tie him back to Ethan's death.

Surprisingly, the drive back home was quiet.

"Mother?" he whispered. Nothing. "Mother, are you here?" No answer. *Could she be gone for good?* He wondered. He remembered his last conversation with her, telling her to leave him alone. Then he smiled. It couldn't be that easy to get rid of her. She'd be back.

Chapter Twenty-Eight

Matthew stood alone in his barn and tried calling for his mom again.

Matt, your mother's appearance is a manifestation of your loneliness. You are missing her, he recalled Dr. Cavanaugh saying during one of their sessions.

What? Manifestations? Loneliness? Why would I want my dead mother to haunt me?

He was offended by the insinuation. Although he remembered thinking, *that's what therapists do, right? Analyze what you are, who you are, and all your issues are blamed on your childhood relationship with your mother.* He shook the thoughts away. All he knew was that he needed his mother at this moment. Maybe Linda was on to something. He wasn't sure if this was how it was done, but he'd seen it in the movie before where they would call for the spirit and all; a bit creepy even for him, but he was desperate to talk to someone, and if he wanted her to show up, then she would show up according to his therapist's theory.

"Mom?"

Nothing.

"Mom, are you here?"

Nothing.

"Manifestation, my butt!"

He looked at his watch and realized he'd been working for hours; he knew he only had a little time before the Sheriff, or the detectives arrived at his house. He lived only a block from the manor and was sure they would be canvassing his area, too; he needed to hurry. He grabbed the debris scattered on the floor from dismantling the Toyota, now stripped of the windshield, hood, and front bumper, and even threw all four tires in the back of his Ford truck with the other parts he'd removed earlier. Working at a car shop in California paid off; he learned to dismantle a car in no time. He opened the glove compartment and ensured everything was out, including the fake registration form; he paused, looked at the paper, and shook his head, not believing he had gotten away with a fake registration. He was about to place the plastic container in the back of the truck when he heard someone call his name. Immediately, he dropped the container, closed the barn doors, and rushed toward the front of the house. Glancing at his watch, he couldn't believe it was already past noon.

"Hey, LT," his partner called out, almost giddy as if they were best friends. She was in her mid-twenties but acted like a teenager. He didn't mind her. She was a bit chatty but nice. He didn't want to work with her when she first arrived at the station, but the captain insisted that she ride with him and *learn from the best,* as he recalled him saying.

"What are you doing here?" he asked as he emerged from the backyard, hoping she would follow him to the front of the house.

He needed to get rid of her fast to finish his tasks and leave Virginia as soon as possible.

"I thought I'd check on you since you missed work. You ok?"

He watched her stare at the beads of sweat on his forehead.

"I'm ok. I was feeling under the weather," he said.

"Fever?" she said, still staring at his forehead and glancing over his shoulder from where he had emerged.

"What were you doing back there? Shouldn't you be resting?"

"Nothing. Was looking for something," he said, trying to move her along. "I hate to rush you, but I really need to get inside."

"Are you sure you're OK, LT?"

"Yes, but I do have to go. I need to get something done before it gets too late."

He tried to lead her to her car without being too obvious, but she continued to blabber and did not pick up on his gesture.

"You missed it, man." She continued yapping. "The guy that got hit by a car yesterday. You know the guy who was staying at Serenity? What a tragedy, man. I heard the detectives earlier saying he must have been targeted. Whoever hit him meant business. It was crazy. I knew he wasn't gonna make it, man. I was gonna tell you when I talked to you from the ambulance, but wifey was there, so I really-------"

"Stop." Matt didn't mean to snap at her, but he couldn't bear to stand there and listen to what had happened to Ethan, thinking of how Hannah must have felt and knowing it was all his doing.

"What's wrong, witcha, man?" she snapped back.

"I'm sorry, I didn't mean to — I don't feel too well, and I really need to go inside and rest. Maybe we'll talk tomorrow?" He needed to get her out of there fast so *he* could get out of there, fast.

"Sorry, LT, I didn't mean to disturb you. I just got off, and I thought you'd wanna know about the incident since you'd asked about it earlier. Guess I'll go now."

"Thank you for stopping by and letting me know. I do appreciate it," he said. He could sense her skepticism, but he wouldn't allow himself to worry about that right now. He went back to the barn and did a quick mental assessment of what needed to be done before he split. *Good Enough.*

He went inside the house, grabbed the bag he had already packed, threw it in the back seat of his truck, and drove away. To where? He had no clue.

He drove south for a few hours, ensuring no one followed him as he stopped at several junk yards to dispose of the evidence. He wanted to be as far as he could before stopping at a gas station to refuel, grabbing a few snacks and a couple of six-packs for the road.

The scene of what he had done flashed back, seeing Ethan tumbling up in the air. He meant to kill Hannah, but he couldn't do it. He killed Ethan instead. Why? He didn't know. It just happened. He grabbed a bottle of beer from the passenger seat and cracked it open as he drove away. After several more bottles, his eyes started to weigh heavily; it was time to get some sleep. He'd entered North Carolina a few miles back and decided to drive for a few more before taking the next exit. He found a motel, and after getting his key, he headed to the bar next to the building called *Chug a Lug*. The name made him smile. Perfect for what he wanted to do. Drown his sorrow. Or was it to celebrate? Either way, the bar was the perfect spot.

The place was small, and though he didn't see anyone smoking inside, smoke permeated the room. A couple was canoodling at one table by the entry door, and an older man was on the other side of the bar. He chose a stool at the bar closest to the entrance.

The bartender simply nodded at him, and Matt answered the unasked question.

"Bourbon, straight," he said.

The bartender placed a glass in front of him and poured him a good amount of liquor.

"Put it on my tab, please."

Matt scoped out the place to see if there was anyone he knew, a habit he'd learned over the years. He took his first sip, and the whiskey sent a warm sensation down his throat; it felt good. It had been a while since he'd had some hard liquor. His therapist had suggested that he abstain from drinking while on his medication. *Tonight wasn't that night,* he thought. He ordered another and asked the bartender to make it a double. Suddenly, he remembered the thud he felt when Ethan landed on the hood of his car. Closing his eyes, he tried to shake it off. Instead, Hannah's silhouette replaced the images in his mind. He took another gulp of whiskey and headed to the back bathroom and splashed his face with water, hoping to eliminate the haunting thoughts. He spent a few minutes trying to regain his composure before returning to the bar.

"You okay, sir?" the bartender asked as he grabbed his glass and drank what was left.

"Another double, please."

The bartender poured more liquor into his glass, set a glass of water, and placed his tab beside it. He gave the bartender a dirty look, but the man shrugged. It wasn't worth it, so he took the glass, downed the whole thing, paid for the tab, and walked out. He walked back toward the motel, seeing each woman he passed looking like Hannah. Her vision made his heart drop as he stumbled over the sidewalk and fell. He fumbled for the key he'd dropped on the ground, got up, and managed to find his room. After locking the door behind him, he flopped on the bed. The room started to spin as he began to hear voices, Andrea's and Hannah's voices echoing on top of each other. *Why Matt, why?*

"I'm sorry. I'm so sorry," was the last thing he remembered saying.

It was almost five AM the following day when a nightmare woke Matt up. Ethan was alive, angry, and his wife, Andrea, was happy next to him, but another woman was crying. It was Hannah. *What is wrong with you? You are crazy.* He heard Hannah bellow as she approached him with her car at full speed. He woke up trembling, soaked in sweat. The effect of the alcohol still lingered as he stood and headed for the bathroom. He turned on the faucet and splashed his face with water, hoping for relief. He grabbed the towel from the rack, wiped his face, and as he looked up and glanced at the mirror,

Hannah's face flashed in front of him. He hit his head on the sink as he fell on the floor.

"Dang It."

He stood but stumbled again. Finally, he flopped on the floor and watched the blood from his forehead drip onto the ground.

"Oh, my boy. Do I need to take care of your boo-boo?"

Great. His beloved mother was back.

"Now you show up. What are you doing here? I thought you were gone for good?" he said as he found the energy to get up, grabbed the towel from the sink, and walked back to his bed.

"And miss all the excitement? Nah." She waved a hand. "I've been with you the whole time. I know everything that has happened," his mother said, sitting on the chair beside the bed.

"Where are we headed?" she asked.

"I'm headed somewhere. *You?* I don't know about you," he replied.

"Oh, son, you can't get rid of me that easily," she said. "I'm here to take care of my baby boy as always."

"Are you kidding me? I needed you yesterday, and you didn't show up."

He stared at his mother, waiting for what BS she would come up with. But he was ready to decline whatever it was.

"You're in pain, son, and I'm here to take away your pain. I told you it was a mistake to move back to Virginia. You never listen. Now, look at the mess you've made."

To his surprise, his mother was making sense, and he couldn't help but listen to her babble for a while, reminding him of how awful of a wife Andrea was, how she'd left him, and that she knew she'd been cheating on him shortly after they were married. Matt knew the entire story; he'd heard it all before but was too exhausted to protest. He allowed his mother to rehash everything, including kidnapping two women who resembled Hannah.

"I thought you got this. That's why I got those two girls in Sacramento for you. You were supposed to practice on---"

"Mom! Stop. I didn't ask for you to do that," he grumbled.

"Yeah, but something had to be done. You weren't prepared. As usual, I had to do it myself. And did I get a *thank you, mom*? No."

"Mom, please."

The effect of the liquor was wearing off.

"You're not real," he muttered under his breath as his mom continued to ramble on.

"Ha. And yet here I am. I know Virginia and Serenity held a special place in your heart, but going back there was a mistake. Why do you think I agreed to move with you to California?" his mother said.

I went back to Virginia to find Andrea, ask her for forgiveness and maybe start over," he explained.

"And where did that get you? I told you; she wasn't worth it. You didn't need her. We had each other."

"You still didn't tell me where the bodies are?" he whispered as he pressed the towel on his forehead.

"There's no need for you to know. Take care of this mess you're in. Don't worry about the past," she said with almost sincere concern for him. He almost believed her.

In the past, he rolled his eyes at the thought. "Ma, I've been wanting to start a new life, ask for forgiveness, see a therapist, take my meds, and live life again. I can't keep hating Hannah. I need to find Andrea. Maybe save our marriage."

"Forgiveness? Are you nuts? Happy? The only way you will be happy is to make Hannah pay for what she did to you. You went back to Green Ridge because you wanted to find your wife. Instead, you found Hannah. That's not a coincidence!"

Matt dismissed the comment even though he thought about it, too.

"Ma, I want to live in peace."

Sounding like a devil trying to bargain for her life, she said, "You want to forget about revenge? You want peace? Come with me."

He thought about the offer as he glanced at the bag on the floor. Inside was his 38-caliber wrapped in a towel.

"Go ahead," his mother said.

Matt got up, unzipped the bag, and took out the gun. With trembling hands, he stared at the silver rod.

"Don't just stare at it. Do it, son. Come with me and end your misery."

"Come on, son, do it. There's nothing left for you here. Come on. Pull the trigger." Matt sat in his room with a gun in his hand, oblivious to his mother's command. In his mind was Andrea; how they used to be happy, how they would have been a family, and how he'd loved her so much. Then, the image of the first woman his mom brought home came to mind. She was beautiful, just like Hannah. *Here, you can practice your revenge on her. She looks like that witch Hannah, doesn't she?* He recalled his mother saying as the image of her stroking the lady's curly brown hair plastered in front of him. He didn't even remember her name. All he could remember was that she was feisty. She fought his mother all she could, but ultimately lost her life.

He'd watched his mother drag the lifeless body with her tiny arms after she hit her head with a pipe. It took one blow, and she was gone. He wanted to call for help but couldn't let his mother go to jail.

"Son, what are you waiting for? You don't want to be a fugitive for the rest of your life, do you? Come on, son, don't be a coward."

He heard his mother's plea this time but chose not to answer. Tears were now rolling down his face. He got up, gun still in his hand, and grabbed a beer from the mini fridge.

"You've always been a coward, you know that?"

Matt took a swig of his beer.

"I am not a coward."

"Really? Prove it," she goaded him.

"I have nothing to prove to you, Mother."

He was unaware of how loud he had become until someone from the next room pounded on the wall.

"Hey, keep it down!"

His mother let out the most excruciating, devilish laugh he had ever heard.

"Shhh. People are sleeping," he said.

She laughed even louder.

Suddenly, he was aware of the gun in his hands. He lifted the cold caliber and pointed it at her.

"Are you serious? You're pointing a gun at me? You must be crazier than I am," she taunted him.

Defeated, he lowered the gun to his side. He leaned against the wall and slid down to the ground. He sat there embracing himself and rocked back and forth. Finally, he started to weep uncontrollably. He lifted the gun to his temple, but quickly lowered it down. He continued to sob, this time even louder.

"You're useless," his mother muttered.

Matt gazed at her and let out a wicked laugh. The neighbor pounded on the wall once again.

"Shut up!" he yelled as he got up to the fridge and grabbed another beer, laughing and glaring at his mother, who sat quietly, trying to assess what he would do next. He knew she was waiting for him to pull the trigger. He gave his mother a mischievous smile, set the gun on the night table, and snatched his cell phone from the bed.

"What are you doing? Who are you calling?" his mother asked.

He smiled at her with the utmost sincerity and said, "I love you, mom, but this has to end."

911, what's your emergency?

"I killed a man. Please call Warren County's Sheriff in Virginia and let them know. My name is Lieutenant Matthew David, Paramedic - Station 18 in Green Ridge, Virginia. I'm at a motel just outside of Exit 138. Room 201." Matt hung up before the dispatcher on the other line could even respond.

"You're crazy," his mother protested, but he knew it was time for him to move on. Alone.

"I love you, Mother. Goodbye."

Chapter Twenty-Nine

It had been three months since Hannah came back to Sacramento without Ethan. Still, she hadn't received any new development regarding her late husband's case. She'd last heard that a certain Lt. Matthew David was the prime suspect. She had been calling Detective Reagan and Sherriff Rodgers daily, but both had nothing new to say except *we are still working on every lead to find him. Don't worry; we are not giving up on this. Same story every time*, she thought.

It was almost noon, and she was just getting out of bed. She had one of her dreams again, but she had no energy to entertain it. She opened the curtain and let some sunlight in. Her phone rang. She'd started answering calls a few weeks back when she'd realized ignoring people's calls meant they would end up at her doorstep later that day.

Her phone continued to ring; one more would have gone to her voicemail. Before she could even say hello, she could already hear Kate's voice on the line. Kate had been religious in checking up on her since she returned, especially after the funeral. *The funeral*, she often thought about that day, as she did again today, trying to recall how it all went. Everything was a blur. All she'd remembered was that it was a gloomy day. The service was brief, just how she'd wanted it. Ethan's family and friends were there. Did she even talk to them? Condolences here and there from people she didn't even know. She felt terrible, but she knew they'd understand. Before she knew it, she was back in her empty home. Oliver's family was there, too. Oh God, Oliver. She wondered how he was doing. She hadn't talked to him for a while. She remembered their last conversation after the funeral. Oliver showed up at her door. He didn't look good. He was in pain just as she was. She could tell he had been drinking.

Can I come in?

No, Ol. You need to go home. You're drunk.

I am not.

Yes, you are. Go home, Ol.

He tried to push the door open, but she surprisingly over-powered him.

Please leave me alone. How am I supposed to deal with you when I don't even know how to deal with myself? Go home! She slammed the door closed.

The next day, he called and apologized. She told him she needed space, and he honored it.

Call me when you're ready. I'll be waiting, he had told her.

The pain was evident in his voice. She should not have pushed him away, but she just couldn't hurt for them both. She didn't have the energy. She needed to be alone. To hurt. To sulk. To mourn Ethan.

A week had passed after their last encounter, and she decided to pick up the phone.

Oliver answered right away.

Are you okay? He asked.

I'm okay. Are you?

I'm okay now. Glad you called. Do you need anything?

No. She started crying. *I'm sorry.*

Shhh. It's okay. I understand.

Are you sure you're okay? she asked.

Yes, Han, I'm okay. I bury myself with work. It keeps my mind occupied.

That's good. I just wanted to call and say sorry.

It's all good.

Okay, I'll--- she sobbed.

Han?

I miss him so much, Ol. I miss him so much; it hurts.

I know. I know. I miss him, too.

Thirty minutes later, he was at her front door, and she immediately embraced him. He let her cry. He didn't ask questions; he just let her cry. That was almost three weeks ago.

"Hey, are you there?" Kate's voice forced her back to the present.

"Hellooo," she shouted over the phone.

"Sorry, yes, I'm here."

"I was about to hop in my car and head over there," Kate said.

"Sorry, *Mother.*"

"We seem to be in a lighter mood this morning. Are your curtains open, at least? You need vitamin D, yah know."

"Yes, Kate, they are. Yes, I've eaten, and yes, I've showered," she informed her friend before she could go through the lists of questions, just as she had done every single time she'd called.

"Is that sarcasm I'm hearing, young lady?"

Hannah laughed. "Hey, why don't you stop by after work? Maybe I'll cook dinner." Hannah was even surprised at her invitation. She'd been home alone for three months, and although she went straight to work a few days after Ethan's funeral, she made sure no one bothered her when she got home. She felt comfortable grieving in her own space. In her way. Closed curtains and in the dark. She screened all her calls and only answered emergencies from the clinic.

"It's about time." Kate chuckled on the line.

"Don't forget to grab a bottle of chard...." She caught herself and paused as she remembered how she used to tell Ethan the same thing.

Kate must have understood her sudden quietness and quickly chimed in, "I gotcha, gurl. Don't worry," she said, trying to reassure her. "By the way, don't worry about cooking. I'll bring Chinese. You might serve me that god-awful chicken casserole you've been getting."

"Hey! They were good... Weren't they?" She gave a small laugh. "Anyway, I'm kind of craving some chow mien. So, I'm in!"

They talked and laughed for a few more minutes before hanging up. Hannah was thankful for Kate's friendship, that's for sure. Kate was a few months younger, but she had taught her so much, and she was always there, ready to help and care for her. Hannah was about to hit the shower when her doorbell rang. She stood still for a while, thinking about who it could be, while she grabbed her phone from the counter next to her to check for missed calls, and sure enough, there was one from K a few hours ago. *How did she miss that?*

She answered the door and found him dressed in his dark denim jeans and black pullover. His emerald-green eyes sparkled. He was a few inches taller than Ethan, with a similar masculine build. His strong jawline and brown skin were a perfect match for his thick, dark, and textured hair. Not how she remembered him last. Suddenly, she found him kind of attractive, like he did the first time they met. She really had been confined in the house for so long that she was noticing crazy stuff. She quickly dismissed the thought.

Awkward Silence.

"Hi. I called earlier, but you didn't answer, so I decided to stop by and check on you. I hope that's okay."

Oliver gave her a smile that made her knees buckle. *What is wrong with me?* She thought as she glanced over her shoulder.

"I'm sorry, you have company?" Oliver said.

She quickly straightened up and let him in. "Oh, no. No one is here. Come on in."

"I brought some of your favorite croissants from Alfonso's bakery and a cup of hot Dirty Chai Latte. You still drink dirty chai, right?"

"Yes, I do," she smiled at the thought of him remembering her drink.

Oliver sat the pastry box and the Styrofoam cup on the dining table as he followed her to the kitchen. She discreetly surveyed the room before sitting at the dining table next to Oliver. She could sense his curious look. She needed to say something.

"Thank you for bringing breakfast," she said finally, hoping to divert his attention.

"Are you Okay?"

So much for being discreet and diverting attention, she thought.

"Yes, why wouldn't I be?"

"You seem jittery."

"Must be the coffee I had earlier," she said. "So, how have you been?"

They talked about how she'd been feeling and the lack of progression in Ethan's case. K reassured her he would do his best to follow up with the case. He had checked up on her often since her return, except for the weeks she pushed him away. Even then, he had texted, and she had ignored them. Yet, he was there for her again.

He stayed for almost two hours and when he left, the quietness made her chest tight. She wanted to cry again, but she told herself it was time for her to get it together. She glanced around the house, deciding what to do. The dishes piled up in the sink. Ethan would not have allowed that to happen, so she started there.

"Sorry, babe. I just didn't have the energy to do it. But I'm doing it now," she said, smiling and looking around the empty house. "That should count for something, right?"

Hannah loaded the dishwasher and was about to put another plate in when it slipped her hand and dropped on the floor. Suddenly, she was aware of the tightness in her chest again. She looked up as if looking up in the sky and groaned. "I'm trying here." Who was she kidding? She wasn't done crying for Ethan. So, she cried. She cried as she picked up the broken pieces from the floor. She cried as she threw the pieces in the trash bin. She cried as she opened the refrigerator. Who cared? She wasn't done crying, so she cried.

There were trays of casseroles from her next-door neighbor - an older woman who seemed to think she could eat the whole thing in one day because another tray would be waiting for her the following day. The idea made her smile. She brushed her loneliness aside and studied the contents of the fridge. What would she do with all these casseroles? Take it to the homeless shelter. That's what Ethan would tell her. Yes, that's what she would do. The thought made her remember Ethan saying, *you can't go there alone. It's not safe.* Someone had to go with her. She would have to call K tomorrow and ask him to accompany her. Thinking of K first made her feel guilty. She supposed she could call Kate, but she was just used to calling Oliver whenever she or Ethan needed help.

Hannah put the broom back in the closet and memories of Ethan chasing her with it made her smile some more. It felt good. She paused, trying to hear his voice. Hannah thought she was all cried out but was mistaken as she allowed a tear to fall remembering Ethan's laughter. She wiped away the rest of the tears, grabbed the vacuum cleaner from the closet, and headed to her bedroom, chasing Ethan's image away. She needed to move on.

Hannah sat on the bed for a minute and caught sight of his nightshirt still hanging on the chair next to his side of the bed. She had picked it up a few times before and hugged it while she cried herself to sleep. The following morning, she would place it back where Ethan had left it. She walked toward the chair and picked up the shirt. She could still smell his scent. Perhaps she should wash it and put it away, but she couldn't bring herself to do it. Not yet. She placed it back on the chair neatly folded.

Hannah examined the room before returning to her chores. The sun was bright despite being winter, so she closed the curtain halfway. She grabbed her phone and connected it to the Bluetooth speaker in the bedroom. Nat King Cole's *The Christmas Song* immediately reverberated throughout the room. Christmas was in a few days, and she needed to feel the spirit despite not having Ethan by her side; *this is what he would want*, she thought. She smiled and was about to plug in the vacuum cleaner when she heard a familiar voice.

"What are you doing? You can't vacuum while Nat is singing. That's sacrilege."

Startled, she spun around and saw him sitting on the bed with his leg crossed, grinning at her.

"Have you been here all this time?"

"Of course. Where else would I be?" he said.

"But I didn't hear you arrive."

"Do you ever?" he chuckled.

Nat's voice enveloped the room, and Hannah could not help but feel the longing for him to hold her. *Was it wrong?*

"Christmas is coming soon. My favorite holiday," he said, staring at her.

Hannah could see the sadness in his eyes as he made the statement. "And mine," she added in a soft voice.

Bing Crosby's voice came next with *I'll be Home for Christmas*. She watched him get up and walk toward her; his hand stretched out.

"Dance with me," he said.

"But--?"

"Trust me."

What in the world was she thinking? No one was there, so she reached for his hand and somehow felt him pull her closer toward him. They danced, feeling their heartbeat in unison. While Bing's baritone reverberated in the air, her heart tightened as she tried to savor the feelings of being in his embrace. The song ended, and she stood there with him in silence. They hadn't spent much time together since he decided to come into her life. His presence in the house seemed awkward for both; she wasn't even sure he should be there. *Should I let this happen?* She'd asked herself several times, but she wasn't about to let it bother her. She liked him being there, so she decided no one needed to know.

Chapter Thirty

Hannah did not want to tell anyone about him yet, though she had been tempted several times to tell Kate; she told her almost everything. She knew Kate could tell something had changed about her lately, and though she wanted to open to her friend, it was not the right time. *They wouldn't understand. One day,* she told herself.

"What's the plan for Christmas?" he asked, gently pulling her down onto the bed to sit.

She hadn't thought about Christmas till today. With Ethan gone, it just wasn't the same. She paused for a while before addressing his question.

"Are you gonna be here?" she asked.

"It all depends."

"Depends on what?"

"On who's going to be here."

She didn't know what to say. Kate had asked her the same question a while back, and she had no answer then.

Before she could say another word, he continued and decided for her.

"You need to be with your friends. You deserve that."

"But---"

"Don't worry, I'll be around," he interjected.

Hannah's phone rang. She pressed decline and when she turned, he was gone. He always left the same way. It irritated her. *Ever heard the word courtesy?* She rolled her eyes and grabbed the vacuum. She paused, trying to make out the song playing in the background. It was Nat again. *Go figure.*

She thought about what he had said about vacuuming and Nat King Cole. *Ah, who cares?* She pushed and pulled the vacuum like nobody's business, drowning Nat's voice. She grinned in satisfaction, then stopped and shook her head; you've *gone loony, Hannah.*

Hannah brought her attention back to her house. Their entire place was decorated in a minimalistic style, just as she and Ethan liked. Looking around the room, she was reminded of the day they'd moved in. At first, Ethan told her that their offer had been rejected. She recalled how disappointed she'd felt upon hearing the news. She had her heart set on the modern 2,500 square-foot house sitting on a cul-de-sac inside a new, quiet subdivision in River Park. They had narrowed their choices between two homes in the same area, but as soon as Hannah had first laid eyes on this 'culdesac house,' she had fallen in love with it and knew it was the one. Looking around now, the house seemed massive without Ethan.

The neighborhood was quiet, she remembered thinking then, and being in the culdesac meant it would have been perfect for their future children – three. That's what they'd both wanted -two boys and a girl. Her heart tightened at the memory and the fact that she wouldn't get the chance to have children with Ethan. Maybe she should not have waited. If only she knew. Tears escaped her eyes again, and she immediately wiped them off. She picked up the wedding photo on Ethan's nightstand and started dusting it. They looked so happy. She smiled, remembering the day she'd said "I do" to the man she loved- *will always love.* She remembered uttering the words without hesitation. There was no question whether she would marry Ethan. *How am I supposed to move on without you now?* she asked silently, stroking Ethan's face in the photo.

"Reminiscing?"

She nearly dropped the photo when she heard his voice.

"You really need to stop sneaking in like that," she whined.

"And ruin the fun?"

"Yeah, you have your fun while I die of a heart attack," she teased as she walked toward him.

"Please don't say that," he said, sounding upset.

"What's wrong?" Hannah wondered what made him solemn.

"I love you very much. You know that, right?"

She nodded.

"Please, just know that I love you. I will always love you," he said, looking straight into her wondering eyes.

"I love you, too, Ethan," she whispered.

Hannah noticed that the sun had set, and the coldness had set in. Time went by so fast when Ethan was around.

Suddenly, she heard a knock on the door. She looked at him as if asking if she should answer it.

He nodded. "I'll be around."

***

Ethan had yet to learn where he was. *Is this heaven?* he asked himself as he glanced around. The surrounding was cloudy. He couldn't make out the place, but there was something very familiar about where he stood. *Hello?* He called out. Nothing. He took a step, careful steps. *Hello, anyone here?* Nothing. He took more steps forward through the dark fog before him. Suddenly he could feel a presence.

"Don't be afraid, son," the man said. "Keep walking toward my voice; I promise you'll be fine."

Ethan followed the voice. Suddenly, his vision cleared, and he finally reached the man standing before him.

"What am I doing here?" he questioned.

The man turned around and smiled. "Come closer. Beautiful, isn't it?"

Ethan stood next to him and saw the most magnificent view. Mountains, hills, and valleys stood firmly and tall before him. Lakes, rivers, falls, and the ocean danced in harmony right before his eyes. There were trees as far as eyes could see. Some he hadn't even seen before. Blooming vibrant flowers scattered everywhere. Birds. There were lots of birds which seemed to sing some beautiful tunes as they flew in the massive, infinite, bright blue sky. The view was unearthly. He glanced behind him and saw his queen-sized bed, his nightstand, his wedding photo. He was glancing back at his beige walled bedroom. How could this be possible?

The man looked back at where he stood. "Relax and just enjoy the view for a minute, son. Everything will become clear later."

Ethan was about to protest, but there was some unexplainable contentment that suddenly enveloped him. "I'm Ethan," he said. "But something tells me you already knew that. The question is, who are you?"

The man smiled as he continued to admire the fascinating view before him. "I'm Daniel. I suppose you can say I'm your guardian angel," he said as he vanished right before Ethan's eyes.

***

Hannah still could not believe that Ethan kept his promise. Ethan being back was the only way she could cope with all the loneliness and sadness the tragedy had brought her. For months she was lost, not knowing how she would carry on. Hannah went back to work, hoping to keep her mind off the fact that they hadn't caught Ethan's killer yet or the fact that Ethan was gone. She had wanted the time to go by fast. She buried herself in work, staying late, but there was no escaping the sadness, the quietness, and the loneliness when she got home. Alone.

For weeks, she had cried herself to sleep. The following day, she would wake up thinking it was all a dream – a nightmare. She would feel the bed next to her, thinking Ethan would be there lying next to her, but reality would hit her again like a ton of bricks. Ethan was gone, so she cried again. She cried until she fell back to sleep. That was her ritual for weeks: no people, no friends, no anyone. The door was locked, the curtains closed, and the phone was off. She wanted to be alone. To cry. Grieve. Yell. Feel. God, she needed to feel, but she couldn't; she was numbed. She was numbed from crying and numbed from the excruciating pain she felt inside.

One night, a few days after the funeral, she walked into her empty house, and the loneliness had gotten unbearable. The quietness was too loud. The cut was too deep, and she couldn't endure the pain any longer. Hannah decided to drown her misery with alcohol. With the curtain shut, she grabbed a bottle of wine and sat on her large, lonely, white, L-shaped leather sofa. With the bottle in one hand and the remote in the other, she had absentmindedly flipped through the channels as her tears started to fall, staring at the tv, not really seeing or hearing anything at all. Frustrated and angry, she threw the remote on the white, wooden, square coffee table in front of her and screamed at the top of her lungs. Hannah sobbed, kicked, laughed. She cried. She punched the air and threw tantrums like a petulant little child. That's when she had felt his presence and saw him sitting by her feet.

She was scared at first, but his presence seemed to calm her. Was she hallucinating? Was she too drunk? She remembered asking herself, trying to make sense of it all.

She eased up to touch his face, but she couldn't. She tried to talk to him, but he was silent. He stood there, staring at her with despair. Despair? How could he look at her with despair? How could he judge her actions when he was the one who left and broke his promise? All the unexplainable feelings deep inside her surfaced, and she was angry. She was mad at him for leaving her.

Ethan stood there watching her. She was determined to make him feel her intolerable pain. She lunged at him, but she had stumbled and had fallen back on the chair. Uncontrollable laughter came as her tears flowed like a river. *You are going crazy, Hannah. You are seeing things;* she had told herself. She walked to the kitchen, grabbed another bottle of chardonnay, and headed for her room and decided that she just needed to sleep it off.

Hannah entered the room and had immediately dropped onto her bed with the bottle still in her hand. Before she closed her eyes, she saw a silhouette of a man standing before her. Though it was hazy, she knew who it was. It was her husband. "Ethan, you're alive. You kept your promise," she whispered, smiling before passing out completely.

That next day, she remembered waking up with a throbbing headache. She was about to get up, but the vague memory of the night before halted her. Rubbing her head, she had remained in bed for a while and had tried to recall the events. She remembered crying and going to her room with the bottle of wine, but she couldn't remember what she had done with it.

Crap.

She'd noticed the bottle on top of the night table and wondered if she had placed it there. She'd picked it up and stared at it for a moment, and that's when she recalled seeing his face.

Can't remember? There's a reason you were only allowed two glasses of wine, sweetheart.

Startled, she had fallen off the bed.

Gosh, I really must be going crazy, she recalled telling herself as she scooted to the floor. She closed her eyes, hoping it was just her imagination, but she'd heard him again.

You're not going crazy, babe. I am here. I will be the first to tell you to see a therapist, you know that, but I'm here. I'm really here. I could not believe it either, he'd said.

Hannah froze with her eyes fixed on him. She was speechless for a long while. She'd tried to touch him but couldn't. That's when everything that happened the night before came flooding back; *it couldn't be,* she thought.

"You were here last night," she said, unsure.

"Yes, I was trying to get your attention, to let you know I was here, and to stop you from getting drunk."

He had a slight grin, but she could sense his annoyance at the same time.

She squinted her eyes. "And I tried to hit you."

"Ha. *That* you did, and you fell," he said, amused.

Hannah had tried touching him again, but it was like touching air.

Since that day, Ethan's visits have become regular, and her days have been easier. Kate noticed the sudden change in her. Oliver had, too. She wanted to tell them, but tell them what? That she saw her husband's ghost. She'd decided to keep everything to herself despite their persuasion for her to see a therapist. *Shutting down is not healthy,* she remembered Kate telling her. *Everyone grieves differently, but I still think you need to talk to someone,* Ol would add. What do they know? She knew what she needed- who she needed. She had *him.* She had Ethan back, and that's all she would ever need.

Chapter Thirty-One

Hannah's phone rang. She ran to the door before answering, knowing it would be Kate.

"Hello?"

"Are you going to open the door or what? I've been knocking and ringing the doorbell for hours," Kate said over the phone.

She opened the door while Kate was still on the line.

"Yes, I am," she laughed. "Sorry, I heard the knock, but I got distracted," she added as she tried to sense Ethan's presence before hanging up the phone.

Kate walked into the room like she owned the place and started looking around.

"Somebody here with you?"

"What? No, who would be here with me?" Hannah asked, trying not to laugh as she noticed Ethan now sitting on the sofa, mocking Kate. She discretely shook her head at him while grabbing a bottle of wine from Kate's hand.

"You are acting weirder and weirder. Which reminds me, have you contacted a therapist yet?"

Hannah stood behind the white island in the kitchen and poured wine into their glasses, not looking up as she answered

Kate, "You sound like Ol, and no, I haven't." She glanced sideways at Kate before saying, "Because I don't need one."

"Says you. Hannah, as your *employee*, I can't tell you what to do, but as *your friend*? I am worried about you. Grief is a serious matter that needs to be talked about."

Hannah understood her best friend's concern, but she wanted to relax today and not talk about grief or anything else, so she simply smiled and said, "I will, but not today."

Kate rolled her eyes and shook her head in defeat.

"Where's dinner?"

"Ol is bringing it."

"What?"

"Oh, you didn't say *not* to bring a plus one, did you?" Kate lifted her brows as if to taunt her.

"This is not a wedding reception, Kate. You aren't supposed to bring a *plus one*. By the way, plus one means a date." Hannah laughed as she teased Kate.

"Oliver Keon Rossi? *My* date? Ha! As if." Kate rolled her eyes.

"As if what?"

"Nothing. I was just kidding. Any who, the bag's right there." Kate spun around the swivel chair she was sitting on and sipped her wine, pointing at the boxes on the living room table.

Hannah giggled as she watched Ethan try to rummage through the bags.

"What in the world are you giggling at?" Kate asked.

"What? Me? I wasn't."

"You need help. Seriously. I think you're going nuts." Kate said, glancing around the room, trying to see what made her laugh.

"Wait. Are you seeing ghosts? Is Ethan here?" Kate said. "Ethan, are you here?"

"What are you doing?" Hannah said.

"Sorry, I know. I know. Not funny."

Hannah loved Kate's sense of humor, but something deep inside made her consider her friend's comments. *Maybe I am going nuts,* she thought. She chased the thoughts away. Instead, she decided to enjoy the moment. "C'mon, grab your plate. Let's eat in the living room and watch a movie."

If she only knew, Hannah thought, looking at her best friend. Would she understand?

***

Oliver sat on the phone in his office with Detective Reagan, discussing Ethan's case. He promised Hannah he would help her work with the detectives, ensuring the case didn't get cold.

"We will inform you as soon as there's an update, Mr. Rossi," Detective Reagan, assured him over the phone. "I promise you; we won't stop looking for who's responsible for your friend's death," she added.

After his conversation with detective Reagan, Oliver gathered his things and was ready to head home when one of his colleagues knocked and peeked through the open door. The young man was known to be a lady's man in their office. He was dressed in black slacks and blue long sleeves. He was not much shorter than Oliver, but he was at least ten years younger.

"We're heading to the new Irish pub down the street. Thought you might want to join us. Heard there are lots of single women looking for fun."

Oliver would have jumped on the invitation, but lately, Hannah's face kept popping into his mind, stopping him from putting himself in a risqué situation. He was unsure why or what, but something deep inside him had changed. Who was he kidding? He knew exactly why. He knew it was not a why but *a who*, but he also knew that he couldn't or shouldn't act upon it. *It's Hannah, for crying out loud.* He shook the ridiculous idea away. He shouldn't be thinking of such a thing. She's his best friend's widow. But he just couldn't help himself.

"Are you coming?" his colleague asked.

Oliver needed to take his mind off his feelings for Hannah, and he knew exactly what he needed for the night - booze. He glanced at his watch: eight-fifteen. "Yeah, I'll be there."

After a few minutes, Oliver walked into the boisterous pub, where people stood shoulder to shoulder, chatting and laughing the night away. If tables and chairs were around, he couldn't see them from where he entered. Some were even trying to dance despite the tight space. The place didn't look like the typical Irish pub he was used to, that's for sure. This place looked more like a club. Finally, he managed to find the bar and squeezed between two guys to order his drink. Hanging behind the bar was the flag of Ireland. *There you go. I guess that made the place an Irish pub.* He laughed at his own thoughts.

"Jack and coke, please."

"Hey, you made it!" his colleague said, grabbing a couple of beers from the bartender.

"This place is packed!" Oliver yelled over the loud music.

"Isn't it crazy?"

The bartender poured some Jack Daniels into a glass, splashed it with soda, and slid it in front of him.

"It's on the lady at the end of the bar." The bartender pointed to a group of ladies smiling at him at the opposite end.

"Wow, that was quick," his colleague joked. "The guys are there, join us when you can," he pointed to a table across the bar as he walked away grinning.

"Yeah, I'll be there in a bit," Oliver replied.

One of the ladies from the group stood from the opposite side of the bar and sashayed in her black mini - dress, working through the crowd toward him.

Oliver was ready to party, or so he thought, until Hannah's image clouded his vision again. *Get a grip on yourself*; she's *off-limits. Is she? Still?* He parted with the questions still lingering in his head as the blonde lady now stood in front of him.

"Thanks for the drink," he said and smiled politely.

"I'm Milena. What's your name?" He heard an accent, *Russian*, he told himself.

"I'm Jack." *Jack? Where did that come from?*

Hannah had invaded his thoughts lately, making him say stupid things out of the blue just as she used to in college. He was a coward then, too, and it had cost him his happiness. Now another opportunity had presented for him to grab the happiness he once let slip away, but how?

Once again, he was fighting the same dilemma he had once fought before, but this time he was fighting with the memory of his best friend. He knew Ethan loved Hannah very much, but so did he. He just didn't have the chance, or perhaps the courage, to tell her before Ethan did.

"Did you hear what I said?" Milena's voice pulled him back from his thoughts.

"I'm so sorry." He leaned closer, pretending to be interested in what the lady had to say.

She leaned in closer. "I said, why don't we leave this place and go somewhere else?"

He thought about it for a moment. Spending time with a lady could help him forget about Hannah, but for how long?

"I'm sorry, I have an early day tomorrow. Rain check?"

Right away, he saw the disappointment on her face. He stood and gave her a respectful kiss on the cheek. "It was lovely to meet you. I'm sorry, but I have to go."

Oliver walked through the bar, bumping several shoulders. Several 'sorries' later, he reached the exit. He patted his phone in his pocket as he left the pub. He pulled it out, went through his contacts, and stared at her number before absentmindedly hitting the call button.

The phone rang only once before Hannah answered.

"Hello?"

Hannah's sweet, innocent voice sent chills down his spine, making him freeze, unable to speak.

"Ol?"

Hannah calling his name with her sweet voice didn't help. He made a conscious effort to shrug his feelings off and finally managed to respond.

"Hannah." His voice cracked a little. "Sorry, I was walking to my car and must have butt-dialed your number. I hope I didn't disturb you," he said, shaking his head as he thought of how dumb his excuse was. *Really? Butt dialed? That's the best you could come up with?* He thought shaking his head,

"Not at all. I just walked Kate to the door. She and I had some Chinese food and binged on Chicago PD." There was a momentary pause; then she continued, "Working late? Or..."

He heard the teasing accusation in her voice. He knew she was insinuating about a girl. "N- N- No. I - I was invited...." *Get a grip, Oliver.* He took a deep breath to settle his nerves before continuing, "By a colleague, not a girl." He shut his eyes closed as he heard his last statement. *Really? Not a girl? Why did you have to say that?* "I meant, I was invited by Carlo, one of our new Real Estate agents. We went to this new Irish pub by the office, and I just left. Wasn't my scene." He was babbling. He wasn't sure why he felt the need to explain, but he did, nonetheless.

"K..."

"Yeah?"

"Are you drunk?"

"Me?"

"Yeah, you," she gave a faint laugh.

"Not at all. I had a couple of drinks, that's it."

She called him K. She had stopped calling him K when she had gotten married to Ethan. It had been Oliver for years, but tonight, she called him K. What does that mean? He paused to check the time – eleven thirty-nine. He hadn't realized he was at the pub that long.

"Are you headed home?" she asked.

"Well... I think I'll try to find an open Chinese restaurant around here. I haven't eaten yet, and now that you've mentioned it, Chow Mein sounds good right about now," he said with a chuckle.

"Actually, we have some leftovers if you would like to drop by."

He froze, and his heart thumped. He wasn't quite sure how to take Hannah's invitation.

"You still there?" she asked.

"Yes, yes. I'm still here."

"So what? Do you want the leftovers?"

"Are you sure? It's kinda late."

"Yeah, I'm sure. You might as well take it; otherwise, it will just go to waste. Anyway, maybe we can talk about you taking me to this shelter Ethan and I used to go to. I need to take all these casseroles there, but I promised Ethan I wouldn't go there by myself," she explained.

"Casseroles are still coming?"

"Yeah. I don 't have the heart to tell her to stop, but I would have to soon. So, what do you think?"

"Sure, as long as it's alright with you."

She snickered. "It's alright with me, Ol."

Now, back to *Ol. You are killing me, lady.* He shook the thought aside. "Alright, I'll be there in a few."

"Wait."

"Yeah?" His heart thumped again.

"Are you sure you're okay to drive?"

"I promise."

She cared. He smiled.

Chapter Thirty-Two

W hy was she excited to see K tonight? Maybe it was her loneliness. Yeah, that's right. She was just lonely. It will pass, but then she called him K. It just slipped out. She brushed the thought aside as she looked around the room.

Forty-five minutes later, K was at her doorstep.

"What took you so long? I was about to call you," she said as she opened the door. "Come in."

"Sorry, I stopped by the liquor store and grabbed your favorite wine," Oliver explained as he walked into the house and handed her a bottle of chardonnay.

"You didn't have to."

"Well, I have had a couple of drinks from the pub and didn't think keeping the *buzz* to myself was polite." Oliver winked and touched her shoulder slightly. "I'm kidding. I know how your mind works, Mrs. Presten, so don't give me that look. I'm not drinking and driving. Well, technically not," he added, letting out another suppressed laugh.

She took some chilled wine glasses from the refrigerator. "Well, I do have a bottle that's already open. I suppose I can have a drink with you. Do you want me to heat the food, or would you rather take it home?"

"If you don't mind me eating here. You wouldn't let a *drunk* man starve, would you? "

"Oh, stop it," she said as she handed him a glass of wine and placed the box of Chow Mein in the microwave, but she could feel his stare from behind. She turned around, "What?"

Oliver smiled. "Nothing. I'm just glad to see you smiling again."

His statement made her feel guilty, and she discreetly assessed the room. She sat the food on the table in front of Keon and took the seat across from him.

"I miss Ethan very much. There are no days that I don't think of him, but I do need to start learning to live without him," she said seriously. She tried to feel Ethan's presence. Nothing. "It will be hard."

"I miss him, too, Han," Oliver said as he held her hand. They both sat quietly for a while as they sipped their wines. Oliver broke the silence first.

"So, you wanted to go to a shelter?" he said, twirling the noodles with his fork.

"Whenever you have a free time. I know how busy you are these days."

He looked straight into her eyes. "I always have time for you. You know that."

Butterflies. There were butterflies in her stomach.

Another moment of silence, this time, she spoke first. "How about tomorrow morning? Say... around ten? That way, they could serve it for lunch."

Oliver took a forkful of Chow Mein in his mouth before responding, "Sure, I'll be here right after the morning briefing at the office."

"No rush."

"So, how's Kate doing, by the way? Is she and Dr. Reed an item yet?"

"You mean *Dr. H?*" Hannah giggled.

"Oh yeah, I forgot. Dr. *Hotness*, as she calls him, right?" He let out a light-hearted laugh and shook his head.

"Kate is still Kate, and yes, still gaga for Dr. H. That girl can't take a hint, though."

"Hint? What do you mean? The doc doesn't like her back?"

"Are you kidding me? What's not to like? She's pretty, she's young---"

"She's crazy," Oliver interrupted before sipping his wine.

Hannah glared at him and crossed her arms. "That's my best friend you're talking about."

Oliver quickly raised his hands as if to surrender. "I'm just kidding."

"Anyway, as I was saying, she's pretty, young, smart, and... crazy." She laughed.

"See, you admit your friend is a nut job." He teased. "So, what's the problem, then?"

"Geez, I forgot how eager you are to hear gossip. Wanna chew your food first?"

"Sorry, I am famished, and I do find Kate's love life very interesting," he said rolling his eyes as he placed another forkful of noodles in his mouth.

"You find Kate interesting?" If Hannah didn't know any better, she sounded a little jealous.

"No. I mean her feelings for Dr. Reed. The fact that she calls him *Dr. Hotness* is adorable, don't you think?" He winked.

Winked. Oh, my goodness, he winked. When was the last time someone winked at her? Something about a guy winking at her made her senses disappear. Then she recalled exactly when that last time was. They were back in college. She and Oliver were playing pool at the bistro.

You're not too bad for playing for the first time, Oliver had told her.

How about we make it interesting? she said.

What do you have in mind?

If I win, you have to take me to dinner, she said.

And if I win? Oliver asked, looking her straight in the eyes with those piercing green eyes, making her blush.

What do you want?

It took Oliver a while to respond, she recalled, then he said, *if I win, you owe me a kiss,* then he winked at her. At that moment, her knees became weak, and her heart pounded. She knew at that moment that she liked him. It had only been a few weeks since they had started hanging out, but it wasn't hard to like Oliver. He was smart, handsome, well dressed, kind and seemed to really pay attention to her. She quickly snapped out of it when he said, *just kidding. If I win, I pay for dinner.* Perhaps he didn't like her the way she liked him, she remembered telling herself. Everything became clear to her after a couple of days when she saw him walking a girl back to her dorm, after not answering her call. Then she met Ethan. She decided to tuck her feelings aside for Ol and diverted it to Ethan. Ethan was sweet. He made sure she got back to her dorm safe one night after she had had a few drinks at a campus party. Since then, it was Ethan who made her feel loved.

But why did his wink affect her the way it did tonight? She felt as if her stomach had done a somersault. *You need to snap out of it, Hannah. He was just trying to make you laugh,* she told herself.

"Earth to Hannah," he said, trying to get her attention.

"Winked," she blurted out.

"I'm sorry?"

Great. How would she get out of this? Her face started to feel warm and her hands clammy.

"I'm sorry. What was the question?"

"Where were you?" he asked, teasingly.

"Stop it. What did you ask me?"

"I didn't really ask you anyhting. I was saying that Kate calling Dr. Reed, *Dr. Hotness* was crazy." He smirked.

Could he tell she was affected by his wink? Gosh, she hoped not. "Oh, yeah! I mean, the guy is basically throwing himself at her, but she's in denial. She says, *'I think he's just being polite,'* Hannah tried to imitate Kate, sounding like an annoying teenage girl.

"She sounds like that?"

"Stop it." Hannah giggled and absentmindedly punched him on the shoulder again. *Okay, I really need to stop that.* "Have I been doing that to him all this time?"

"What? Punching me? No, this is new." He smiled and winked.

She immediately felt her face heat up again. There was no way of explaining that or taking it back now. "I'm so sorry. Don't know what came over me. Must be the grieving," she babbled as she watched Oliver's green eyes twinkle. *Stop it,* she told herself. But the wink. He winked at her again. *Get a grip, Hannah. Get a grip.*

He stood and ruffled the top of her head. "You've always been weird, kid."

Ol was being Ol. He was again trying to save her from looking like a fool. He'd always been so sensitive to other people's feelings, especially hers.

"Thanks for dinner," he said, holding his plate.

"Let me take that from you."

Oliver was quick to move the plate above his head, away from her reach, and gave her a wicked grin. He walked past her, took the plate to the sink, and washed it.

"I'll let Kate know you said *thank you*. It was *her* leftover, after all," she said from the living room.

He didn't look up. He continued washing the dishes and yelled out to her, "You need to give it up, lady. I am *not* Kate's type. I'm not *hot* enough. She told me so," he added as he turned around and rolled his eyes as if to show how offended he was.

There was a time when she and Ethan had tried setting him up with Kate, but Oliver didn't want to entertain the idea. Not that Kate was thrilled about it, either. Even if she was, she couldn't. Hannah knew that.

K finished putting the dishes away and glanced at his watch. "You should get some rest if we are to go to that shelter tomorrow."

"Gosh, I didn't realize it's that late."

She walked him to the door. "Are you sure you're okay to drive?"

"Yes, ma'am. I had *one* glass of wine and a plateful of Kate's leftover noodles. I think it soaked up all the alcohol in my system," he said.

She watched him from the door as he walked to his car.

"Make sure you lock everything before you go to bed," he called out over his shoulder.

"Yes, sir." She saluted.

Hannah waited till he drove off before closing the door behind her.

K's presence tonight left her with some unsettling feelings. She was just lonely, she told herself again. Oliver was a friend, that's all. Besides, it's only been three months since Ethan passed away. *Ethan.* She stood in the middle of the empty and quiet living room and looked around." Ethan...are you here?"

Nothing.

After locking the door and closing the window shades, Hannah went straight to her bedroom, where she found Ethan waiting.

"Goodness!" she exclaimed, holding her chest. "You really need to let me know when you're here."

"I told you, babe, I'm always around." He glanced toward the open door. "Geez, you had visitors all night. I never thought your friends would ever leave."

"My friends?"

"Yeah, *your* friends," he replied.

"*Our* friends, you mean?"

"What? I've never seen them before in my life."

"Ethan, did you not recognize Kate and Ol?"

"Who?"

"Those people were *our* friends? I've never seen them before in my life... or *death*, for that matter," he said, furrowing his brows.

She stared at him blankly.

"You're asking lots of questions again, aren't you? I can smell the smoke coming out of your ears." He grinned.

"You knew who they were! Gosh, stop scaring me like that."

"I was just kidding. Of course, I remember. What's their names again?" He laughed.

"Stop it, Ethan."

"I'm just pulling your leg," he said and gestured for her to come closer.

She pouted like a little girl. "Tell me you remember who they are first."

"Oh, c'mon, babe."

She didn't budge.

"Okay, okay, here it goes. Kate is your assistant and *your* best friend. She has a crush on *Dr. Hotness*. Are they together yet, by the way?"

She shook her head and crossed her arms, waiting for him to continue.

"Oh, sorry. Oliver? *K*, is *my* best friend, *our* friend, *my* roommate in college, and the guy who has feelings for *my* wife."

"Ethan."

"Just teasing."

Long silence. Could he have seen the way she felt about Oliver earlier? Was she that obvious? That's preposterous. Ethan was joking, but she could sense that he meant that last part.

"Alright, alright. I was just pulling your leg," he said.

She pretended to be annoyed and walked toward the bath-room.

"I can't believe you. Why would you joke like that?" she mumbled through a mouthful of toothpaste.

"You didn't actually believe I had some kind of amnesia, did you?" He chuckled.

She emerged from the bathroom in her nightshirt and climbed onto the bed. She grabbed a pillow and threw it at him. "Whatever." Of course, she couldn't actually hit him, but it was an instinct. "By the way, pulling my leg? Better be an idiom. Don't you *ever* pull my leg when I'm asleep. I will kick the Casper, the friendly ghost, out of you or whatever you are."

"Whatever I am?" He was bemused.

She smiled. She still missed him so much, despite his presence in the house. It just wasn't the same. She wished she could feel him completely, touch him, embrace him, sleep with him, and wake up the next day right next to him. Her heart throbbed for him to be alive. That whole thing with Oliver was just loneliness, she reminded herself.

He broke her trance. "Did you have fun today?"

"Yes, it was good unwinding with Kate tonight."

She could tell he wanted to say something else but held back. So typical of him to keep his innermost feelings buried inside.

"I'm going to the shelter tomorrow to bring some food," she announced.

"Someone going with you?"

"I asked Ol," she said, hesitantly.

Did she just hear him sigh?

"Is that okay?"

"Of course. That's good. I told you not to go there by yourself. It's too dangerous. Glad Ol can take you."

It was just the answer she expected to hear from her husband. Despite how great Ethan was at concealing his true feelings, she was always aware of it. She knew he wouldn't tell her if Oliver's presence was bothering him. Well, not until it really did. She yawned and shifted to get a better look at Ethan's expression. He smiled. A faint smile. She decided to change the subject. "Are you going to watch me sleep?"

"Do you want me to?"

Another enormous yawn escaped her. "I want you to stay, but don't be creepy. None of that pulling leg crap." Another yawn. She sensed Ethan moving, but she was already half asleep.

Ethan planted a kiss on her forehead, and she let out a quiet moan.

"Good night, sweetheart. I'll see you in the morning."

"I love you, Ethan," she said as she drifted asleep.

Chapter Thirty-Three

E than watched his wife sleep. She looked so beautiful, peaceful, and so fragile. He brushed a strand of hair away from her face. Watching his wife made him wish she could feel his touch completely. He hated the thought of her hurting. Yes, he was there. She could see him, but eventually he would have to leave her again, and he knew it would hurt her again. He recalled Oliver's presence in *his* house earlier. He was thankful that his best friend was there to take care of his wife; he had always thought Ol would. He had expected that, but there was an uneasy feeling in his heart about it this time. His mind wandered and remembered the day Oliver told him about Hannah. They were still in college and were in the middle of a basketball game.

Guess what? I met a girl yesterday at the café. We hung out last night and we're hanging out again tomorrow, Oliver had told him as Ol dribbled the ball next to him. *Her name is Hannah. She's studying to be a vet,* he added before shooting the ball. He recalled being excited for him, but he was more focused on guarding Oliver and swatting the ball. A few days later, he'd attended a party on campus and had also met a girl named Hannah. She looked like she'd partied and drank more than she could take and needed assistance. He couldn't just leave her on the side of the road, so he walked her back to her dorm. He held the door for her, but as she walked in, she leaned in and kissed him. He kissed her back until *she* pulled away and apologized. He never thought he'd hear from her again until the next day.

Hey, thanks for last night and sorry for that temporary lapse of judgment. I guess I had more than I could handle, she said over the phone.

No need to apologize. How are you feeling today?

I'm okay. I think I just need something to eat and take a couple of aspirin.

Probably a great idea, he had told her.

There was silence for a while.

Would you like to get breakfast? he finally asked.

Before they knew it, they were a couple. He had told Oliver about Hannah and recalled him being aloof about it. He didn't know why. A few days later, they both met with Oliver, and that's when he found out Hannah was the woman Oliver had met a few weeks before. Oliver eventually gave them his blessings to marry, and that was it. He had stopped worrying about Ol's feelings for Hannah, but as time passed, he realized Oliver may have not gotten over his feelings for his wife. Would Oliver take advantage of his death and finally make a move on Hannah now that he was gone? The thought infuriated him. But then again, if anyone deserved to take care of Hannah, he would rather it be his best friend. He was confused; his feelings were all over the place, then it hit him. *Why am I thinking of all this? I'm not going anywhere. I made a promise.*

***

Oliver drove home in silence and thought about how the night went. There was something different about her lately, and he couldn't tell what it was. Maybe Hannah was right; she was just grieving. He was worried about her, especially with her mental state. She was smiling again. He was happy about that. Each time she smiled, his chest tightened. Then there was the blushing. She blushed when he winked at her, and she got flustered. Did his wink affect her? He tried to brush the thoughts away. He shouldn't assume. But what if it did?

He finally pulled into the garage, and instead of getting out of the car, he sat there remembering the voicemail Hannah had left him years ago. *Hi Oliver, it's Hannah. There's a party I was invited to tonight, and I was wondering if you would like to go with me. Call me back.* If he'd just checked his phone, then. If he had just told Ethan to back off, that he couldn't stop thinking about her, that he liked her very much, if he had just fought for her. All the *ifs*. What was he doing that day, anyway? Where was his phone? Why didn't he check it? All these questions haunted him for years. Hindsight and regret always did go together. So did cowardliness and pain. He should have fought for Hannah. Then what? Risk his friendship with Ethan? So many unanswered questions, ifs and buts, would've, could've, and should've.

He knew it was too late, or was it? Suddenly, he felt something powerful deep inside him. *Lord, please guide me.* The prayer felt good, even though he hadn't attended church for a long while.

"I was at church! Oh my gosh, I was at church!"

He didn't answer her call because he was at church, had switched his phone off and must have forgotten to turn his phone back on. Oliver sat there in silence. *Could this be a sign? An answer from God?* He thought. Despite the reputation he'd received over the years, he was always a believer. He made people believe he was a partier – a womanizer. Sure, he'd partied and dated girls in the past, but he'd never intentionally disrespected them or broken their hearts. He'd always been a gentleman, treating all women with respect and honor as his mother taught him. His lack of a serious relationship was not because he was a womanizer and could not settle with one, it was because the one he wanted to settle with had settled with his best friend.

There was just something about Hannah that kept him from moving on. Oliver tried to stay away from Ethan and Hannah when they'd started getting serious, but Ethan was so excited about R&P Real Estate that before they knew it, the business was thriving. Oliver wanted to leave California and start a new life somewhere east, but he couldn't, not when the company had just taken off. He'd always wondered if that was the only reason. Now and then, he would go out of town to have a break from seeing Ethan at work or Hannah's photos plastered all over their office. One day, he had gone MIA for a couple of days, and when he got back, Ethan had assumed that he had hooked up with a girl in Reno, so his reputation began. Every time he'd leave, they had automatically thought he was partying with some girl somewhere when he was in fact fishing or spending time with his sister, Olivia, and her kids. Olivia was the only person he'd talked to about his feelings. Olivia knew his pain. She'd even tried to set him up on a blind date to help him move on, but none worked out.

After Hannah married Ethan, he tried his best to forget his feelings. He tried to convince himself that if anyone should have her, it might as well be his best friend. He knew Ethan was a good man - no, a great man - and he knew Hannah would be happy with him, but he also knew that he would have made her happier. After a while, he thought he had finally let her go, but his heart just wouldn't allow it, and so he continued to endure the pain of watching the love of his life build a life with another man.

Oliver didn't know how to take what just happened. Why couldn't he remember what had happened to his phone for the longest time? Why didn't he call her when he didn't hear from her? Now, with everything that had happened, suddenly, he'd remember. *This must be a revelation*, he told himself. *It must be God's plan; it must be. So, what now? What should my next move be?* He decided he needed to pray some more. He wanted to make sure that this was, in fact, a divine intervention. *He has a plan for you,* was the last thing that entered his mind.

Chapter Thirty-Four

After finding out about a guy named Matthew David – a local paramedic from Green Ridge admitting to Ethan's death, Reagan's team had rushed to his house. At the same time, she drove to North Carolina to meet with the guy only to be told by the Sherriff in charge that David was nowhere to be found when they got to the motel. The team back in Virginia, however, found traces of blood in the shed at the back of his house confirming his connection to the incident, but without David himself, there was not much she could do. Her frustration started to creep in, but she was not one to give up that easily. She needed to find this guy, bring justice to Ethan's death, and close this case.

"I still don't understand why Matthew David would call 9-1-1 in North Carolina, say what he said, then go on hiding," Reagan mumbled as she rummaged through Ethan's file.

"Impulse? Probably realized he wouldn't last in jail," Shikadans answered.

"Or he could be toying with us. Psychopaths like to play games." Reagan swiveled her chair to face her partner, standing before her, "I received a call from Oliver Rossi on my cell last night asking if we had any leads. I need to find this guy, Ard."

"Who's Rossi again?"

"Oliver Rossi, Ethan's business partner."

"Oh, that's right, I knew that."

"No sleep again?"

"Baby was up every hour," he said.

"Oh, man so sorry."

Her phone rang.

"Detective Reagan."

Silence.

"Hello?"

"It -- now, detect--ive I can't -- this anymore. Please tell Ha—I'm --sor"

"Sir... Who is this? Where are you calling from? Sir, are you okay?"

Another long silence.

"Flor—d."

Emily gestured for Ardy to trace the call, but she was too late, the call was disconnected.

"Dang It." She pounded on her table.

"Who was it?"

"I don't know. The line was mostly static." Reagan paused, trying to make sense of what was said. "I think he said he was calling from Florida."

"Anything else?"

"I think he said something about telling someone he's... *sore*?" She knitted her brows together.

"Sore? He wants you to tell someone he's sore?"

"Yeah, weird," Reagan said.

She tried to call the number back, but there was no answer.

"Could he be telling you to tell someone he was *sorry*?"

"What?" She spun around. Her eyes wide.

"I think the man could be saying he was *sorry*. You said the line was choppy. Maybe 'sore' was actually sorry?"

"Oh my gosh, I think you're right. He wanted me to tell---" Her skin crawled.

"Son of---" She finally realized who the caller was.

"What?" Shikadans blurted.

"I think he said... *'Please tell Hannah. I'm sorry.'*"

Reagan and Shikadans went through David's file again to see if there was anything they missed. She needed to find where David was when he called. After almost an hour of reading David's file line by line they didn't find anything that would lead them to his location. Suddenly, her phone rang, "Detective Reagan," she answered as she started pacing.

"*Detective?*"

The caller sounded surprised.

"Yes, this is Detective Emily Reagan from Green Ridge Police Department."

"Detective Reagan. This is Detective Angelo Gallardo from Jacksonville, Florida. We responded to a shot fired at one of the residences here an hour ago. We believe the victim's name is Matthew David. Ring a bell?"

Was David calling her because he was in trouble and was asking for her help? Reagan took a deep breath and shut her eyes tight before answering. "Yes, he's a suspect in an ongoing investigation."

"We found his phone next to his body, and it looks like your number was the last number he called. Did you speak with him?"

"Not really. The line was choppy. I could barely understand him. I didn't even know who it was. You said he's a *victim* of a shooting? Is he dead?"

"Initially, we thought he was a victim. Would you mind telling me why he would try to call your cell minutes before he shot himself?"

"Suicide?"

"Looks that way," the detective replied.

David had her cell number and had tried to call her again. She'd been in the force for nearly ten years and had seen many cases, but this case had her perplexed. The thought that she could have prevented David's death will haunt her forever.

Silence.

"*Detective*," Detective Gallardo called out.

Regan regained her composure. "The connection was poor. I tried to decipher what he was saying, but he was cutting in and out, then the call was cut off completely," she explained.

Both detectives talked for several minutes, piecing all the puzzles together.

"Are you sure it's Matthew David?" Reagan said.

"We're pretty sure. Easy way out, if you ask me," Detective Gallardo said.

"You got that right. Now, I must inform the victim's wife. I hate this part."

"You probably should hold off for a while before you make that call."

"What? Why?"

"There's a sealed brown envelope here addressed to you."

"To me? What the hell?"

Stunned, she wondered what it could be. A letter? Why was it addressed to her? For all she knew, David did not know her. There's only one thing it could be.

"A confession?"

"Not quite. Two other envelopes were inside addressed to a Hannah Presten and a lady named Andrea David. His wife, I'm guessing."

She had to handle this herself.

"We'll be on the next flight out, detective," she said before finally hanging up.

Chapter Thirty-Five

Hannah was still unsure what to think about the information she received from Detective Reagan a couple of days ago. Now, the detective was at her house. If the killer was dead, what else was there to discuss?

"Please have a seat, Detective. Would you like something to drink? Coffee? There's hot water if you want tea instead." She was blabbering and knew it. It was her coping mechanism whenever she got nervous, at least that's what Ethan used to tell her, and the fact that Detective Reagan flew from Virginia made her very nervous. Something was up.

"Tea is fine, thank you," Reagan responded.

Hannah poured some hot water into the Detective's cup and threw a nervous glance at Oliver, who was now sitting next to her across from the Detective.

"I called Oliver to come. I hope that's okay. I just don't think I can handle this alone," Hannah said.

"That's totally fine. I'm glad he's here."

"So, you flew to California just to hand me a letter from my husband's killer? Something else is wrong. I can feel it," Hannah said sharply.

Oliver placed a hand on hers.

"Take a breath," he whispered.

"I'm sorry. I'm a bit nervous."

"Don't worry, Mrs. Presten, I understand. Like I've mentioned to you on the phone. David had left a letter for you. I wanted to make sure I was here when you read it in case there's something helpful to our investigation."

"But I don't understand. David is dead. Shouldn't the case be closed?" Hannah said.

"Yes, you're right. Ethan's case *is* closed, but we're looking into another open case that might be tied to this, and we could use your help," Regan said as she pulled the envelope out of her bag and handed it to her.

Hannah's heart pounded as she felt the Detective release the envelope into her hands. Though Ethan's death would no longer get justice, deep inside her, she still wanted to know why he was killed. Why did this David guy choose her husband? Maybe knowing would give her closure. But another case? Related to Ethan's death? Her heart thudded some more.

"I don't know if I can do this," she mumbled, glancing at Oliver.

"You can do this; I'm right here," he reassured her as he tightened his grip on her hand.

She took out the letter from the envelope with her shaking hands, unfolded the paper, and began to read:

Dear Hannah,

I have no idea where to begin or what to say, even. I could tell you my reasons, but you probably won't understand.

She paused, her heart beating like a drum. *Damn right, I won't understand*, she thought to herself. She wiped a tear that had escaped. She felt all sorts of emotions. She felt angry, she knew that for certain, but she almost felt sorry for this man. Why? Why would she feel sorry for this monster who killed her husband mercilessly? The monster, she reminded herself. Anger quickly replaced her empathy.

"This is an apology letter? A sorry for killing my husband?" she said, addressing the Detective. She wasn't expecting an answer. An apology letter for human life? Her anger rose, and she wanted to scream. She wanted to confront the man, but the beast was now dead. What would she do with that?

"Would you like to take a break?" Reagan asked.

She glanced at the crumpled letter in her hand, took a deep breath, shook her head, and smoothed the paper before reading the rest.

I loved you. I loved you for a very long time, but you never even noticed. Instead, you thought less of me; even so, you consumed my every thought. Your smile, your lips, your laughter occupied my mind day and night. Then there were your last words to me. I bet you won't even remember, but I do. I remember every single word you said. I remember how you said it. Most especially, I remember the pain and humiliation I felt when you said, 'He's no one.' Your words consumed me, Hannah and I became a monster because of it. I became a monster because of you. I couldn't even love my wife the way she deserved to be loved because for the longest time, I thought of myself as NO ONE. I learned to hate myself because of you.

She felt herself heated up. "Is he for real? I'm to blame? He killed my husband because of me? Because of what I said to this man? Who is this guy anyway? I don't even know him!" Hannah said, frustrated at what she just read, but she continued.

I'm sorry for what I did to your husband. It should have been you.

Matt David

P.S. I bet you won't think of me as "no one" now.

Chapter Thirty-Six

*I*t *should have been you.* The words hit her like a ton of bricks. Who is this guy? Why did he want to kill her? *I've loved you for a very long time.* That's when it hit her. "He'd been stalking me. Oh God. He'd been stalking me, hadn't he?"

She looked at Detective Reagan for confirmation.

"I'm afraid so. Do you have any idea what he meant by his last statement?" Regan asked.

"That I wouldn't think that he was *no one* now? I don't know what that even means! You think that's connected to your investigation?"

"Maybe. I was hoping you could shed some light," Reagan replied.

Oliver shifted in his seat as if to make sure he didn't miss the answer to what he was about to ask Detective Reagan. "What's this new investigation you are working on? What does this have to do with Hannah? Is she in danger?"

"No, Hannah's not in danger. David is dead and he can't hurt her now, but we are led to believe that he and his mother were responsible for the missing two women here in Sacramento; Joy Mason - 26 and Kerry Carlson - 35. Kerry left a husband and two little girls," Regan explained.

"My gosh," Hannah sighed, shaking her head. "How can we help?"

"I was hoping you could give us more insights as to why David did what he did to you or to Ethan, and maybe it will give us some answers that could help us find the missing women."

Hannah looked at the letter, trying to make sense of what she just heard. Suddenly, something struck her. The signature. Something about the signature was familiar to her.

She repeated his name in her head several times. The way it was written. There was something about the way the letters were written, especially the last letter of his last name. The *d* had a distinct swoop at the bottom. She still could not put her finger on it. Yes, she'd heard the name mentioned repeatedly; she'd said it often, but why was it suddenly screaming at her now? Like she'd known this name all along. She couldn't stop staring at his last name; she thought that was unusual when she first saw it, but where?

"Are you okay?" Oliver asked.

"Matthew David. I've heard or seen this name before," she finally said.

"Good. We're getting somewhere. Where do you think you've seen it?" Detective Reagan prodded.

"Of course, you have. Detective Reagan had mentioned his name several times during the investigation," Oliver said.

She shook her head adamantly, looking at Detective Reagan. "No, I've heard this name even before we went to Virginia."

She could sense Oliver tensing.

"Are you sure?" he said.

She squinted her eyes and rubbed her head as she tried to remember. "Yes, I would have to call Kate to look at our records at the clinic, but I'm pretty sure I saw this last name in the file."

Detective Reagan spoke, "Mrs. Presten -"

"Hannah. Please call me Hannah," she interjected.

Detective Reagan handed her a folder.

Hannah opened the folder and inside were two photos. "Oh, my god." Her heart sank as she inattentively touched her curly hair, scanning the picture in her hands.

"They look like me."

"That's what we thought, too," Reagan said. "Have you seen these women before?"

She shook her head and her chest tightened as the thought of her being the real target sank in. Ethan wasn't the intended target. She was. *It should have been you.*

"That's why we think there's a connection. They also resembled his ex-wife, Andrea," the detective added. "David seemed to be obsessed with you. If we find out why, we might have a chance at finding some answers about these missing women. Are you sure you don't recognize David? Maybe you've met him before. He was born and raised in Green Ridge, Virginia. Didn't you used to visit Green Ridge when you were a kid?" Reagan added.

"What? He lived in Green Ridge? My gosh. Maybe I *did* know this man. Yes, I used to visit my grandparents in Green Ridge when I was a kid," Hannah said, her head spinning. *Who was this, David?*

"We also know that he and his wife left Green Ridge with his late mother a few years ago," Reagan announced.

"He moved to California, didn't he?" Oliver blurted out.

"Yes." Detective Reagan nodded, then shifted her attention to Hannah. "Here in Sacramento, in fact."

Hannah stood up fast, holding her stomach. "I think I'm gonna be sick."

"Do you want to discuss this some other time?" Oliver asked.

She spun around to face Oliver, trying to control her anger. "Absolutely not. I want to know everything about this guy. Who is this, Matthew David? Why did he follow me here? Why was he stalking me? Why did he kill Ethan. God, Ol! He wanted to kill me! Not Ethan! ME! Now, there's two other women out there. We don't even know if they are still alive!"

Oliver stood and wrapped his arms around her.

"It's okay, Han. We'll figure this all out," he said as he glanced at the Detective. "Right, Detective?"

"That's why I'm here. To help make sense of it all, and hopefully lead us to these women. Alive."

Hannah slowly sat back down and tried to regain her composure. "I'm sorry. I didn't mean to snap at you." She grabbed Oliver's hand, pulled him down next to her, and gave him an apologetic look.

"Please continue. What else do you know about him?"

"His wife left him two years after they were married. Apparently, he had a mental breakdown shortly after. His mother, who was also in and out of the psychiatric facility, died last year. I'm sure that didn't help. We are led to believe Mr. David decided to go back to Virginia to search for his wife, but from what we gathered, she'd moved on with another man somewhere where he couldn't find her."

"Where in Green Ridge did he live?" Hannah asked.

Reagan rummaged through her notes and found what she was looking for.

"101 Chonokis Road."

"That's a few houses down from my grandparents, but I don't recall meeting a Matthew David."

"Are you sure? Sometimes we forget people we meet along the way. I understand it had been a while but try. Try thinking about the time you were in Green Ridge. Most of the time, irrelevant things can spark a memory," Reagan said.

Hannah pondered for a while, recalling the people she'd met in Green Ridge when she was a kid.

"There were these two girls I met there. I think their names were Ressa and Abbey- no, Ressa and Anne. Then, of course, Jody," she glanced at K. "The guy I told you I dated for a few months."

K nodded.

"Anyone else? You were there every summer for years, Han. There's gotta be others you might have met. Maybe there were other guys who liked you. How about Jody's friends?" Oliver said.

"Wait...There was a boy I saw one time when I first visited. I think the same boy worked at an ice cream shop a few years later, but I can't seem to recall whether I got his name."

"Good. That's good. Think about that time. What does the boy look like? Think, maybe he said his name," Reagan coached.

Hannah stood up, trying to relax the tight muscles that had suddenly formed on her shoulders. She paced and tried to recall the name of the boy. Nothing.

She closed her eyes, trying to recall his face.

"This boy was quiet," she finally said after a few minutes. "Awkward. Skinny. That's all I remember," she added.

"That must have been David," Reagan said.

"Even if it was, I'm sure the police had already searched his home, right? If you guys suspected that he was involved in these women's disappearance."

"Yes, the police did, but did not find anything pertinent that could lead us to the women's whereabouts. Your connection to him could be our last hope," Reagan explained.

"If that boy *was* David...what's his beef with me?" Hannah asked.

"What else do you know about this guy?" Oliver said, addressing Reagan.

"We were told that David suffered from mental issues. We've subpoenaed his medical records, and it looked like he was suffering from hallucinations. Apparently, he'd claimed to have seen and talked to his dead mother."

The detective's statement took her by surprise. She couldn't help but question herself, thinking about Ethan's visits. Was she also hallucinating? She looked over her shoulders to see if Ethan was around. She felt a surge of sudden guilt.

"David came back to Sacramento sometime last year. Maybe you've spoken to him then?"

Hannah shook her head.

"Wait, he was here? How did he know Hannah would be back in Virginia?" Oliver asked with a stern look on his face.

"We don't know," Reagan said.

"You're telling me it was all a coincidence?" Oliver said, astounded.

Hannah shook her head as she thought of the connections.

"No, it wasn't. I told you I've seen this name before," she blurted out. "Kate called me with an emergency a few days before we left for Virginia. A kitten was struck by a car. A guy brought the cat in, but never came back. I think the record said something David. No contact information. That's got to be him. I'm calling Kate."

"I think that's a great idea. If you don't mind, I'd like to wait and see if I could also talk to your friend and ask her few questions," Reagan said.

Oliver stood and grabbed his phone from his back pants pocket. "I'll call her,"

Within a few minutes, Kate was at Hannah's door. Her friend took one look at her and pulled her in for a tight hug. "I'm here. Please tell me what I can do."

K had already given Kate the short story over the phone. Hannah introduced the detective to her friend and had Reagan take over the conversation as they all sat in the living room.

"Kate, can you tell me about the guy who brought in an injured kitten to---"

"Maroon," Kate said before the detective could finish her thoughts.

"I'm sorry?" Detective Reagan said, confused.

"Maroon. That's my Kitten's name," she said as she claimed the chair next to the Detective. "I'm sorry. I'm a bit nervous," Kate said, giving Hannah a pleading look.

Hannah reached out to her friend and held her hand, telling her it was okay.

"No need to be nervous," Reagan reassured her some more. "I just need you to tell me what you know about the guy who brought...Maroon to the clinic."

"Yes, ma'am," Kate answered.

"Go ahead, please tell me what you know."

"Not much, really. A guy came in with an injured kitten, told me he found it on the side of the road and left the poor thing with me, but the guy never returned. He left a number, and I've called it several times, but there was no answer."

"Did you get his name?" Detective Reagan questioned.

Kate handed the Detective a paper. "Only what he put down on this form."

"*M. David*." Reagan said the name aloud before addressing Hannah. "That's probably the first time you've seen the name."

"Yes, and come to think of it now, the way he wrote his name in the letter was what jogged my memory. I thought the swoop at the end of the letter *d* was unusual."

"Would you remember what he looked like if I showed you a photo?" Reagan asked Kate.

"I think so."

Detective Reagan pulled out her phone and showed Kate the photo.

"Is this him?"

"Yes, that's him. He's a paramedic?" Kate furrowed her brows seeing the man in uniform.

"Did you ever mention the doctor's trip to Virginia? Maybe by accident?" Regan asked Kate.

"Oh gosh, no. I don't think so." Kate darted a sideways glance at Hannah. "Gosh, I hope not. You know how I can talk up a storm sometimes. My goodness, do you think I did?"

"Relax, I'm sure you didn't tell him anything," Hannah said. Suddenly, she felt chills up and down her spine. "Oh, my gosh. I did."

"You did what?" Detective Reagan questioned.

"I mentioned our trip. I was excited and mentioned it to someone at the clinic. Gosh, it happened so fast, but now I remember a guy talked to me that day. That must have been David. He must have overheard me telling someone about Virginia and started a conversation. He had mentioned he used to live there or something like that, I'm not sure." Hannah was now frantic.

"Wait. I think I remember that. He was kind of lurking around the front desk while I was taking care of other people. It was pretty busy that day, so I just didn't pay attention," Kate added.

Hannah held her temples with both hands, "Why couldn't I remember his face?"

"Doc, you had a lot of things on your mind that day. You were planning a trip, had back-to-back appointments, and had several emergencies that day. You can't beat yourself up for not paying attention to the man's face. Besides, he was in a hurry to leave."

Hannah grabbed the letter from the table and stared at Matthew's last name, hoping something else would jog her memory. Suddenly, it all flooded back. She was eighteen years old. It was her last year in Green Ridge. Mamala had passed on a year before, and they had just found out that Papalo had colon cancer. They had decided to spend one more summer before they sold the house and moved Papalo back with her mom. It was also the summer Jody had broken her heart, but right before that. She recalled the incident at the ice cream shop.

"*No one,*" she mumbled.

"Excuse me?" Reagan said.

"That's what I called Mattie when he tried to ask me out. *Mattie.* The boy at the ice cream shop. *Mattie.* As in *Matthew David.* Oh my gosh," Hannah said as her heart raced a hundred miles per hour.

"But why? Why would he try and hurt you for that?" Oliver asked.

"I don't know. Maybe he didn't take the rejection well. Maybe he thought I called him *a no one. A nobody.* This is all too much to take in." Hannah shut her eyes.

Suddenly she remembered a familiar face. "Detective, can I see that photo again, please?" The detective handed her the phone. Her skin crawled instantly as she looked at the image. "What's David's mother's name?"

Detective Reagan went through her notes and found it, "Matilda Severrano. Severrano was her maiden name. Matthew took his father's last name."

Hannah was speechless, suddenly realizing the connections.

"What is it?" Kate asked.

"Han?" Oliver called out, trying to get her back from her trance.

"You're right. There's no such thing as coincidence," she whispered.

"I'm sorry?" Detective Reagan looked puzzled.

"Matilda...I knew her." She gave the phone to Oliver. "She worked at the shelter where Ethan and I used to bring food."

"Are you sure?" Reagan said.

"One hundred percent. I could not forget those eyes. I've seen them before but never put them together until now. In fact, I saw David at the hospital the night Ethan died. He talked to Mrs. Clark." She could barely speak right. Her heart pounded, and her voice quivered. "Something about his eyes reminded me of someone then, but I was lost that night. I was confused. Now, I know he reminded me of Matilda," she said. Hannah's voice trembled as she continued, "I will never forget Matilda's eyes; there was emptiness in them. There was something very disturbing and terrifying about them. I saw that exact emptiness in David's eyes the night... Ethan died at the hospital. My gosh, he was there."

"They followed you here. Stalked you," Oliver murmured then raised his voice as he continued, pacing around the living room. "Now you're telling me that the mother f... ugh! The guy was back in Virginia when Ethan died, and no one knew he was responsible. Really?"

"Excuse me, but I have to make a quick call," Reagan announced and walked to the other side of the room.

They all listened to her conversation.

Hey, this is Reagan. I think we got something. Matilda, David's mother used to volunteer at the shelter where Mrs. Presten used to visit. Maybe there's a connection there with the women somewhere. Really? Do you need me there? Are you sure? Yes, I'll head there as soon as I'm finished here. Thank you, Detective.

"A team is on their way to the shelter," Reagan announced.

"Do you think they will find them there?" Hannah said.

"If not, at least now we know where to start."

Reagan wrapped it up with them and was about to head out the door when her phone vibrated. She immediately answered it.

Give me some good news, she said. *Dang. Both of them? Three? Who's the third? Son of a ---That's too bad. Alright. Heading there now.*

"That was the Detective in charge of the case here. They may have found the ladies. The manager of the shelter had informed SAC PD that Matilda had mentioned about a warehouse not too far from the shelter and the team rushed there immediately."

"Please tell me they're okay," Hannah said instinctively, though she knew the likelihood of them still alive was very slim.

Reagan shook her head. "They found their bodies. The Detectives think they've been dead for a while."

Hannah felt like her world was collapsing. She knew there was nothing she could do about David and his mother. They were dead, and Ethan would never get the justice he deserved, but she at least hoped the ladies would be found alive.

"You are right, Hannah. The shelter's manager informed the Detectives that both Joy Mason and Kerry Carlson had been in the shelter. Joy had just started working there when she went missing, and Kerry dropped food there every Saturday."

Hannah felt her knees buckle. She realized that this could have easily happened to her.

"I knew there was something odd about Matilda. She was *too* friendly. A couple of times I went, I caught her staring at me then asked if she could assist me somehow, but it was the way she asked, though. It was almost... forceful," Hannah said.

"You were probably next," Reagan offered. "Sometimes, these people would do a trial run and see if they can get away with it, perfect their crime before pursuing the real target," Reagan finished.

Hannah's skin crawled.

Oliver pulled her next to him. "Let's just be thankful that she didn't get to you."

"That's right," Reagan concurred.

Hannah parted with the frightening scenario, realizing it didn't matter anymore. She was alive. Matilda and Matthew were dead, but so was Ethan. She felt a sudden stab in the chest. Again, she was alive because of Ethan. Ethan protected her. Even now, he still protects her. Ethan kept his promise. She couldn't help but study the room again to see if he was there. Reagan was staring at her, and she could sense the detective wanted to say something else as if what she just told them wasn't bad enough. "Oh, God. Please don't tell me *he's* alive?"

"No, David is dead, but they did find three remains."

Oliver's eyes widened. "Three?"

"Oh, God." Hannah intuitively placed a hand over her mouth, dread coming all over her as she realized who the third person was.

"*Andrea,*" she said, shocked even as she uttered the words.

"No, Andrea is safe and sound. She had moved to New York with her boyfriend. The third body was placed on top of the other two and was not as badly decomposed. Which led them to believe that—-"

"She was killed recently," Hannah finished.

"Yes," Reagan confirmed.

"If it's not Andrea, then who's body, is it?"

"It's a woman by the name of Linda Cavanaugh. She was David's therapist in Virginia. We're not sure how she got to Sacramento, but there had been speculations that they had some type of a relationship."

"Oh my God, that's terrible," Hannah said, squeezing Oliver's hand.

She could not believe how it all played out, how she got tangled in all this craziness. Three women were dead and no one to answer for their deaths. Ethan was dead and no justice. What was she to do with all this information now?

Reagan placed a hand on her shoulder. "At least, now, you have closure."

"It sure doesn't feel like it," she said.

Chapter Thirty-Seven

Hannah thought about Andrea. Good for her. She dodged a bullet, but she couldn't help but feel awful for the family of the other victims. One lady had two children and Dr. Cavanaugh. What did she do to deserve death? I'm sure she was just trying to help him. Her heart sank. She felt helpless. She wanted to connect with the victim's families, but what would she say? That she was the target? That if it weren't for her, their loved ones would still be alive?

The day came and went. So much was discovered while Detective Reagan was there. It was nearly seven o'clock in the evening when the Detective left.

Kate stood from the chair. "I better get going. I still need to stop at the clinic before I head home," she announced.

"Thanks for coming, Kate. I know this is hard for you, " Hannah whispered as she walked her best friend to the door. Oliver trailed behind them.

"I'm okay. It's you I'm worried about. You sure you're okay?"

She nodded.

"I'll stay for a while. You shouldn't be alone," he offered as Hannah turned to go back inside.

"Thank you. I could use some distraction," she said as she glanced around to see if Ethan was there. Shouldn't he be there? Shouldn't he have been listening to everything the detective was telling them? She walked to the kitchen and grabbed two glasses and a bottle of wine. "I could use a drink right now. Join me?"

"Absolutely," K replied.

Hannah handed a glass to K, who quickly took her hand in his.

"Hannah, I'm here as long as you need me. You know that, right?"

"I know. Thank you," she said, rubbing his arm.

He looked deeply into her eyes, then decided to give her a hug. "Anytime, kid."

The hug felt good. She wanted to release all her frustrations and cry, but she was too exhausted to even do that. She flopped on the leather sofa and sighed deeply after sipping the cold wine in her hand. The whole thing did not make sense. People were killed, and no one paid for those crimes. She never thought all this could happen to her. She felt drained.

K joined her on the couch. He looked as exhausted as she was. "Well, I guess we now have our answers," she said, then slammed whatever wine was left in her glass down like a shot of tequila.

"Not the kind of answers I would have liked. I think David took the cowardly way out if you ask me," K grumbled.

Hannah nodded, but deep inside, she knew that David was troubled - sick. As much as she wanted him to pay for what he had done, it wouldn't bring Ethan back.

"Yes, he did. I wish he was alive and took responsibility for what he had done. What he had taken from me." She looked at Oliver. "From us. He should have at least gone to a treatment facility," she said.

Ethan would have agreed with her, or *would he?* Once again, she inspected the room. Nothing.

Oliver's jaw dropped. "What? Are you kidding me? Jail is where he should have been. If he weren't a wuss and didn't off himself, I would have done it myself."

"Don't say that."

"I'm serious," Oliver confirmed.

"I know, but the man was mentally unstable. He was talking to his dead mother for crying out loud," her last statement caught her off guard. She rubbed the back of her neck as she lowered her head and thought, *What about her? Where did she belong*? The longer she spent time with Ethan, the more she was convinced there was more to his existence. She couldn't help but think about what Papalo had said about angels. He always talked about angels. What if Ethan was, *in fact,* her guardian angel? She remembered what Ethan had said. *I believe in guardian angels, don't you? I will always be watching over you.*

She felt K's icy hand as he tried to pry hers off and started rubbing her neck. She wanted to protest, but it felt good.

"You have a good heart, Hannah. No wonder Ethan married you right away."

She was taken aback by his statement, unsure how to respond.

"So, Christmas is in a couple of days. Are you spending it with your family?" she asked as she straightened, pulling herself away from his hands. She faced him.

"Olivia wants me to spend the holidays with her family, but I thought...."

"Thought what?" she prodded.

"Well, Kate told me she was going back to San Diego, so I thought I'd stay here." He hesitated, then continued. "With you."

Chapter Thirty-Eight

K wanted to celebrate the holidays with her. What was she to do with that offer? Since she got married, she'd never celebrated Christmas with anyone else but Ethan. She wondered whether Oliver wanted to hang out as a friend, or could it be more than that? She shook her head. Of course, he was there as a friend. What was she thinking?

K swallowed the last drop of wine from his glass and leaned closer.

"I don't think you should be alone for Christmas. We should--"

A loud noise interrupted their conversation.

K rushed up, ready to check. "What was that?"

She knew exactly what it was. Who it was.

"It's probably just the wind. Something must have gotten knocked down. I left the window open earlier," she prattled on.

"I should check and make sure."

"Oh, no. There's no need. I got it," she said, hoping K would just let it go. She rose and slowly headed toward the front door. "I think I'm going to get some rest, K. I'm exhausted."

She watched K's confusion as if to question what had just happened.

"Of course. You call me if you ever need anything, you hear?"

"Yes, I will."

"K?"

"Yeah?"

"Thank you for being here. I don't know if I could have survived the day without you next to me."

K smiled. "Anytime, kid."

She gave him a quick peck on the cheek.

"Get some rest. I'll wait for your call."

After K left, Hannah shut the door behind her and leaned on it, lingering on K's last statement: *I'll wait for your call.* She wasn't quite sure why it affected her the way it did. She pushed the feelings aside as she rushed to the bedroom to find Ethan. He stood by the window, staring into the darkness outside.

"The night seems to get longer and longer, doesn't it?" he said without looking at her.

She wondered if there was more to that statement.

"Hi," she greeted.

He turned around to face her. "Hi," he greeted her back with a half-smile.

She didn't understand why she felt nervous. Was Ethan upset about the detective's news, or was it because K was there? She wrestled with those thoughts as she walked toward him.

"Where have you been? I've been looking for you."

"Here and there," he said casually.

"Here and there? What does that mean? Were you here the whole time? Did you hear the news about David?" She paused. "David, Lieutenant Matthew David was the guy who...." She took a deep breath, staring and studying him, not knowing whether she should say it aloud.

"The prick who killed me? Yes, I heard everything."

"Is everything okay?"

"No. Everything is *not* okay, Han. The man who killed me just took the easy way out. What a coward."

"That's what K said." She regretted the words the moment they came out. Hannah wasn't sure how he felt about Oliver lately and her calling him K. Or was it her own conscience bothering her?

Ethan sat on the bed, silently watching her. For the first time, she couldn't read his expression.

She sat next to him. "Detective Reagan said he had a mental illness like his mother." She placed a hand on his lap. Then she remembered Matilda. Her voice jumped an octave. "Can you believe his mother was a woman who worked at the shelter? Do you remember that night when we dropped off some clothes, and this one woman kept staring at me and was insistent on helping us?"

Ethan nodded. "Yeah, I remember."

"Okay, what's going on? You've been quite aloof."

Ethan took a deep breath. "I'm sorry, babe. I just didn't know how to take this whole thing. Hearing the entire story from that detective just made it real for me. I wish I could see this David guy, but I'm sure he's in hell. I hope he rots there."

Hannah felt a pang in her chest. There she was, worried that it was about Oliver. She kissed him on the forehead, or at least attempted to, but she still couldn't feel him fully. She wished sincerely that she could. She wanted to hug him and feel him return her embrace. Then she remembered what

Detective Reagan said about David. He was hallucinating. He *claimed to be talking to his dead mother.* Was that the reason she couldn't feel Ethan? No, there's something different about it. Ethan's presence felt real. In fact, she'd felt these feelings before. It was the exact same feeling she felt whenever Jean was around. She felt peace. *Oh my God, could he really be an angel?*

"What is it? "

"Nothing. I just wish you didn't hear everything that was said," she said, trying to process what she had just realized. *Does he know?*

Ethan brushed a strand of hair off her face and stared straight into her hazel eyes. "I needed to hear it," he whispered, then planted a kiss on her forehead. How she wished she could feel his kiss the way she used to.

"I just don't know why he needed to kill me," he said without looking at her.

Hannah felt another jab to her heart and fell apart. "I am so sorry. It's my fault. I was his target. I should have died. Not you." She rushed toward the window wiping the tears that were clouding her vision The thought of her being alive instead of Ethan made her hate herself, and she could not bear to look at him.

"Look at me, Han," he said, and she did. "Don't blame yourself. This isn't your fault. Do you hear me? This was done by a maniac. Someone with no regard for people's lives."

"But----"

"No buts, sweetheart. This is not your fault. What happened to me was how it was supposed to be. Do you understand? Please tell me you understand."

Hannah nodded. "Ethan... I *miss* you so much."

"I know, baby, I know. Come on," Ethan gestured for her to go to bed. "Why don't you take a quick nap, so you feel better?"

She could use a nap after the day she just had. "Will you stay with me? Please stay with me," she pleaded as she lay on the bed and pulled the cover halfway over her body.

"Yes, baby, I will be here, I promise."

***

Ethan was unsure about everything that went on; the fact that the man who killed him was dead, that he wasn't the target all along, that his best friend seemed to be spending more time with his wife, and the fact that he could now sense Hannah's feelings toward Oliver. She's back at calling him *K*, like she did in college. He didn't know how to process all the information. The only thing he was sure of was how much he loved the woman in front of him. He didn't want to leave her, but he knew sooner or later he would have to. He looked up to heaven. *More time please.*

Chapter Thirty-Nine

Hannah's phone vibrated and woke her up. She grabbed it and looked around, but she could sense the emptiness in the room. *I'm always here,* Hannah recalled Ethan reminding her. She looked at the phone as it continued to vibrate and noticed the tiny numbers on the top left of the screen- it read 10:34 pm. She must have really been fatigued. Who wouldn't be?

She thought of how the day had gone from the Detective's visit to Oliver's proposal to stay with her for Christmas to her conversation with Ethan. Yes, one would be exhausted for sure. The phone continued to vibrate. She glanced at the unknown number and answered it, hoping it was not one of those telemarketers she'd been getting a lot lately. She didn't have time for that.

"Hello, this is Dr. Presten."

"Dr. Presten, I'm glad I reached you. This is Molly Murphy. I have a dog named Chika. You saw her months ago for her annual checkup?" The young lady said in between heavy breaths.

Hannah tried to recall the name, but her mind was foggy. "Hi, Molly, what can I do for you?"

"I'm sorry to bother you, but Chika is having difficulty breathing. She's not eating, and she's very lethargic. She's just lying on the floor staring at me," the lady said frantically. "I wasn't sure whether you do house calls. I know it's late, but I didn't know what else to do."

"Molly, where do you live?" Hannah could hear the panic in the young lady's voice, so she immediately changed her clothes and got ready to go. She never turned down a patient so she got in her car and headed to the address Molly gave her. Twenty minutes later, she was scrambling for coins to drop in the parking meter in front of Molly's fifteen-story condominium. Then she heard Molly yell her name. She was standing by the entrance waving at her.

"I took care of parking, Doctor. Please hurry."

Hannah grabbed the black bag containing all her veterinary instruments from the passenger seat. She followed Molly into the elevator, and before she knew it, Molly jumped out and rushed to an open door where a young man was waiting. Hannah could only assume he was Molly's boyfriend.

"Where's Chika?" Molly cried out, rushing past the young man. "This is JR my fiancé," she quickly added.

"She's in your room. Nothing's changed. She's still lying on her bed panting."

She followed Molly and found the winded heavyweight English bulldog.

"How long has she been panting like this?" She bent to check on the dog, who was clearly distressed. The bulldog was surprisingly calm and didn't show any aggression. Either she was well trained or in too much pain. Before anyone could answer Hannah's first question, she asked another, "How far along is she?"

"I'm sorry?" Molly stammered.

From Molly's intonation and the shocked look on the boyfriend's face, she was sure none of them knew their pet was pregnant.

"We didn't know she was---"

"She was always on the heavy side, even for a bulldog," the fiancé interjected.

Hannah wasn't surprised; this wasn't her first encounter with owners unaware of their pet's pregnancy, especially with big dogs like Chika.

"I brought her to the clinic a few months ago. Wouldn't you have told me she was pregnant?" Molly said.

Hannah continued to check on Chika slowly feeling her belly, and she could almost feel her own uterus reacting. She wondered how it would have felt to carry her own baby. Ethan's baby. The thought made her miss him suddenly. The bulldog gave a soft growl, and Hannah quickly pulled her hands away, addressing Chika with her puppy voice. "Aww, I know, sweetheart, you're in pain, huh? Don't worry. It'll be over soon." She smiled and got back to Molly's question. "Well, that depends on exactly when you brought her in. Dogs carry their pups for about sixty-two to sixty-five days. I'm guessing by the way Chika looks right now. It was a few months before then." She glanced at Molly, standing next to her fiancé with her hand to her mouth. "Don't worry. She'll be fine."

"What do we do now? Do we wait till she gives birth?" the fiancé asked.

"Unfortunately, because of the size of the puppies, Chika will need a C-section. We need to take her to the clinic to make sure she's comfortable and make sure the pups are okay."

"Can we come with?" Molly asked.

She could tell Molly really loved Chika. Suddenly, she remembered what Papalo used to tell her about pets. It made her smile.

"Of course. Let's get her ready, and you guys can follow me to the clinic." She patted Molly on the shoulder to ease her concern.

***

By the time Chika recovered from the surgery, it was already well past seven in the morning. She told Molly and her fiancé to go home and rest and that she would call them once the bulldog woke up from her anesthesia, but the young couple decided to rush over; they had been in the clinic for a few hours waiting to see Chika and the new addition to their family.

"Chika is doing well. All three pups are healthy," she said. "Here's a pamphlet on what and what not to do in the next few days and also what to watch out for," Hannah told the couple.

They smiled and nodded while holding hands. Watching pet owners react to new puppies made Hannah wonder how she would feel when she first saw her own child. The thought sent a sudden knot to her stomach, knowing she would never have one with Ethan.

She stayed at the clinic till noon and decided to go home for the rest of the day. It had been a long night for her. While driving home, her conversation with Detective Reagan flooded her thoughts. *You were the intended target, Dr. Presten. Ethan was a victim of David's lack of impulse control. He was apparently talking to his dead mother. He was delusional and was hallucinating.* Her eyes were suddenly clouded with tears. Detective Reagan's words kept bellowing in her head. She glanced at the window, and her heart suddenly stopped. Matthew David stood by the crosswalk, staring at her. Suddenly, she heard a loud screech, and everything went dark.

Hannah woke the next day, not realizing where she was. She glanced around the room, still disoriented, and noticed a bouquet on a table beside her bed. Next to the vase was a tray with a glass of orange juice, and what she assumed was hospital food covered with a white plastic cloche.

She turned her attention to the other side of the room, the door was open, and she could see people passing by. She noticed a man in a white coat talking to a lady wearing blue scrubs. She finally realized she was in a hospital, but what was she doing there? She tried to sit up, but a pounding headache stopped her. She noticed the IV connected to her arm and the button beside it. Before she could press it, Kate came in holding a Styrofoam cup.

"Hey, Hun... You're awake. How are you feeling?" Kate set the cup on the table next to her and fixed Hannah's blanket.

She rubbed her right temple and felt the bandage on her forehead. "Aside from a pounding headache, I think I'm okay. "What am I doing in a hospital?"

Oliver, who stood at the door, chimed in before Kate could reply. "You got into a car accident on your way home yesterday. Don't you remember?"

She tried to recall what had happened. All she could re-member was that she did an emergency C-section on a bulldog the night before and had gone home early to get some rest.

"Was it my fault? Was someone else hurt?" Her heart raced as she waited for Oliver to answer.

He came and stood by her bed. "Relax, Sweetie. No other car was involved, thank goodness. No one else was hurt."

"Thank God," she said sighing.

"According to the first responders, you apparently swerved, ran onto the curb, and flipped your car. You don't remember why? How?" K asked.

Hannah shut her eyes, trying to retrieve some information. What could've made her swerve like that? Did she fall asleep? She did have a rather long day. And night. There's gotta be an explanation.

"Did you fall asleep at the wheel?" Oliver's voice pulled her away from her thoughts and opened her eyes.

"I don't think so," she said, furrowing her brows. She turned her attention to the doctor who had just entered. The gray-haired man looked like he'd had a long day himself.

"How are you feeling, Hannah?" The doctor asked.

"Just a bit of a headache," she replied.

"Aside from cuts and bruises and a hairline fracture on your ankle, your images look good. There are no other injuries that would prohibit you from going home today."

"That's great news," Kate blurted from the corner.

"We can both go home today." The doctor chuckled.

"Long day, Doc?" K asked, casually leaning on the wall with one hand in his jean pocket.

"Let's just say I could use a couple of hours of sleep before I have to be back here again." The Doctor smiled. "Anyway, the nurse should be coming in soon to give you the release form, and then you can take your wife home shortly."

K was about to correct him, but the doctor continued, now addressing Hannah as he walked toward the door. "Just make sure you take it easy for the next few days."

"Thanks, Doc," Hannah replied trying to ignore the awkwardness in the room.

"Your wife? Hi-*laa*-rious." Kate chuckled, teasing Oliver, but quickly backed off when she saw Hannah knitting her brows together, instead, she grabbed her purse and stroked Hannah's arms. "Anyways, I better get back to the clinic. I told Dr. H that I wouldn't be long." She nodded to Oliver. "I'll call you guys later. Take care of her," she said jokingly, widening her blue-shadowed round eyes at him as she walked out the door.

Hannah sat up and grabbed her folded clothes from the table next to her bed. "Don't listen to her. I can call an Uber or something."

"Or something. Are you crazy? You're not calling an Uber," Oliver protested. "I'm here to take care of you for the next couple of days till you get back on your feet."

She was too tired to argue. She didn't even know why she said what she'd said. Call an Uber? Did she really expect K to let her get into an Uber after what she'd been through?

"I'll go get the car," K announced. "Unless you need my help." He saw the look on her face and immediately corrected himself, "I meant, need my help to get you up. Not getting dressed." he rolled his eyes.

The ride home was quiet. Hannah stared out of the window for the most part. K slowly swerved, avoiding the pothole ahead as they hit a red light at one intersection. The sudden movement jogged her memory as they sat there waiting for the light to change. When she realized where they were, she clamped her hands over her mouth, but her eyes were fixed on the sidewalk.

"Oh, my gosh."

"Are you okay? What's wrong?" K said.

She remained silent for a while trying to find the words.

The light turned green, but she had not moved. In the corner was a small hole-in-a-wall Italian restaurant. K pulled into the parking lot to check on her.

"Are you okay?" he said, trying to gently pry her hands from her face.

Her voice trembled. "I remember what caused the accident," she mumbled. "David." "David?" Oliver said, perplexed. "As in Matthew David?"

"Yes, I saw him standing across the street. Right there by that light post." She pointed toward where she'd seen Matthew. Her voice cracked. "He smiled at me," she said, her voice trembling. "He smiled at me, Ol. He smiled at me."

"Are you sure? David is dead. Maybe the man just looked like him."

"I don't know... All I know is that I saw him. He smiled at me like he was taunting me." Hannah considered the fact that she might be hallucinating. "Maybe I'm going crazy," she cried.

"Of course not. I'm sure there's a plausible explanation for all this." Oliver unbuckled and reached over her. He pulled her closer to him, letting her head rest on his shoulder.

She couldn't keep her eyes off the sidewalk where she'd seen David standing tall, smirking at her, very much alive or was he? She recalled the day Detective Reagan delivered the news of Matthew's death. His letter. His mother. His mental illness. What if he's playing a sick game with her? She tried so hard to remember what she saw - who she saw, and suddenly she wasn't sure anymore. "I don't know," she mumbled under her breath and buried her face deep in K's chest.

"Tell you what, I'll call Detective Reagan as soon as possible and ask her to check on David to make sure," K reassured her.

"Okay," she said, sniffling.

K kissed her forehead as he shifted into drive with Hannah's head still resting on his shoulder. Though the ride was short, she fell asleep. He pulled in front of her house and woke her up with a gentle kiss on her head. She slowly opened her eyes, forgetting where she was, and with David's smile being the last thing she'd remember before falling asleep, she shot up, startled, and pushed Oliver away.

"It's okay, Hannah. It's me."

"Oh my gosh, I'm so sorry. I must have been dreaming." She straightened and unbuckled her seatbelt while Oliver made sure she was feeling alright before getting out of the car. He ran to the passenger side to assist her.

"Really, K... I'm fine."

K pulled back, placed his hands on his hips, and glared at her. "I'm sure you are, but I'd like to help you, anyway."

His reaction made her smile.

"Now, don't be stubborn," he said, trying not to smile.

She walked in the door, and for a minute, she felt guilty that she hadn't thought about Ethan while she was at the hospital.

Ethan wasn't at the hospital at all. How could that be? Why would Ethan not be there to comfort her? That's so out of his character. It must have been the accident. There was no other reason for it. Perhaps he was there, she just didn't see him, but why?

She made a mental note to talk to him about it when she saw him. She wondered if she should mention Ethan's presence to K or maybe Kate. *Absolutely not.* Not yet at least. She knew Kate would tell her to see a shrink. Not that she was against seeing a therapist, but she just never thought she would ever need one. Despite her childhood upbringing, she thought she'd turned out okay and was happy and content. Well, till Ethan's death.

Chapter Forty

O liver's heart pounded. He didn't know why he suddenly felt nervous around Hannah. He took a deep breath, straightened himself, and dropped his shoulders. Ethan was gone, and it was now his obligation to take care of Hannah. Hannah's accident scared him. He could have lost her. He wouldn't know what to do if that ever happened. He was supposed to make sure she was safe.

If anything happens to either one of us, we take care of each other's family - no matter what. That was the promise he and Ethan made to each other the day Ethan got married. Naturally, he was Ethan's best man, and granted the promise was made during their drunken bachelor's night, he still took it seriously. The next day, right before Hannah walked down the aisle, as Oliver stood by his best friend's side, Ethan reiterated the promise, and Oliver nodded, remembering the oath they'd made the night before.

He needed to put his feelings aside. He needed to and *would* fulfill his promise to his best friend. The question was, how long could he set his feelings aside?

He went to the kitchen and opened the cupboard where Hannah kept the cups.

"Why don't you sit and relax while I get you some tea? What kind would you like?"

"Green tea would be nice," Hannah replied.

He made sure the water was boiling, knowing that Hannah liked her tea extra hot. It was one thing he found out about her the day they'd met at the coffee shop.

Hannah sat on the couch. She looked to her left, then glanced to her right. She seemed to be scouting the room.

"Something you need?" He inquired as he handed her the hot tea. "Be careful."

Hannah slowly took the cup from him, holding the saucer beneath, and peered to the side, avoiding his stare.

"Just trying to see how much cleaning the house needed."

He felt like she was hiding something but decided not to press.

"Lady, you just got out of the hospital. The last thing you need to worry about is cleaning your house. Besides, the house is clean," he pointed out as he pretended to assess the condition of the house. "You should see my apartment. Now... *that* place needs cleaning."

Hannah smiled at his attempt to humor her.

"Thank you for being here, K. I don't know what I would have done without you and Kate." She blew on her tea before taking a slow sip. "Now, this is hot tea." She winked at him. "Not like the one Kate brought to the hospital this morning. How could someone drink that lukewarm tea? It's disgusting." She smiled.

He rolled his eyes. "You'd think Kate would know how you like your drinks by now," he teased.

"Hey, you're making me sound like a diva. For *your* information, I have never asked her to do a drink run for me. She does it out of the goodness of her crazy heart," she chuckled.

"The hair, what's up with the different colored hair? One day it's red the next day it's purple. If I didn't know any better, I'd say she's hiding from someone, especially with those glasses she wears," he said, laughing.

Hannah just shrugged and they both let out a hearty laugh. Gosh, he loved the way she laughed. He could sit there all day and listen to her sweet laughter. Another one of the beautiful traits he'd noticed the first time they'd met. His mind wandered as he stared and smiled at her, pretending to hear everything she said. *How in the world am I going to ignore these feelings?*

She started glancing around, and he was suddenly brought back to their conversation, and was audible again. "Besides, not too many people know about my preference in beverages, except for..." she said while absentmindedly rubbing her temple.

"I do," he interjected. "And Ethan, of course."

Hannah didn't respond, instead she started checking out her surrounding, and when she didn't find whatever she was looking for, she tilted her head side to side as if trying to loosen a knot on her neck.

"Are you okay?"

"Yeah, I'm fine. I think the medicine is wearing off. I should lie down and sleep it off," she said, closing her eyes with force and then opening them again.

"I think that's a good idea. I'll stay," he announced.

"Oh, no, no. There's no need. I can take care of myself. I promise." She gave him the sweetest smile that made him remember why he had fallen in love with her in the first place.

"I'll stay till you fall asleep. Call me when you wake up, I'm just a phone call away."

Hannah laid on the sofa as he grabbed the white blanket and placed it over her, tucking her in like a child. He put a pillow under her bandaged, wrapped ankle. "Comfortable?" He smiled, trying hard not to lean down and give her a passionate kiss.

"Yes, thank you." She smiled before closing her eyes.

Oliver kissed her on the forehead, sat at the dining table, and waited for her to fall asleep. What was he to do with his feelings? He was still madly in love with this woman.

Chapter Forty-One

S till groggy from the medicine she had taken earlier, Hannah fumbled for her phone as it rang.

"Hello," she managed.

"Well, good morning, sunshine."

She immediately realized her best friend's voice was too upbeat for her pounding headache. "What time is it?"

"It's seven forty-five, Doc. I thought I'd check on you before I head to the clinic."

"Clinic?" Hannah asked, confused.

"Yes. Clinic. The place you work at. Are we still out of it, Doc?"

"Softly," Hannah mumbled under her breath.

"What?"

Hannah pulled the phone away from her ear and spoke at it, "I said, speak softly," she repeated as she put the phone back to her ear, touching her forehead and feeling the bandage she'd almost forgotten about. She slowly stood and noticed the sliver of light coming from the window. She couldn't believe she'd slept throughout the night. Oliver, who tucked her in before she fell into a deep sleep, flashed before her eyes.

"Hello? Anyone there?" Kate whispered on the other end.

"Yes, I'm here. I didn't realize I slept this long."

"You sure did. Ol was paranoid. He called me last night asking if I had spoken to you last night.

I told him you were probably asleep and that you needed the rest, but he said you were talking crazy when he left you. The man's worried."

"Crazy?" She wondered what he meant by that.

"Yea, he said you saw *David*? And that's why you crashed your car? What's that about?"

"I'm not sure. Perhaps I was exhausted. Let's talk about it later. I have a migraine from sleeping too long."

"... Or from that cut on your forehead," Kate replied, then continued blabbering before Hannah could argue. "Alright, call Oliver, will you? Let him know you're up before he goes nuts. By the way, have you noticed something odd about him?" Kate asked.

"What do you mean?"

"He seemed very aloof; distracted you could say," she explained.

"I really didn't notice," she lied. She had noticed a shift in Oliver's demeanor, but there was so much going on she never had the chance to ask him about it. "Maybe he's just preoccupied with work."

"Anyway, call him so he stops pestering me."

"Will do. Thanks for checking on me. I'll try to stop by the clinic later," she said before hanging up.

She was about to dial K's number but decided to get some aspirin for her massive headache first. She opened the refrigerator, grabbed the carton of orange juice, and just as she was shutting the refrigerator, she felt his presence.

"Good morning," Ethan greeted her.

Still facing the refrigerator, she shut her eyes before turning to see if Ethan was just a figment of her imagination. The word, *crazy* just kept creeping in her thoughts.

"What are you doing? Are you okay?" Ethan asked.

She took a deep breath, opened her eyes, and slowly turned around, and there he was, sitting on the barstool behind the counter, looking at her, confused.

"Hi," she managed to say in the middle of her racing thoughts.

"Everything alright?"

"Yes, I'm fine. You startled me, that's all."

"Wait, what's that on your forehead?" he asked as he came closer.

"Oh, I had a minor mishap," she explained, touching the bandage. She walked past him to the bathroom, where she opened the medicine cabinet and grabbed a bottle of pain reliever.

He followed. "A mishap? What kind of mishap?"

She nodded as she hobbled past him to the kitchen, poured orange juice into a glass, and popped two aspirins into her mouth.

"Babe, are you going to tell me what happened?" he pressed.

"Yes, after my headache subsides."

Ethan let it go. "You must have been wiped out. I watched you sleep all night."

She spun to face him.

"You were here?"

A wrinkle formed on her forehead, wondering if he saw Oliver with her.

"Yeah, I told you, I'll always be here. I promised, remember?"

"Yes, I know. I mean, I knew you were here, but I didn't see you. I fell asleep early." He'd been asking what had happened to her. Did that mean he didn't know about the accident? Is he confined in the house? That did not make sense. Was he really an angel or was she going insane?

"So, what are you up to?" Ethan asked.

"Me?"

"Yeah, you. Who else would I be talking to?" He knitted his brows together. "Don't tell me... you're seeing another ghost?" This time, he let out a chuckle.

She did not find Ethan's joke amusing. She was not in the mood for his usual jests.

"So... you *are* a ghost."

"What? No."

"You're not?"

"I told you, I'm your guardian angel, remember?"

She dismissed the insanity. She didn't want to sound crazy.

"I'm sorry. I'm a bit confused today. Must be this massive headache," she said, trying to avoid the conversation as she walked to the living room, but Ethan tailed behind.

"I'm sorry, but could it be from that cut on your head? Are you going to tell me what happened?" he said.

She halted and felt a sharp pain in her ankle but ignored it.

"You really don't know?" She felt annoyed.

"You're head, your ankle? No, I don't. How would I? You haven't told me."

"I am not in the mood for one of your jokes, Ethan."

"I am not joking, Hannah. I am totally confused here. I really don't know what happened to you."

She studied his face. No expression. He stood there waiting for her to explain.

"I'm sorry. I didn't mean to snap at you," she said, lowering her tone as she sat on the sofa. She dismissed a dozen questions in her head and just explained. She was too tired.

"I got into a minor car accident the other day. I---"

He scooted closer. "Car accident? What happened? Are you okay?"

The shock in Ethan's voice confirmed her suspicion that he wasn't with her when the accident happened. She should have known. If he were there, he would have protected her as he always did or, at the very least, been in the hospital comforting her after, but he wasn't.

"I'm okay," she said calmly. She stared into his eyes and said, "I just thought you... you would have known."

"I'm sorry, babe, but I didn't," Ethan said, mystified, obviously bothered because he wasn't there with her.

"How did it happen?"

She decided not to bother with the truth. She thought it would only bring more confusion or questions about his existence, or even confirm her hallucinations. "I must have dozed off at the wheel. Really, it's not a big deal. No one else was hurt, and I'm fine."

Ethan shook his head and tried to touch the bandage on her forehead. "I'm sorry I wasn't there. Are you sure you're alright? Nothing else hurts?"

Many emotions flooded all at once. Ethan didn't witness the accident. He wasn't at the hospital. She could only see him in the house. Why? Hallucination was the only logical explanation, but nothing was logical lately. The fact that she had just lied about seeing David to Ethan made it more difficult. It was all too much. "I'm okay," she whispered, trying to withhold her tears.

Ethan planted a kiss on her forehead, and it stopped her. She suddenly felt chills all over her body. "Do that again."

"Do what?" He smirked. *"This?"* Ethan kissed her forehead again. She waited, but she didn't feel anything. The chills she felt earlier were quickly replaced with disappointment.

"What's wrong?"

"Nothing." She shook her head.

"Are you sure you're okay? Maybe you need to lie down again. You look a little pale."

"No, I'm all good." She touched the bandage on her forehead.

"I'm worried about you."

"I promise I'm okay, Ethan."

"Alright, I trust you. So... Christmas is in a few days. Do you have any plans?"

He was always great at making her forget whatever bothered her. She remembered what Oliver said about staying with her for Christmas.

"Nope, no plans. I think I'll stay home and binge-watch something on Netflix," she said, trying to avoid the topic. There it was again, the lie. *Lie by omission is still a lie,* she recalled him saying. *Gosh, would he be hurt? Feel betrayed? Would he feel anything at all?*

"Sweetheart, you can't celebrate Christmas alone."

"I won't. You'll be here, won't you? You'll be here, right?" She didn't mean to sound like a little girl, as she absentmindedly laid her head on his shoulder. She shot right up, realizing her head had actually rested on his shoulder. This could only mean one thing, what she felt earlier was real. She *did* feel Ethan's kiss.

"Are you okay?" he asked.

"Kiss me," she said.

"What?"

"Kiss me. Again. Please."

"What are you---"

"Trust me. Please."

Ethan leaned in and kissed her.

Her heart pounded as she anticipated his lips on hers. She closed her eyes. The chills she felt earlier were back. She could feel it along her spine. She took a deep breath in anticipation. Would she feel it, or would it confirm she was going crazy? Then she felt the warmth of his lips touching hers. Her heartbeat quickened, and she instinctively parted her lips to welcome the familiarity of it all. Tears rolled down as she felt his kiss - almost for the first time. She couldn't believe what was happening. She felt his kiss.

The overwhelming feeling, she thought she would never feel again, rushed through her veins, sending unexplainable incredible sensations throughout her body- her soul. She slowly opened her eyes, making sure she wasn't dreaming. She watched him kiss her while his eyes shut, full of hunger and longing. Him. Ethan. Her husband was kissing her, and she could feel him with all her heart. She shut her eyes closed, savoring the moment, afraid for it to end, fearing that it could all be her imagination.

They kissed till they both forgot the peculiarity of their situation. She didn't care, she felt him, and that's all that mattered. She couldn't be hallucinating, she felt him, and for now, she would relish the entire experience, however odd or impossible it may be. All she knew was that she could feel Ethan again. His kiss. His love.

After what felt like an eternity, both emerged from their euphoric journey.

"Is this real?" she asked as she nuzzled on his chest.

"Did you feel it?" Ethan asked, looking intoxicated.

"Did you?"

"Yes, with all my heart," he mumbled.

"Then... it's real," she said.

Chapter Forty-Two

Why didn't he know about Hannah's accident? There were so many things that couldn't be explained. Where in the world was Daniel? Daniel said everything would become clear later, but Ethan was more confused than ever. Daniel was the answer. He needed to talk to him and get his explanation, but he would have to deal with this man later. There were more pressing matters, like Oliver. He seemed to be spending more time with Hannah lately, and he didn't like that.

Yesterday, he watched Oliver and Hannah walk in through the door after waiting for her all night. He'd stood in the corner watching Oliver tuck his wife to sleep on the couch.

Ethan could see Oliver's longing for *his* Hannah. There was no hiding it. He sat next to Oliver, watching him watch Hannah sleep. So many mixed emotions were brewing inside. He was angry. He was thankful. He wanted to scream at Oliver and tell him to leave. He wanted to hug and tell his best friend he missed him. He was overwhelmed. He was jealous. Yes, jealous. Now that he was dead, and Oliver was alive *with* his wife. Yes, he was jealous.

Oliver sacrificed his feelings so *he* could be happy with the girl Oliver fell in love with. He knew that, but he didn't do anything about it. His best friend gave up the love of his life to give him his. That's when he heard him. *I should have fought for you,* Oliver whispered as he kissed Hannah on the forehead before walking out the door. After Oliver left, he sat there alone as Hannah slept, thinking of what he had done. Ethan could feel Oliver's heartache, he had seen it before, but he had chosen to ignore it. Ethan recalled the first few weeks he began seeing Hannah: *Oliver, is your friend? Where's Oliver? How's Oliver?* Oliver was all Hannah could talk about then. *Ol is great. He'd just started seeing a girl from his class,* he had conveniently announced to her one day, and all the questions about Oliver ceased from then on.

He suddenly remembered what had happened earlier. Hannah could feel him. She could feel his kiss, and he felt hers. It almost felt like the first time they'd kissed. Oh, how he'd miss his wife's affection. Her kiss. Her love. What he would give to make the moment last forever. They'd ignited their passion again, but something about it made him uneasy. Something wasn't right. He decided to let it go for now, knowing his entire existence did not make sense. He ignored the thoughts and focused on what had just happened. He could feel his wife's kiss, and she could feel his. That's all that mattered. At least for now.

As he sat there, satisfied with Hannah resting her head on his chest, he heard a man's voice.

"We don't have much time."

He turned toward the voice. Daniel stood behind them.

Hannah looked up. "What?"

266

"Did you hear that?" Ethan asked.

"Hear what?"

He looked at Daniel, who was waiting patiently.

The man shook his head letting him know that no one else could see him.

Daniel motioned for him to follow and then walked toward the bedroom. His quick gait told Ethan this was urgent. He gave Hannah a soft kiss on the lips. "I'll be right back."

"Where are you—"

Ethan walked into the bedroom and was again enveloped by a magnificent view. The place looked familiar, but he couldn't quite place it. The site was picturesque and tranquil. There was a lake in front of him, waves moving smoothly, making him feel a surge of calmness. Surrounding the beautiful lake were sturdy trees and vibrantly colored flowers. He noticed the lush green grass swaying softly under the sun. A golden-orange oak leaf loomed before him, climbing higher and higher. There was a black, wrought-iron bench where Daniel sat next to the oak tree. The man sat with his back to Ethan, basking in the splendor of this wonderful place.

Ethan approached him. "Where am I? What do you want from me?"

Daniel ignored his questions, smiling as if Ethan wasn't in front of him, blocking his view.

"Sit with me, son," Daniel said as he patted the space next to him before taking his hat off and placing it on his lap.

Ethan hesitated but obliged.

"I'll address your questions soon." The man smiled. "Isn't this beautiful?"

They both sat in silence for a while just like the first time they'd met. He was once again mesmerized by the splendor of the place. The breeze picked up, the leaves began to sway, and the golden orange leaves on the ground were carried away by the wind with poise and elegance.

"Doesn't this give you peace?" Daniel asked, gazing past the lake. His focus went farther than what was in front of them. Suddenly, it dawned on Ethan. The place reminded him of Serenity Manor in Virginia.

"Are you really an angel?" he asked.

"Do you doubt?" Daniel replied.

"Remember the promise you made?"

"The promise?"

"I was sent here to make sure that you fulfill your promise before---"

"My promise?" Ethan asked, puzzled. "Wait, before what?"

"Before you go where you're supposed to be." The man looked up at the bright blue sky as the breeze picked up again, and the white clouds started to dance with the wind.

He felt the coolness of the breeze brush along his arms. The feeling was unexplainable. Whatever it was, it felt good. It felt... welcoming. "Hold on; you *are* an angel." It was meant as a question; it came out as a revelation.

Daniel smiled and nodded. "Son, do you remember the promise you made to your wife?"

"I've promised a lot of things," he mumbled, trying to figure out what promise Daniel was referring to.

"You promised to love Hannah, didn't you?"

"And I always will," he answered without hesitation.

Daniel looked straight into his eyes. "Didn't you promise to stay with her forever? To make her happy? To make sure she's loved?"

"Yes. And I plan to."

"Well, I'm here to help you fulfill that promise, but in the right way."

"The right way? What are you talking about?"

"You didn't expect to be earthbound forever, did you, son?"

He glanced toward the lake before answering, as if to look for an answer. "Actually, I have no idea. I didn't expect to...." He looked down. "You know, leave her so soon."

"We all leave unexpectedly," the man said, as if he'd said the words many times before.

"See, son. Usually, no one stays back unless something unfinished is pulling them back. You weren't supposed to be here, but deep in your heart, you felt guilty for not fulfilling your promise. You held on and couldn't let go, but you are going about it the wrong way."

"That's why I'm still here?"

"And that's why I was sent here to... kind of move things along." Daniel winked at him.

He sat there pondering what he had just heard.

Daniel smiled. "You are trying to make sense of what's going on, aren't you?"

Ethan nodded.

"Don't, because you won't. No one does. Trust me, you'll go crazy if you try," Daniel patted his shoulder like a father encouraging a son. "There will be things you'll be able to see and understand. Things that will make sense to you, but there will be many that won't, just like when you were still alive.

That's just how it goes, we're not supposed to make sense of everything, instead, we are supposed to trust, so I suggest you let it go and start trusting. It's all for the greater good," the man reassured him.

"You said we don't have much time. What did you mean by that?" Ethan asked.

"Yes, we are all allotted a short time to let go of things before we move on – a time to fix our mistakes and some things we have not fulfilled. You've lived a glorious life, son. You loved and took care of your wife, but you also made some mistakes. The only way you will fulfill your promise of loving Hannah is to fix your mistakes and let go of your guilt."

"I've made so many mistakes in life. Which one are you talking about?" he said begrudgingly.

"Deep in your heart, you know which one I'm referring to, the only one that matters."

Ethan knew exactly what it was. *Who* it was. "What do I need to do?"

"Forgive yourself and let go. Let your loved ones - the *living* take care of each other."

"Then I'll be gone?" Ethan choked on the words.

"Well, you'll be around watching them as you promised, but..." the man lifted his head to the bright blue sky. "This time, it will be from a distance." Daniel searched Ethan's eyes. Then picked up his hat, placed it on his head, and stood. "Everything will be alright, son. Trust me. Hannah took after her Papalo. She is resilient. She will be fine. You must let go." Daniel smiled.

"Papalo," Ethan whispered the name. "You're Hannah's grandfather. I knew I'd seen you before. I just couldn't place it. Hannah's childhood album."

Daniel smiled. "You did great, son. You took great care of our Hannah, now let go and let someone else take care of her," he said as he nodded, walked towards the lake, and vanished.

Chapter Forty-Three

It had been almost an hour since Oliver left the little boutique inside the mall, and he still couldn't figure out what to get Hannah for Christmas. He rode the escalator, unknowingly humming along with the loud Michael Bublé song, 'It's Beginning to Look a Lot Like Christmas.' An older man on the opposite side going down caught his attention. The man, who appeared to be in his late seventies, nodded and smiled.

"It's great to see people smiling this holiday season, isn't it?" the man said.

The man looked sharp in his dark brown trench coat. His gray hair was visible under his black hat, and his salt and pepper mustache and white goatee were neatly trimmed. He was a handsome man with a positive disposition. Oliver couldn't help but notice his buoyant demeanor and felt somewhat connected to the man. Not fully aware whether the man was, in fact, talking to him, he turned around as the man reached the ground floor and yelled out, "Merry Christmas to you, sir."

The man tipped his hat and vanished into the crowded space.

He stepped off the escalator with unexplained satisfaction and happiness. Perhaps it was the man's contagious personality. The smell of perfume once again permeated the air as he stood on the second floor scanning the surrounding stores. He thought about getting Hannah a bottle of perfume, but it just didn't seem the right gift for her. A quaint gift shop caught his attention, and he entered. On the corner was a small table with several devotional books. He picked up a sky-blue spiral journal with the words 'Promises and Blessings' on the cover. Perfect. As he was about to pay, a figurine behind the counter also caught his attention. Among the mother and child, father and son, and family figurines was a beautiful porcelain of a woman in a white long-sleeve dress. The woman wore a white Panama hat with pink flowers, carrying a white umbrella, and a long-haired, brown cocker spaniel sat beside her. The lady behind the counter informed him that it was a Lladro called *Lady with Shawl*. The figurine's stature, grace, and beauty reminded him of Hannah. A few minutes later, he was out of the gift shop and into the center of the busy mall, carrying the boxed figurine.

Rocking Around the Christmas Tree greeted him full blast as the escalator descended. He was rocking along with the song when he felt his phone vibrate.

"Hello?"

"Hey, Ol. It's Kate."

"Hey, Kate. What's up?"

"Where in the world are you?"

"I'm still in San Francisco. I stopped by the mall to finish my Christmas shopping."

"I see. I wear a small, in case you're wondering. Favorite color is pink, and I don't mind something blingy,"

Oliver made a fake static noise over the phone.

"Can you hear me?" He grinned as he waited for her response.

"Haha. Very funny."

He chuckled as he hurried and brushed around the chaos inside the mall, looking for the exit.

"Anyway, should I call you later instead?" Kate asked.

"No, no, I'm out now." The music ceased as soon as he stepped out.

"What can I do for you?"

"Wow, how professional?" Kate teased. "Well, Mr. Rossi, I wanted to ask if you were staying in Sacramento or going to your sister's for Christmas."

"I'm staying. Why?" Oliver said nonchalantly. "Wait. Weren't you supposed to leave today?"

"Yeah, but I decided to stay."

"Why?" He didn't mean to blurt it out, but it was too late.

"What do you mean, why?"

"I mean, is everything okay?"

"Yeah, everything is fine."

Somehow, he got away with it.

"I talked to my mom on the phone the other day. She'd asked about Hannah, and we talked about her being alone for Christmas."

Oliver fell silent. He knew where this was going. He wanted to protest and tell Kate that Hannah wouldn't be alone, that he would stay with her, but then again, he hadn't confirmed that with her.

"So, I thought it would be the best friend thingy to do, you know? Stay with her and keep her company. "

"Thingy?" He snickered. "What's a thingy? Is that even a word?"

Kate's voice rose an octave higher. "Yes, it's a word. *Anyhow*. I was wondering what your plans are--"

"I'm staying." He didn't mean to sound blunt, so he continued with a softer tone. "I also think Hannah shouldn't be alone for Christmas." He paused to give her time to respond, but she didn't, so he took his chance and continued. "I actually kind of mentioned it to her about me spending Christmas with her and all, but she hasn't said anything yet. I was going to ---"

"Great. We can all spend Christmas together. I have a plan."

Kate had a plan...Great. He waited for her to continue, but the line was quiet.

"...and your plan i-i-i-s?"

"We could bring Christmas to her since she didn't want to decorate or celebrate Christmas. What do you think?"

He wished to be alone with Hannah for Christmas, but the thought of the three of them, made him realize that this would be what Hannah would want.

"So... how are we going about this 'Christmas operation?' Tell me the plan," he said as the old gentleman he saw earlier inside the mall smiled at him from across the street.

Chapter Forty-Four

Oliver was coming out of Vallejo on I-80, heading back to Sacramento, when his phone rang again. The volume reverberated through his car speakers, interrupting the authoritative male voice on a podcast he was listening to. *"Knowing others is intelligence. Knowing your true self is wisdom-"* the motivational speaker quoted Lao Tzu.

He pressed answer. "Hello, this is Oliver Rossi."

"Hello, Mr. Rossi, it's Detective Reagan. Did I catch you at a bad time?"

"Hi, Detective. Not at all."

"Sorry it took me a while to get back to you," the detective said.

"No worries. Did you find anything new?"

"Well, as I mentioned to you last time, according to the coroner, they had Matthew David's body, so whoever Hannah saw that day was not David."

"That's great news."

"Well, I did more digging into David's family, and we found something else."

He didn't like the sound of that but waited for Reagan to continue.

"We found out that Matilda gave birth to two boys- twins, But---"

"Did you say twins?"

"Yes," Reagan answered.

"Where is the brother now?"

"He was given up for adoption, but we could not find any records of it."

"So, the man Hannah saw could have been David's twin brother?" Oliver said, irritated with the idea that another madman could still be lurking around.

"Possibly, but according to the records, Matilda lived overseas and only brought one son when she moved to the United States."

Oliver could feel a headache coming on and pulled over to the side of the road. "What do we do now?"

"I wish I could tell you. I know how hard this must be for you, but in all honesty, I don't think it was the twin; that's just too much of a coincidence," Reagan said.

"I am worried about Hannah. I don't want her to worry anymore."

"I understand. There could also be another explanation for what Hannah experienced."

"And what's that?"

"Mr. Rossi, if you don't mind me saying, I've seen some pretty odd stuff being in the force all these years. Based on my experience, it is not unusual for victims to sometimes imagine seeing people they aren't supposed to see anymore. Some even claim to talk to them."

"Like a ghost?" Oliver asked, bemused.

"Well, I guess to some. That's their belief."

Could her grieving be playing tricks on her or was there really a possibility that Hannah saw David's brother?

"Please go on," he said, hoping for a better explanation.

"Some imagine their assailants' faces on some random person," Reagan said. "I'm not saying it's the case here, but has Hannah seen a grief counselor since Mr. Presten's death?"

"I don't think so."

"I would suggest you encourage her to see a therapist. It might be helpful for her grieving process."

He supposed grieving was much better than knowing it was David's brother she saw, and even if it were, who was to say he was a lunatic like David? He decided to keep the information to himself.

Reagan ended the call. Something about another case. He continued driving in silence, deciding that Hannah needed him now more than ever.

***

Hannah was surprised when Kate arrived at her front door unannounced, carrying boxes of Christmas decorations. A few minutes later, K came knocking. When she opened the door, there he was, standing tall with a massive tree on his right shoulder, muscles visibly penetrating through his gray sweatshirt. She forgot her manners as she stared into his sparkling green eyes. She absentmindedly brushed the strands of hair that had fallen down his face.

"Thank you. But this tree isn't getting any lighter. Are you gonna let me in?" he asked, smiling.

"Oh, my goodness. What is wrong with me? I am so sorry. Come on in," she said, stepping aside to let him pass.

He winked as he walked into the living room, and instantly her knees buckled.

"Where do you want this?"

"Right there." She pointed at the space next to the fireplace, and Oliver immediately dropped the tree.

"I can't believe you guys are here."

"Hey, if Oliver gets to stay, so should I." Kate said then, like a petulant child, stuck out her tongue at Oliver.

"Wait, What?" She knew K wanted to stay with her, but they had yet to really discuss it. "K, you're not going to Olivia's for Christmas?"

K shook his head and gave Kate a dirty look.

"K?" she pressed.

K walked toward the kitchen and picked up a cookie from the platter. He toyed with it as if buying time to come up with the proper explanation.

"Didn't want you to be alone for the holidays, so I told Olivia that I wouldn't be coming this year, and she understood; in fact, she encouraged me to stay," he said between chews.

"How are the cookies, Ol?" Kate asked.

"Good. Want some? Quick. Catch," he yelled before throwing one in her direction.

The cookie landed on the floor.

"Hey. I'm not cleaning that up," Kate protested.

Hannah picked up the crumbled pieces from the floor. "Stop, you two." She smiled, shaking her head at them like a mother scolding her children. "You guys, I would have been okay. Really."

"We know *you* would, but *we* wouldn't. Knowing that you're going to be alone for the holidays. Not cool," Kate said.

K nodded in agreement.

"You guys are the best," Hannah said, feeling rather sentimental.

Kate tried to break the awkwardness by circling her index finger in the air several times before finally pointing at the Christmas tree. "Fyi,this whole thing was my idea. Okay?"

"Of course. Wouldn't wanna take credit for it," K said, rolling his eyes.

Kate threw a pinecone and hit K right on the forehead.

"Hey." He winced as he picked up the cone and motioned to throw it back at her, but he didn't.

Their laughter made Hannah realize she needed all this. She couldn't remember the last time she laughed - really laughed. No, she did remember; it was with Ethan at Serenity Manor. She tried to hold her emotions together but could no longer resist them, so she let go and allowed her tears to flow.

She could tell Oliver was about to comfort her, but she needed Ethan, so she rushed to her room. She sat on the edge of the bed and sobbed. "I can't do it, Ethan. I can't. I miss you too much."

"But I am here, sweetheart," Ethan whispered.

She lifted her face from the pillow, happy to see Ethan beside her. She buried her face in his chest, just as she used to do. She closed her eyes and savored his scent, which had been stronger and stronger over the last few days.

Ethan gently lifted her face.

"What's wrong?"

She shook her head, not looking at him, tears flowing. He brushed them away.

"Sweetheart, you're supposed to be having fun with our friends."

"It's not the same."

"I'll be next to you."

"You promise?"

"I prom--"

"Hannah? Are you alright?" Oliver's voice interrupted them.

She ignored the knock. "You promise?" she asked again.

"I promise," Ethan whispered.

She wiped her tears and kissed him. Then, just as she was about to stand, she felt Ethan's tug.

"Hannah?"

She spun back around, and his lips covered hers before she could say anything. The passion ignited like it always had, as if Ethan had never left. It was real. She could feel it. She could feel his longing, his love. It was all back. She could feel it. Her heart ached for him so much. They were imprisoned by their hunger for life, lust, and love. She had forgotten about K behind the door.

The pounding on the door released both from the shackles of their vehement hunger for each other. Ethan pulled away first, but she could still clearly see his longing for her. She didn't want to part from him. She stared into his eyes and studied his face. He nodded, wiped her trickling tears, and let her go.

"Hannah, can I come in?" K pounded on the door some more. There was panic in his voice.

Ethan gave her a comforting smile and gestured for her to open the door. Hannah could hear murmurs behind it. She was sure Kate had joined K outside the room, so she turned around to address Ethan, but he was gone. Not ready for him to disappear again, she sighed. "Give me a minute," Hannah called out as she headed to the bathroom and splashed water on her face before opening the door.

"Are you okay? We were worried about you," Kate said, her voice cracking.

She glanced at Oliver, who remained silent, watching her intently. Not wanting to address the situation, she pulled her eyes away from his gaze.

"I'm okay. I just needed to let that out... I'm sorry," she replied. "But I'm okay." She reassured them as she walked out to the living room.

Kate and Oliver trailed behind her without a word.

She nudged K playfully. "You okay?"

He nodded and gave her a weak smile.

***

It was almost ten in the evening, and Oliver waited for Kate to leave so he could talk to Hannah alone. He wasn't going to let the night end without talking to her. For crying out loud, she was having a conversation alone in her room. *Has Hannah seen a grief counselor since Mr. Presten's death?* Detective Reagan's voice had been in his head since.

"You okay?" Hannah said.

"Can we talk?"

"Sounds serious," she said as she turned to sit on the leather sofa. "What's wrong?"

He sat next to her and went directly for it. "Have you seen a grief counselor since Ethan's death?"

His question took Hannah aback. She took a deep breath and gave him a defensive smile.

"I'm okay, Ol. I know I had a little off moment earlier, but I'm okay..." She paused and sighed. "I haven't really cried out like that, you know. I guess it was bound to happen. It's the holidays."

He knew she was searching for understanding from him, but he didn't offer an expression that would indicate he understood. He wasn't trying to be mean, but he needed to be firm to get to the bottom of the situation.

"If you are worried about my mental health, don't. I didn't have a breakdown; I won't have one... Well, not anytime soon, at least," she said, trying to keep her tone playful, but he heard a slight edge. She stood, but he grabbed her hand before she could walk away.

"Hannah, I'm serious here. I'm worried about you. You are not acting like yourself. First, this whole thing about David, which detective Reagan confirmed that he is in fact dead. I think---" Hannah's blank gaze interrupted his thoughts. Suddenly, he questioned whether it was the right move.

She sat back down and faced him.

"The body was David's?"

"Han, you're grieving, it's normal, but I think—"

"Ol, I was overwhelmed, okay? As you can understand, Christmas is Ethan's favorite holiday, and ---"

"*Was*."

"What?" she scoffed.

"Was. Christmas *was* Ethan's favorite holiday," he said, holding his irritation in.

The annoyance was visible on Hannah's face. "Yes. I meant Christmas was his favorite holiday, and it's just hard."

He could tell he was upsetting her, but she kept her composure. He understood but could not dismiss what he had heard earlier, especially knowing that her mind may be playing tricks on her. "I'm worried about you, Han. There's nothing wrong with seeing a grief counselor. As you said, you are overwhelmed," he said, touching her hands slightly.

"Thanks for your concern, but I think I'm good. Especially after that cry earlier. I needed that."

He didn't know how else to convince her, so he went for it. "I heard you."

"What?"

"I heard you talking to yourself, Han. Have a full-on conversation in your room."

Hannah snatched her hands away from him. He could tell she was irritated, staring at him blankly. He stood and started pacing, trying to control his emotions.

"You can talk to me. Please talk to me, Han," he begged, gripping his hair in frustration.

"You don't...You *won't* understand," she replied, turning away.

He rushed beside her and gently pulled her back to face him.

"Then help me understand. I'm here for you, Hannah."

Chapter Forty-Five

I t was a tough day for Hannah. Christmas Eve. Though Oliver and Kate did their best to make her forget about the tragedy, it didn't ease the pain of her loneliness, so she buried her mind in something else and cooked dinner. She baked her famous Filipino dish *cebu chon* - a slab of brined pork belly, patted dried, seasoned with salt and pepper. Hannah lined the slab with stalks of smashed lemongrass, chopped onion, garlic, and ginger, rolled it like a log, and tied strings around to hold it together. It was appetizingly beautiful-the perfect centerpiece for their Christmas Eve dinner. She was not much of a cook, but there were a few dishes she'd learned from her mother, and *Cebu chon* was one of them; it was one of Ethan's favorites. Oliver brought a green bean casserole, and Kate graced them with her famous creamy coconut peppermint pie for dessert.

After dinner, K suggested they play a card game called Three Thirteen while enjoying some eggnog K had prepared earlier that night. Kate proposed a toast. As they clinked their wine glasses together, she caught a glimpse of Ethan standing by the fireplace, watching them. Though she could see his loneliness, he gave her his brightest smile. She gave him a faint smile back, raised her glass slightly, and nodded, while trying to conceal her interaction with him from her friends.

K handed her a gift bag and she immediately took out what's inside and unwrapped the gifts. She loved them all, especially the figurine. "You know me so well, thank you!" She was about to get up and hug K, but he got up first, forcing her to sit back down.

"Hold on. I have another one for you. I'll be right back," he said. He walked out the house. She and Kate exchanged glances wondering what it would be. Kate shrugged.

K returned carrying a long wooden stick of some sort with a red bow tied around it. Hannah's eyes immediately welled up upon closer look, realizing what he was carrying.

"You didn't," she whispered as she stood to touch the gift K was carrying.

"I remembered you telling me about your Papalo and how you wished you had taken this door jamb before you guys sold the house. I know Ethan would have gotten this for you if he had the chance. So, I thought---"

"Thank you! Thank you! You have no idea how much this means to me." She kissed him on the cheek. "Best gift ever. Ethan would have appreciated this. I know he would." She looked at Ethan as she hugged Oliver. He was smiling. She could tell he was sincerely grateful for what Oliver did. They continued exchanging gifts and talked the rest of the night. It was a fun evening, just what she needed.

***

It was almost five in the morning before Kate and Oliver left. Hannah stood in the middle of the living room, waiting for Ethan to show up.

"I remember how much fun we had hanging these together," Ethan said as he stood by the beautifully lit Christmas tree toying with some ornaments. He gestured for her to come closer. She walked toward him and reached for his hand. Somehow, she felt the urge to say something. What? She wasn't sure.

"My best friend did well," Ethan said with a faint smile, not looking at her and continued toying with another ornament on the tree. "I'm glad he got it for you, I know how much that meant to you. I just wished I could take the credit." He chuckled slightly.

"I think Ol did it for you."

"For us," he said softly as he smiled and squeezed her closer. "Shall we celebrate *our* Christmas now?"

Bing Crosby's *I'll Be Home for Christmas* started playing in the background, and they began to dance. She could feel his embrace, his heat, his love. He lifted her chin and right away claimed her pulsing lips. She responded by parting them for him, welcoming his warm lips onto hers as they ignited their passion once again. She was back in Ethan's embrace, and everything that bothered her melted away. She let her hair down, releasing a fresh scent of lavender and berries. They swayed in silence, feeling each other's heartbeats.

Ethan planted soft kisses on her bare shoulders, thanks to the red off-shoulder mini dress she decided to wear that night. She could feel each kiss he planted and each nip he made; it was making her crazy. *Could this be real?* Again, she wondered, she just couldn't wrap her mind around the whole thing, but he was there, and it felt good. Ethan moved to her neck, exploring every inch of it, caressing it with his lips. He gently nipped on her earlobe, making her cry in excitement. Ethan twirled her around, pulled her swiftly back to face him, and again claimed her lips. She let out a soft moan. Ethan pulled away. He studied her, brushing the tears from her face. She leaned into him. She felt his resistance.

"Ethan?"

She waited for him to say something; instead, he stared back as if looking into her soul, and just like that, he claimed her soft lips once again. They danced. Kissed. Danced, and they kissed some more. By the end of the night, they were on the floor, holding each other next to the Christmas tree. She didn't want the night to end. Suddenly, she felt an icy breeze and woke to the sun glaring through the window. Alone.

That Christmas morning was the last time Hannah saw Ethan. It had been almost a month. Was he gone for good? Was that memorable night his way of saying goodbye? Did that really happen? The thoughts were unsettling, and Hannah didn't know how to take it all in. Ethan needed to come back; that couldn't be the end.

***

Daniel told him he needed to move things along. That didn't sit well with him. Did that mean he was leaving Hannah soon? That he would be gone forever? He needed to see him. He sat on the bench where they first met and decided to wait for him to appear. As he sat watching the birds in the sky, he was reminded of Christmas night. It was bittersweet. The feelings he had watching Hannah getting more comfortable with Oliver that night came flooding back. It was disconcerting, but Daniel's voice kept reminding him to forgive and let go. Easy for him to say was his thought every time he was reminded. Hannah was the love of his life. How could one let go? He recalled forcing a smile whenever Hannah looked in his direction that night. He watched her when she wasn't looking. Gosh, she was beautiful. The way she moved, the way she smiled, the way she laughed, God, she was laughing again. She seemed happy. How could he take that away from her? He didn't want her to suffer, but was it wrong that he almost wanted her to be sad for him instead?

Lately, he saw Oliver and Hannah's connection getting stronger, and Hannah looked happy. He also noticed the longing on his best friend's face every time he looked at his wife. Maybe he should have stepped aside from the very beginning. Perhaps they were meant for each other all along. All the thoughts became heavier to take in. Watching the exchanges between his wife and Oliver over the past few months hadn't been easy. He could see how Oliver had been trying so hard to be there for Hannah since his death, to comfort and take care of her. It must have been hard for his best friend to do that, he thought, knowing he still had feelings for Hannah. Oliver loved her from a distance. He also knew that Oliver held his feelings back because of their friendship. That's how Oliver was - always sacrificing his feelings for those he loved. A sudden surge of unexplained emotions came over him. Was this what Daniel meant by letting go? Letting go of Hannah and accepting that Oliver was there to watch over her now? Even love her? It made sense. Hannah looked happy with Oliver, happiness Ethan couldn't any longer give her. Still he didn't like the revelation one bit. He wasn't ready.

Ethan brushed the thought aside, and Christmas night flooded back again. The heaviness in his heart was unbearable as he watched his wife in the arms of another man. Hannah's feelings for Oliver were back, he could see it. The revelation was like a sharp knife digging into his already pained heart, yet there was also something relieving about it, as if a heavy burden had been lifted off his shoulders, knowing that Hannah would be taken care of. He couldn't explain it.

He had wished Daniel was there that night to explain all the confusing emotions he was feeling, but celebrating Christmas with his wife one last time was more important. He wanted to give everything to Hannah that night. Give her the best Christmas gift he could have ever given her. He wanted to make sure she felt his love, that she would always remember the feeling even when he was gone. He wanted them to connect as they'd never connected before and feel alive again. But as time had passed, the pain of the realization that he would never have Hannah again, brought so much pain.

He recalled Hannah walking out of the room in her red off-shoulder mini dress and he fell in love with her all over again, as if that could have been more possible. He knew she chose that dress for him. *I hope you like this, babe.* He'd heard her mumble to herself as she was getting dressed earlier that night.

Even after his death, she still tried to please him. How did he ever get so lucky? God, she was beautiful. He remembered admiring her from a distance. Her simplicity was intoxicating, and that night, she was exquisite. He couldn't wait for Oliver and Kate to leave, but he was also satisfied just hanging around to see his wife happy and not alone. He still could not wrap his head around the bizarre situation, especially the fact that their connection had been getting stronger and stronger, especially that night. Their touch, their kiss, their love, they were so natural, almost eternal. He never wanted that night to end because he knew this whole thing wouldn't last long. A new and better place awaited him, that's what Daniel said, and he didn't have much time. He watched her sleep on his lap, taking every inch of memory he could. She looked peaceful, and at that moment, he knew what he needed to do. He kissed her forehead as always; his heart aching at the thought that this could be the last time he'd ever get to do that.

Chapter Forty-Six

February 17, 2022

E than needed to clear his mind and make sure he was doing the right thing. He watched Hannah the whole time. He knew she was upset but he needed to give her space to make things easy for everyone. He needed to provide space so *she* could let go.

He was back at the lake, where he had his first talk with Daniel. They have spoken a couple more times since Christmas, and each time they met, Daniel brought him one step closer to understanding how to fulfill his promise. He needed to let go and let love take its course once again. *Hannah is a strong woman, my son, but we both know she is stronger when loved,* Daniel reminded him. Ethan sat on the bench, watching the peaceful sky above him. He felt a surge of powerful emotions he couldn't quite explain. The wind picked up, and the lake waves crashed before him. There was a beauty to the way the waves danced together, as if urging him to cast his fears into its depths. Ethan could not explain what he saw, but he let his feelings wander with the waves, trusting God.

Finally, he let go. He let the currents carry his emotions out, and he let the wind carry his thoughts into the sky. The bright blue sky caught his attention, noticing the soft milky white clouds moving slowly and rhythmically as if opening their arms, welcoming him into its fold. He felt the breeze touching every inch of his body. He took another deep breath and exhaled. Each exhale carried another piece of him, releasing them into the air. As the lake became still, he smiled. He could feel himself almost elevating, a heavy burden lifted off his entire body. He found clarity. He felt contentment. Freedom. Ethan found peace. He let go.

***

Hannah was still at work when he arrived at the house, and though Ethan was sure of his next step, he couldn't help but feel nervous. Daniel clarified he needed to let Hannah love and be loved again. Hannah will always love him, and he will always love her. Their love for each other will always live on. The reminder made him feel better and made things easier.

The doorknob turned, and he knew Hannah was home. He decided to put on some music. Frank Sinatra's *The Way You Look Tonight* started playing. Hannah walked into the bedroom with misty eyes. She stood at the entrance but didn't say a word. He feared she could be upset, but her facial expression told a different story. There was longing in the way she looked at him. There were questions. He knew he had hurt her by leaving her without a word. The poor gal must have been so confused about his existence. Even he was confused, but all he knew was that God had given him a second chance to fix his mistake and had given him the opportunity to show how much he loved Hannah by letting her go and be loved again.

Hannah tilted her head to the side as if asking where he had been. She stood still, unable to speak, he could sense the worry and pain in the way she breathed. His heart became heavy. He didn't want to do what he came there to do. He didn't want to cause her pain. Again. But it was time. It was time for her to be happy and to be loved the way she deserved to be loved. He gave her his warmest smile as he stood in the center of the room; his heart raced, his breath rapid. He lifted his hand and gestured for her, asking to dance.

"I've missed you," she whimpered, her eyes heavy with welled-up tears. Then, finally, one escaped and dropped.

"I've missed you, too, honey," he replied.

They held each other without saying a word for what felt like an eternity. Their bodies swayed together with Sinatra in the air as they held each other tightly, fully knowing that it would be the last. He felt the wetness from her tears on his chest, and his heart constricted. He took a deep breath and forced himself to keep his composure. *She needs to love and be loved. You need to let go,* he reminded himself. The music switched to a different song, and he took advantage of the moment.

He pulled her away to see her beautiful face one last time. She smiled and welled up tears thudded on the ground. They were always tuned in to each other's feelings; he knew this time was no different. He knew that Hannah could tell that this was goodbye. Ethan brushed the tears off her face, but her eyes immediately welled up again, replacing the many teardrops that had already fallen. He guided her to sit on the bed, but he remained standing.

With the sun threatening to set, he faced the window. "I'm afraid it's time," he said, trying not to choke on his words.

"No," she whispered. "Not yet. I'm not ready," she added as she shot up and wrapped her arms around Ethan's back.

"Remember the time we talked about guardian angel?" he said.

"Yeah," she managed to reply between soft sobs.

"Believe, Han. Believe that I will be watching over you." He wiped her tears away. "Do you know who told me so?" He smiled a little.

She stared into his glistening eyes.

"Papalo told me. He misses you, he said, but we will all be watching over you."

"What? You saw Papalo?"

"Yeah. He is quite a man." He gave a faint laugh.

"All?" she said, tilting her head quizzically.

"Yeah, Mamala and Jean are there waiting for me. They are full of love, Han. I can't wait for you to see them again, but please..." He smiled through his tears. "Take your time."

He could not help but let his tears fall as her arms wrapped around him tightly, her tiny hands barely reaching together around his waist. He placed his hands over hers and continued watching the quiet street outside. The lamp post was now shining its light in their cul-de-sac. One last time, he envisioned little Ethan and little Hannah running around while they watched them from the sidewalk, just like he and Hannah had envisioned. Finally, the tears threatening to escape fell, drop after drop. Each drop seemed heavy, carrying all the pain he had inside him.

He faced her. It didn't matter to him anymore if she saw him cry. He wanted to be free with his emotions, to be vulnerable and raw. He wanted her to see his heart, his pain, his regret. He also wanted her to feel the peace and the love he was leaving her.

"I will always love you, Han. Keep those words in your heart."

With those last words, they both let go.

Chapter Forty-Seven

I t had been several weeks since Ethan said goodbye, but it took Hannah time to heal. She missed Ethan every day but talking to Dr. Marcel had helped ease her loneliness. Whether it was grief or some unexplainable powerful being, her borrowed time with Ethan was worth it. *Remember, this is real. You hear me? Real,* she remembered Ethan telling her before finally letting go. She knew it was real and didn't have to justify it to anyone. She didn't even address it with K. However, she realized that Keon was right to suggest the grief counselor. Dr. Marcel's guidance through the five stages of grief was beneficial.

Hannah stood in front of the rectangular stainless-steel table inside the examination room, absentmindedly petting a honey-colored mini lop bunny she hadn't noticed was trying to break free from her grasp. As she inattentively felt for lumps on the furry animal's body, she ruminated over what her therapist had told her about grief. *There are typically five stages of grief, but everyone handles grief differently. Some go through all the stages, some experience a few and some... well some just choose to move on,* he told her. Did she go through the stages? He did suggest that denial may have explained her visions of Ethan. Hannah did not detail her encounter with her late husband, only that she had seen and spoken to him once or twice. They'd explored her anger. She *was* angry, no, furious, that's what she was; furious that Ethan had died. Furious because *she* was the cause. She was also livid that David took his life. Ethan was right, the coward took the easy way out. *Perhaps, you needed David to be alive so he could be punished?* She recalled Dr. Marcel asking. Of course, she wanted him alive. She wanted him to pay for what he'd done. She didn't want him dead. She wanted him to rot in jail.

Progress - We're making progress, Dr. Marcel said during their last session. What now? It had been a few weeks since she'd last seen Dr. Marcel. She considered the five stages again as she continued to pet the bunny. *Denial, anger, bargaining, depression...* She paused, trying to determine if she had gone through the phases. According to Dr. Marcel, hostility, helplessness, and running away from the problem were a few of the things she would feel if she was depressed. She didn't remember being hostile. Helplessness... maybe. Running away? Definitely not. So where was she in the stages? She let it go. Everyone grieved differently, she told herself.

Whatever she was holding got away, and the chubby bunny leaped toward the other side of the table, before jumping down, bringing her attention back to the task at hand. "Goodness. I'm sorry, Mr. Thumper. I was daydreaming," she said as she gently grabbed the bunny form the floor and back to the center of the table. She gave him some love, nuzzling and petting his belly before she restarted her examination.

***

Oliver and Hannah agreed to meet downtown at a new Japanese fusion restaurant called "Kawai." As Hannah walked into the restaurant, Oliver stood and waved. He chose one of the round tables in the corner.

"Hi," He greeted first.

"Have you been here long?" she asked as she glanced at his drink on the table.

"Soda. I got thirsty, and no, I have not been here long," he answered as he offered and pulled out the chair across from him for her to sit.

"Have you tried the food here?" she asked, glancing around the room, and placing the white linen on her lap as she sat.

"Once. I tried the sushi platter, and it wasn't bad."

"Fancy place."

The restaurant was small but elegant and full despite being early in the evening. The bar area was packed with men in suits and well-dressed women.

"Can I get you something to drink?" the server asked.

They ordered and had their usual *'How was your day at work'* conversation.

"So... according to my therapist, I'm making progress," she said as she took the last gulp of her second glass of chardonnay.

"Really? That's great."

"I was depressed for a while, but I'm better now. I think," she said nonchalantly as she looked around, waving her empty glass.

"You *think*?" he said.

"No, *I know*. I feel a lot better." she smiled.

"Glad to hear you feel better. I'm---" He got distracted by her trying to get the server's attention. "Han, are you wanting another drink?"

"Yes. It's the weekend. I need to unwind."

"Hannah, that's your second glass."

"Geez, K, relax," she teased.

He knew about her low alcohol tolerance way before Ethan did, she told her. He took her empty glass from her. "Okay, but maybe slow down a bit? I think you're already tipsy."

"Me? Nah. How could I?"

"The fact that you are asking that question tells me you are," he said, smiling.

"But I ate."

"You had a few sashimi. I don't think that constitutes a meal," he replied. "Plus, you're driving."

"Oh crap. I forgot."

He shook his head and grinned. She was getting loose with her words.

"So, I was saying... Dr. Marcel thinks we're making progress. I'm unsure what that all means from here, but I wanted to tell you."

"Glad to hear that, Han," he said. One, because she is progressing and two, because she seemed to think it was vital for him to know. It had been a while since they had spent time with each other, and he missed her terribly each day he didn't see or talk to her. He knew she needed time to heal, so he gave her space. "You look good, by the way," he said.

"Thank you, K. So do you. I like the new do. And the facial hair..." she beamed. "It suits you."

He toyed with his perfectly groomed goatee. "Really? It's not weird?"

"No, not at all. I think it's very *debonair,*" she said, smiling as she enunciated the last word.

"I wasn't sure about it, but I thought I'd try a new look. I'm glad you like it," he said, satisfied by her reaction.

Hannah smiled back.

Gosh, he thought he would never see that smile again. He didn't realize how much he'd missed her. His heart fluttered.

"K, can I ask you a favor?" she said, snapping him out of his thoughts.

"Of course. What is it?"

"Do you think you can drive me home tonight? I really want another glass of wine. Kind of celebration for my progress, you know?" She batted her eyes, "Ple-e-ase?"

She was so damn cute, pouting her lips like a little girl.

"Stop that," he said as he let out a deep breath.

"What?" She pouted her lips and batted her eyes again. "Th-i-i-s?"

"Oh, hell. Fine. But on one condition."

"What's the condition?"

"You're going to eat more of that bread on your plate. I'd hate to carry you out of here."

Hannah stuck her tongue out at him before tearing a piece of bread. "Fine." She tore another piece and ate it. "Happy?" she teased as she smiled, chewing the bread.

God, I love you.

***

It was a quiet ride back to her house. Hannah's mind wandered. She discreetly stole some glances at him as he drove. He was so handsome. She giggled in silence at the thought. What in the world was happening to her? It was the wine. She glanced at him again. Keon had been very patient with her.

After her last day with Ethan, K called every day, checking up on her. A few weeks later, he had started asking her to go out, but she'd refused every time. She needed to take care of herself first, but as time went by, she started missing him. Tonight, she felt ready. It had been a while since she felt free and relaxed. She wasn't drunk, but she felt good by the night's end. It was just what she needed. She was confused. She felt many emotions she had never felt before, not even when she was with Ethan. There was something about Keon that made her feel at home. Of course, she loved Ethan and always would, but her attraction to Keon was different. She thought she had gotten over him after she had met Ethan, but the feelings came flooding back. She found herself missing him when he didn't check on her. What was going on? It had been almost a year since Ethan passed away. Was it too soon for her to feel this way? And with K? She glanced over at him again. He seemed to be lost in his own thoughts. She wondered what he was thinking.

He glanced at her, she smiled, and he smiled back. She felt another unexplainable feeling deep inside. Confusion came whenever she confronted her newfound feelings toward Keon. Well, maybe not new. She recognized these feelings; they were the same feelings she had when they first met in college. Suddenly, she realized what it was. It was love. First love. Ethan was not her first love. It was Keon. Her heart pounded, and her palms sweat. She rubbed them together, trying to find the courage to speak, to tell him how she felt. What if he rejected her?

"K?" she said, her voice cracking.

"Yeah?"

She looked out the window. "Nothing." *C'mon, Hannah. You need to find the courage.* Before she could say another word, the car stopped.

"Why did we stop?"

"Cause we're home?" Keon caught his mistake and cleared his throat. "I mean, we're here. *You're* home."

The drive home seemed short. She didn't realize she was that deeply lost in her thoughts and feelings, for that matter.

Neither of them moved. She gave him a side glance and for some reason, he was looking more handsome as each minute passed. The moonlight radiating inside the car hit his face at just the right angle, making his emerald, green eyes sparkle. It made her heart pound some more.

"Are you okay? Was there something you wanted to say?" he said.

For a moment, there was an awkward silence. She wanted to tell him how she felt about him, but something held her back. She didn't know what. They sat, waiting for each other to say something - anything. As she tried to muster the courage to tell him, she heard Ethan's gentle voice. *Promise me you will love and be loved again.* That was all the confirmation she needed. She wasn't confused or scared anymore. Perhaps her heart wanted to make sure it didn't forget Ethan. Hannah glanced at K, and before she could tell him her feelings, he leaned over and claimed her lips. He took her by surprise, but she was ready. Boy, was she ready for his soft and warm lips, his gentle touch, his undying love. She closed her eyes at the sudden revelation. He loved her. Somehow, she knew that deep in her heart, and *she* loved him. She always had. Keon's breathing intensified, matching hers. She unbuckled her seatbelt and leaned in closer to him. He welcomed her and pulled her close again. She could feel his heartbeat as if his heart was jumping out for joy. He kissed her hard as he caressed the back of her head, running his fingers through her hair. She held his face and kissed him equally hard, leaving them both breathless. When they finally surfaced from their blissful journey, Keon smiled, gazing straight into her eyes. "You have no idea how long I've waited to do that."

"Me, too," she whispered.

He planted another quick, soft kiss on her lips.

"K," she whispered.

"Yeah?"

"You're right. We're home."

EPILOGUE

Hannah wasn't dreaming any longer, yet the man in her dreams stood before her. There was joy in her heart as she watched her husband and child. She wanted to pinch herself to make sure she *really* was awake, but she knew. Hannah knew that this was real, that her new family was real. It was a beautiful Saturday afternoon, and it was time to visit Ethan at the cemetery. As they stood there in front of Ethan's tomb, her son broke away and ran next to the pine tree not far from where they were. There he stood and smiled. She watched her son play around the tree, singing, talking, and laughing. After a few minutes, the toddler's tiny feet galloped, jumping into his father's wide-open arms.

"What were you looking at, son?"

"I was saying bye to Uncle Efan, Daddy."

She knew what she heard and she and K exchanged smiles.

Keon threw Michael Ethan up in the air, and their son squealed in delight.

"More, Daddy, more."

Little Mikey raised his tiny arms to the sky as if reaching for the clouds.

"I can't reach him, Daddy. Uncle Efan is so far away."

Keon kissed his son on the forehead before putting him down. "He's closer than you think, son."

She couldn't help but feel blessed at the sight of her husband and child. Her heart was whole. She touched the marble tombstone in front of her and a slight wind picked up. Hannah lifted her head to the bright blue sky and whispered, "Happy Birthday, Ethan."

Author's Note

Creating stories has been something I have enjoyed since I was a kid. However, embarking on a writing journey is a different story; it can be daunting. I am so glad a few family members joined me in this endeavor. Having English as a second language made it a little scary to write a novel, but thanks to my two daughters, Haley and Kayla, who were my first critiques, they made it a little easier for me with their suggestions and gave me the courage to proceed. Their feedback was invaluable, and I am deeply grateful for their support. To my sister-in-law, Gina Star, an avid reader, thank you for being so supportive, encouraging me to pursue publishing, and helping with the final proofread.

I am also blessed to have my family and friends by my side. I am always grateful to my husband, who encourages me to reach for my dreams. I remember a particularly tough day when I wasn't feeling well and was doubting my writing abilities; he would remind me of my strengths and encourage me to keep going. To my mom and dad, who always cheer me on, and the Cabagnot family, thank you for always remembering what Papalo taught us: to be happy for others and celebrate. Most importantly, I would not have been able to do what I do without God's presence in my life; every day, I thank Him.

About the author

J.J. Marcel is a passionate writer who also crafts children's books under a different name and has a keen eye for capturing the beauty around her through her camera lens. Her love for travel and exploration fuels her creativity, and she often discovers fascinating subjects right in her own backyard. Currently, J.J. is working on the second book of the Green Ridge Series.

A Tiny Sneak Peek into Book Two

The Protector

He found me. Again. I had no choice but to run.
Again.

Made in the USA
Middletown, DE
06 February 2025